THE
RAVEN
SPELL

THE
RAVEN
SPELL

LUANNE G. SMITH

Published by 47North, Seattle

www.apub.com

Amazon, the Amazon logo, and 47North are trademarks of Amazon.com, Inc., or its affiliates.

ISBN-13: 9781542034043
ISBN-10: 1542034043

Cover design by Shasti O'Leary Soudant

Printed in the United States of America

Where corpse-light
Dances bright,
Be it day or night,
Be it by light or dark,
There shall corpse lie stiff and stark.

—Sir Walter Scott

Chapter One

Edwina and Mary, quite contrary.

The boy's taunt stuck in Edwina's mind as she stooped to inspect a promising glint embedded among the mud and stones. Her quick eye had spotted the exposed metal despite the gray overcast creeping in with the dawn. Had to be gold to catch the starlight the way it did. She poked a finger in the mud after her sister had tramped off to inspect a hump of rags beside a fisherman's boat stranded by the low tide. Edwina dug deeper in the muck, stirring loose the stench of fish and rotted seagrass. Still, the boy's comment rankled like a herring bone caught in the back of the throat. It simply wasn't fair. They'd done everything they could to blend in, she and her sister. But no one respected the old ways anymore. The magic had to be hidden, disguised, renounced. At least in public.

Edwina pulled the metal free. A gold ring, as she'd suspected. Lost or tossed? In the end she supposed it didn't matter. Gone was gone. She gave the ring a rinse in a tide pool and inspected the band. There was a scratch or two, but after a little polish with a soft cloth and gentle spell, the ring would fetch a handsome penny in the shop.

She glanced up shore to check on Mary. Neither she nor her sister could resist collecting the shiny trinkets that churned up with the river's tide. Rings, bottles, spoons, keys, combs, bones—there was always something new coughed up on the bank, as if the water grew perpetually ill on the taste of human detritus. Sometimes, too, they'd snatch up the dropped coin or snuffbox that had fallen through the hole of someone's pocket to land in a gutter. Of course, it wasn't the scavenging that made them contrary in their neighbors' eyes. Others trampled the same shores and streets searching for treasure without scorn, albeit with less success than the sisters. And it wasn't that neither had married, or that they now lived a reclusive life in the tiny aerie flat above their corner shop on Old Bridge Road, or that neither was ever seen without her black shawl. No, what made them contrary was their apathy toward other people's opinions about them. Well, outward appearances were one thing. Inside, with only each other to confide in, they felt the cold shoulder of rejection the same as anyone.

"Found another ring," Edwina called in the loud whisper they'd perfected on such predawn outings. She wiped it dry with the corner of her shawl as she walked in the direction Mary had gone. "Gold this time. The setting is missing its stone, though." Empty as a tooth socket, she thought, and slid her tongue over her own tender molars. She dropped the ring in her pocket, then squinted as her sister ran toward her with her skirt hiked to her knees and her shawl fluttering off her shoulders.

Blessed Mother, what trouble has she found now?

"It's a man," Mary said, breathing hard from the exertion.

"Dead?" He'd have to be for Mary to exude such enthusiasm.

"Near enough." Mary pressed her lips tight together, as if it might make her wish come true. "His is the shiniest one yet. Come see."

Edwina followed along the rocky shore nearly as far as the railroad bridge. There, she leaned over the man's body and noted his skin appeared pale to the point of being bluish around the lips. Edwina drew her skirt up to avoid the mud and crouched beside him. Barely a wisp of air escaped his lungs. By Edwina's reckoning, he had only a fingertip grip left on this world. Pity. He had a noble sort of face with a firm jaw, though it hadn't been cleanly shaved in days. She was making a quick scan of his clothed body to look for an obvious wound or cause for his predicament when her fingers hit a slick spot at the back of his head that suggested a blow. A criminal most likely. Or a brawler. Or maybe a drunk who'd lost his footing on the embankment above. Poor man. Either way, he wasn't long for this side of the veil. To be sure, she tapped her foot against his shoulder, giving him a nudge. Not even a groan. She leaned the back of her hand against his cheek and felt the chill of death gaining in his blood. If he'd shown just a spark of fire under the skin, she might have given him a remedy. She always carried a little camphor oil with her for emergencies, but there was no use wasting the drops on this one.

"Cold as Christmas, he is," Mary said, leaning over her shoulder. "Might be a mercy to help him pass through the last part to the other side."

"Maybe we should wait a few more minutes to make sure he's dead," Edwina said, but then her sister gave her that aloof glance just short of an eye roll that insinuated she was being a prude. "All right, then. Take your bauble, but we'll need to find a policeman to report the body to on our way back."

Mary squealed with delight and knelt beside the man's chest. Edwina, a touch uneasy since the man still took breath, kept an eye out for any stray fishermen hitting the shore before the sun was up. There was nothing wrong, necessarily, in taking a man's memories when he was on the verge of death. After all, he had no more use for them. But those who didn't understand the unique attraction the rising memories floating off the dead held for her sister might misinterpret her intentions. To some, such a scene might appear as if they were robbing the poor dead fellow of his earthly belongings. True, Mary might yet pluck off a brass button or slip loose his wedding ring, if he wore one, but that wasn't the same as stealing. Not really. Not when it came to the dead.

Mary leaned over the man and held one hand against the left side of his forehead. There might have been a twitch of discomfort, but it wasn't enough to erase any doubt he'd be dead soon. With her other hand she pressed on the man's chest. An instant later an aura of blue light rose out of his throat to form a tiny cloud above his body. Quick as a bird after a moth, Mary grasped the thing with both hands. Cupping the memory between her palms, she blew air into the hollow space inside to preserve it.

"Come, Mary. The tide's rising. We need to head for home."

Her sister stood with the man's memory cradled in her palm, an orb of iridescent cobalt and gold that could pass for a fisherman's glass float. Edwina pinched her brows together, inspecting how brightly the multispectral memory glowed. She could see why her sister had been drawn to the shiny thing.

"All right, pocket it and let's be off," she said. Edwina waited, eyes on the shoreline, while Mary shrank the shimmering orb of energy in her palm down to a solid sphere by clasping her hands together and whispering her preservation spell. Edwina peeked over her shoulder and saw that the memory had retained its iridescence so that it resembled a precious stone or a piece of sea glass rather than a child's marble, as was often the case with Mary's finds. "Pretty," she said and hooked her arm in her sister's.

"I'll store it with the others," Mary said. "I must have over a dozen such gems now, each a deeper shade of blue and gold, though none so dazzling as this one. Someday I hope to discover what all the different veins of color mean."

Not without finding a way to speak to the dead, thought Edwina, but she let it go. She didn't wish to spoil her sister's good find. *Both* their good finds, actually. If the right buyer entered the shop, the gold ring might bring in enough to tip the scales toward a profit for the month. All in all, it was a good morning of scavenging along the foreshore. Well, perhaps not for the unfortunate man they'd left lying on the riverbank.

North of the embankment they spotted an officer making his rounds. Naturally, it wouldn't do to speak directly to a member of the police force. Not with a dead body involved. Or even a nearly dead one. And definitely not when those who had found the dead body were considered by some to be contrary. *Curse that boy.* They'd learned that lesson well enough before.

Instead, Edwina nudged a thought toward the officer by singing the message in a melody. Her sister might have a talent for spotting shiny corpse lights rising off the dead, but she could sing a spell better than any woman in her clan.

Her song trilled through the morning mist, and the officer, cocking his ear, headed for the river. At least the authorities could retrieve the poor man's body before it was swallowed by the rising water. Edwina patted her sister's arm and trotted up the cobblestones toward their third-story flat, a good deed done in the early morning gloaming. But before they turned the corner at the top of the road, a shrill call from the officer's whistle pierced the morning calm, shrieking loud enough to shake loose her denial. She peered at the dark line of the embankment, at the moving lights of men rushing to answer the call to save another human being, and knew.

Chapter Two

Edwina's feet touched down on the wood floor of their attic bedroom. She threw off her shawl, letting it drape over one of two single beds. Mary followed and remembered to shut the window behind her before bounding on top of her quilt.

"Light the lamp." Edwina caught her breath as she braced her hand against the chest of drawers.

Mary blew on her fingertips, illuminating the barely suppressed smile on her face before she touched the flame to the wick. She blew across her fingers, and a curl of smoke and sulfur floated up to the rafters.

"He may yet die." Edwina tried to convince herself as much as Mary. "Things go wrong even in hospital. Complications. Infections." She caught herself pacing the floor and forced herself to sit and take off her muddy boots. And yet her mind still whirled. Had he seen her face? Mary's? Mortals have terrible night vision. Why on earth hadn't he died?

"For all we know, he's laid out in the mortuary already," Mary offered.

Possibly, thought Edwina. But if not, they'd left a man alive in the world without a memory, one precious enough to him that its aura shone brightest at the moment death nearly took him from the world. It was wrong to wish for a man's demise, but if Mary was right and the man had already gone stiff with rigor mortis, there was no question his death would make life simpler.

"I'd been so sure," she said, opening and closing her hands as if they were suddenly foreign to her. "He was cold to the touch. Not a spark of life left to feel."

"Do you want to see my treasure in the light?"

Mary was her fraternal twin, yet sometimes it felt as though the biological gap between them were years wider than the minutes that had lapsed from one birth to the next. Since childhood, Edwina had been forced to behave almost parentally to a sister with a penchant for games and cunning laughter. Never a care for the consequences, that was her Mary.

"Go on, then." Edwina undid the laces on the secondhand men's work boots she used for scavenging the foreshore and slid them off. Later she'd bang them against each other in the alley to get the worst of the mud to fall off. And Mary's, too, when her sister was too preoccupied with the city to do it herself.

"The colors are even more vivid than I dreamed." Mary held the gem under the lamplight, biting her lip the way she did when she had a secret to tell but knew she mustn't.

"'Tis a beauty," Edwina said. "Look at the way the line of gold shimmers against the blue." She couldn't imagine what final thoughts might leave such a mark. She hoped for the man's sake it didn't hold the memory of a loved one still roaming the world. She'd always maintained there was something ignoble about a person's last thoughts not being allowed to travel to their final destination with the rest of the soul. But then Mary's nature was not some abomination either. Their father had explained such talent was a gift, and so it, too, must have a purpose.

Mary let the orb roll across her palm as she admired her newest bauble before snatching it up in her fist. "Now, let's see what you found," she said and nudged her chin.

Edwina emptied her pockets. A handful of brass buttons, a pipe with a carved buffalo's head for the bowl still black with mud, twopence coins, and the gold ring. She placed the gold under the light so that, even without a proper polish, its value shone.

"Must have been exquisite when the gemstone was in it." Mary picked up the band and turned the ring around to better see the details under the light. "Old, judging by the handiwork."

"Maybe even Grandfather Merlin old," Edwina said. She gave the ring a rub with the corner of her discarded shawl, then handed it back to Mary for further inspection.

"A raised bevel held up the stone."

Edwina nodded. "Garnet would be my guess."

Mary's eye glinted with the shine of mischief. "I could replace it," she said and reached for a scarlet ribbon from the nightstand. "Make the ring whole again."

She could. Mary's unique magic made it possible to render such gemstones nearly out of thin air. But then to ask a price for the ring to match the worth would raise suspicion in their little shop. No, 'twas best to pass the ring off as something more akin to pawnbroker gold and get what they could, minus the misgivings.

Her twin understood without her saying a word, though she gave a little sigh of regret before setting aside the ribbon and retrieving the mahogany jewelry box atop the dresser. The box, which they shared, had three compartments inside, each lined with velvet. Edwina kept a few keepsakes inside the first partition—a pressed flower given to her by a promising young man, which she'd saved between sheets of wax paper, a ruby teardrop earring missing its partner, and a silver thimble that had once belonged to their mother—but the other two compartments were taken up with the shiny orbs Mary collected. Edwina had lost track of how many there were now, but her sister removed them for inspection, all in a row, each and every Sunday evening after their tea. Always comparing and evaluating one against another, trying to determine why one might be more attractive to the eye. Some were dull like storm clouds and others as bright as a peacock feather, but whether that was due to the quality of the person's memories or some other influence, she had yet to figure it out.

Mary gave the shiny new remembrance a final approving glance, then shut it away in the box with the others. "Thirty minutes," she said, putting the box away.

Edwina didn't need to glance at the cloisonné clock on the pedestal table by the washbasin to know her sister was right. She'd often wondered how the cogs and gears ticked away in that clockwork brain of her sister's to be able to announce the precise moment each morning exactly thirty minutes before the shop was to open. But she imagined it was akin to her own ability to understand the rise and fall of the tide in conjunction with the phase of the moon. Another odd tic of their nature.

"Right, we better get on with the day, then," she said and slipped her feet into the black ankle boots she reserved for shop work.

Mary sat and did the same, doing up the buttons with a small hook. "We'll have customers today," she said and tossed her muddy boots in a wicker basket at the foot of her bed. "Wednesdays are always good for selling tin and brass."

"And hopefully a little gold." Edwina scooped up the ring and followed her younger sister down the corkscrew staircase that led to a modest kitchen and cozy snug. There, two upholstered chairs faced the stove while two hard-back chairs made of oak sat tucked beneath a crude wooden table. Edwina had draped white lace, a secondhand tablecloth she'd accepted in exchange for a pair of wrought-iron finials a month earlier, over the bare wood. It went against her nature to barter away shop merchandise, but the idea of a real tablecloth with a vase full of roses atop was too tempting to deny. And, too, it distracted from the exposed bedsprings of the folding bed against the wall where their father had slept before he left.

The sisters shared the flat above the shop with their absent father. He wasn't dead, merely gone walkabout for a time. Before he left three months earlier with a curious tip of his hat, he'd rented the odd three-story corner building that sat at the point where two diagonal streets met at an acute angle in the shabby end of a semirespectable street in the city proper. He'd left money enough to cover one month of living expenses, but the sisters had run the shop on their own ever since with the expectation their gray-headed father would one day walk back through the door. Or perhaps not. When their mother had left in similar fashion with a wave and a hand-blown kiss one year earlier, they'd never seen her again. Not a letter, a telegram, or even a whispered word carried on a trail of smoke.

The sisters each cut a slice of brown bread and smeared it with boysenberry jam while their tea water came to a boil on the gas stove.

"Ten minutes," Mary said, scooting her chair closer to the table.

Edwina agreed with a nod. When they finished their breakfast, they descended the main staircase to the small storeroom behind the shop. A curtain divided the back room from where the merchandise was sold, keeping Edwina's personal books and a small cupboard stocked with jars of dried bits of this and a wing or whisker of that out of view. Up front in the shop, most of the semivaluable and easily stolen objects were displayed in glass cabinets, while most everything else was stacked on bookshelves or arranged atop the pair of end tables their mother had left behind. But because Edwina and Mary had been avid collectors of lost items for most of their lives, there were a number of finds that simply had to be hung on the walls. After three months of the sisters hammering nails into the plaster to display yet another object, the walls of the shop had taken on a mosaic quality from the mishmash of small frames, round-faced clocks, skeleton keys, trivets, belt buckles, spoons, and assorted gardening tools. Mary had even managed to secure a brass elephant with glass jewels embedded in its caparison on a hook above the back curtain.

The shop front had curved paned glass windows trimmed in black, which their father had insisted made them appear a respectable business to mortals. Gold lettering that had been painted on the woodwork above the door a decade or more earlier read MERCIER & SONS. The lettering had also proclaimed the shop to be an apothecary at the time, but their father had that part painted over, though he never bothered to remove the rest—either out of a sense of transience or perhaps because he thought people would trust the original name more than "Blackwood and Daughters." Inside, the shop had become a sanctuary for the sisters, but from the outside, as the eye traveled up, Edwina often remarked that the top floor, which overhung the other levels below, was reminiscent of a cage balanced there by a child tempting the laws of gravity. One little nudge, she thought, and the whole thing would topple over. But it was a comfortable home and shop and not one she had any plans to vacate anytime soon, stars willing.

The sisters slipped their work aprons over their skirts and entered the shop. Mary blew life into a pair of oil lamps to chase away the natural gloom, while Edwina took out her polishing cloth from under the front counter to work on her new ring. Though now it was filled with finds similar to the one she polished, she often imagined the oak-and-glass case had once held jars of elixir and foot cream, or perhaps salt cures and bundles of rosemary with instructions for how to be rid of a stomach ailment. Or, more likely, the apothecary had been owned by a mortal and the case had held only brown bottles filled with small, round painkillers and stuffed with wads of cotton. Curing headaches seemed to be the only magic mortals were capable of.

Outside, the city streets thronged with the noise of ordinary people hurrying to and fro. Their dull energy thudded against the buildings until even the highest-flying spirit was drained sober by the end of the day, if one wasn't careful. Mary watched out the window as a wagon rolled by, drawn by heavy-footed horses. Though she denied it, Edwina's sister showed more of a fascination with mortals than etiquette permitted. There was a firm boundary that must be main-tained, at least metaphorically, between the clans of the old bloodlines and those descended from nonmagical lineages. Especially when one had already been forced to move too many times before because of a sister's impropriety.

"Will we be going to the hospital this evening?" Mary asked once the wagon passed.

Edwina looked up from the ring, which was quickly showing off that enviable yellow shine only real gold has. "I don't think that would be wise, do you?"

Mary turned from the window. "Whyever not?"

Edwina stilled herself as the callousness of her sister's question struck. Mary had only that morning taken a memory. There was little need to volunteer to sit and read to the dying again so soon. "What if he didn't die? What if he's there? What if he recognizes us? Says something?"

"I would think that's why we should go and check on him." Mary propped the OPEN sign against a bottom windowpane and unlocked the front door. "So we can be sure."

Edwina thought again of the policeman she'd directed to the shore. Would he come calling? Had they been seen? A tiny fluttering wing of panic took flight in her chest. Then she thought of the man. What if he lived? What would losing a memory bright enough to float to the surface at the moment of death do to a person? Memories were made up of intricate interwoven strands. Each attached to another in delicate spiderweb threads that created emotional patterns, each one affecting and tugging on the next. What kind of withered existence would that be to carry no past, no connection to anyone or anything? Was that the condition the numbed souls who wandered the streets mumbling to themselves lived in, eyes half-vacant, clothes tattered beyond repair, and their tether to reality stretched to the point of madness? The memories holding one's place in the fabric of society scattered to the four winds?

The fluttering panic inside her chest alit on a branch of conscience and transformed itself to guilt.

Mary needn't go, but perhaps she should visit the hospital. Just to be certain. Dead or alive, she needed to know so she could put this fretting to rest. The police would have taken him to Saint Basil's Hospital. She knew the doctors there, knew their skill to be above average for mortals, but even an accomplished physician could never appreciate the gap in his understanding of the patient's condition should the man recover.

Edwina polished the gold ring until it gleamed as bright as the vein in the stolen memory. Brilliant, valuable, and worth stealing. Yes, she understood her sister's desire to own something so precious. But taking from the dead or dying was an altogether different matter than taking from the living. She should never have allowed it. No, she saw that now. There'd been the chill of death under the man's skin, but perhaps she hadn't accounted for however much time he'd lain unconscious in the cold river mud. Could that have stilled his blood so it pooled away from the skin? As much as she wished to indulge her sister, they should have stuck with the sick and elderly who they *knew* took their last breaths at Saint Basil's.

She threw the cloth down on the counter. How could she have been so stupid? Perhaps she'd better pop in at the hospital after all. Better to be sure the man had died properly and wasn't wandering the halls missing half his mind.

Stars above, helping mortals is rarely a risk worth taking.

Chapter Three

"Seeing stars" was no mere idiom. When the blow had come, the inside of his head had exploded with shattering white light that temporarily blinded his vision to all but the spangled stars that floated on the insides of his eyelids. The savagery of the hit slashed across every crevice of his brain, laying waste to his neck and spine before he'd blacked out. The pain had stolen his breath, his consciousness, and any recollection of what had happened afterward, except for the one odd vision that seemed to be imprinted on his irises. But that part wasn't real, was it? He'd been clouted before plenty, but not to the point he couldn't shake loose the rattling inside his head and get on with it. He rubbed his hand over his face as though he could wipe the slate clean, but all it brought was a reminder of his bruised condition.

He blinked, and his vision switched from middle-space staring to locating the source of the person speaking to him.

"Sir, I need you to try and pay attention." A man stood at his bedside with one hand in his lab coat pocket while the other held a pipe to his lips. A doctor, yes, that's what he was. Newly settled in his profession, by the look of him, having only just crossed the line from stout youth to the first soft edges of middle age. The doctor's broad cheek whiskers reminded him of someone, his own father or employer perhaps, but he couldn't be certain. He couldn't even recall if he had a father, or a job for that matter, though he knew he must.

"As I said, you've had a nasty blow to the head, resulting in a serious subdural hematoma. Indeed, you've been unconscious for"—the man in the lab coat checked a giant clock mounted on the wall—"hmm, going on two hours now."

"A subdural . . ." He tried to mimic the doctor's words, but his mouth would not cooperate. "Will I be all right?"

"Think of your brain like a wooden crate filled with jelly. You've taken a hard smack against the outside of the crate, and all the jelly inside got slammed against the opposite side of the crate from the force. It's very likely you have a traumatic brain injury, which will require observation."

"Traumatic . . ."

"Yes, that's right. And we'll need to watch for signs of psychosis." The doctor held up a fountain pen and tracked it in front of his patient's face. "But you're showing remarkable and steady progress, I dare say." The doctor put his pen away.

For a moment, while he'd watched the pen being waved from side to side in front of him, he'd half expected the point of the exercise was to make something materialize out of thin air, which baffled him completely. And yet he had the awareness to know he ought not say so out loud.

"Now, let's try something else." The doctor, still new enough in his profession to yet bear some patience for the infirm and indigent, peered through his pipe smoke, squinting as he studied the man before him. "Can you tell me your name?" He awaited the answer to his elementary question with apparent optimism, which eventually soured into disappointment.

There were half a dozen men lying in similar cots beside him in the long room. Vagrants by the look of them. Common sense suggested that every one of them had a name. Some of them had it scrawled on a board at the foot of their bed. He shifted on his cot, trying to remember what he was called but was met with an empty void that yielded nothing. "I dinna think I have a name," he answered, though he knew that couldn't be right.

"Of course you have a name. We all have a name. Mine is Dr. Samuel Jones. Head physician on duty."

When he didn't respond, the doctor exhaled and put a hand atop his patient's head, as if feeling for a deviation in the skull. He flinched when the doctor explored too close to the throbbing wound at the back of his head. To his relief, a woman wearing a white apron and pointed white hat approached his bedside to stand next to the doctor. She carried an enamel tray. No, a bedpan. That was the word for it. He clutched his blanket higher, hoping her arrival didn't mean what he thought it meant, but then she pulled a card out of the pan and handed it to the doctor. A distinct rust-colored stain had spread across the backside of the paper. There was something poetic about the shape it left behind, something that urged him to want to form meaningful words together, but they fizzled in his mind before they could find his mouth.

"This might help. The card was in his coat pocket, sir."

"Very good." The doctor held the calling card at arm's length as he read, squinting through his pipe smoke. "Does the name Henry Elvanfoot mean anything to you?" He turned the card around to display the print—a rather ornate script done in garish green ink with an embossed thistle at the top. A reddish-brown splotch sullied the front of the otherwise professional card as well. "Is that you? Is that your name?"

The name Elvanfoot, once spoken, seemed to fill in some blank spot he'd been oblivious to before. Like a shadowy image coming into focus in his mind. Was he Henry? He must be, and so he said so. And yet nothing else arrived with the name. No memory of home, no relations, no job. These were things he must have, and yet none of it would coagulate in any cohesive history of *him* he could recall with clarity.

Disappointed, perhaps, that his patient wasn't the career-making amnesia case he'd hoped for, the doctor tossed the card back in the bedpan and pronounced him a lucky man after coming within a hair's breadth of permanent damage from his injury. Out of an abundance of caution, though, the doctor ordered him to remain in the hospital for a night of observation, seeing how there were a few coins among the rest of his belongings lining the bottom of the bedpan to cover the cost.

The nurse set the tray on the table beside the man's bed, then turned to follow the doctor down the row of cots to attend to the next helpless bugger.

"Wait," he said, gripping her forearm. "I . . . it's like my mind isn't part of my body anymore. My head feels like it's floating up along the ceiling instead of sitting on my shoulders." He swallowed. "Will it get better?"

She pitied him with a solemn look. "You've had a nasty hit to the head," she said. "You've only just regained consciousness." He let go of her arm, and she tugged her sleeve back down before sorting through the contents of the bedpan. "There are some personal belongings here. Maybe one of them will help jog your memory."

He could see only a glimpse of what the bedpan held inside, so the nurse made a space for it on the blanket beside his hip. Though he recognized none of the contents, the nurse's instincts proved correct. The items did stir his curiosity back to life. So much so that he didn't take notice of her leaving until she was halfway down the row of cots and assisting the doctor with a man whose arm was elevated and wrapped in white linen.

Left alone to examine his purported belongings, he tentatively reached in through the pan's slotted opening—sparing a moment's thought as to when the damn thing had last been used for its intended purpose—and retrieved the coins. Though he had no recollection of how he'd obtained the money, he did know its value. Enough to live on for a week in the city, if he was careful. Yes, that was something. He could build on that. Like the card, maybe the other items would ring a bell of recognition. Bullheaded determination backfilled the space under his rib cage until his chest heaved with new resolve. To what purpose, he didn't know, but it was as though his body was prepared to remember what his mind could not.

He dug through the rest of his items, a man on the hunt for answers. There was a broken pocket watch that wouldn't open. As plain as porridge on the outside. No decoration of any kind on the cover, but there were the initials "I.C." along with the number "#03" inscribed on the back that made him wonder if his name really was Henry Elvanfoot. Was the card his? He'd absorbed no sense of connection to the shape and feel of the name on it as his own, but it carried a sense of the familiar. But the watch *was* his. As with the coins, his body announced the truth of it with the solid sureness of a thumping, strong heartbeat that made him nod in confidence. But then what did I.C. stand for?

Having no idea, he sorted through the rest of the items to hunt for another clue. There were a few scraps of paper, a skeleton key, and a rosewood pipe with interlocking stag horns around the bowl, the color tarnished black around the rim. He sniffed the charred tobacco and recognized the scent of cherries. The scent pierced his ignorance. It had once been attached to a memory of a room with a high mullioned window, but his mind couldn't hold the rest. A wisp of smoke that dissipated before he could grasp the damn thing and make it solid in his thoughts. He set the stem of the pipe in his teeth, for that's where it felt most comfortable, and flipped open one of the folded-up pieces of paper. A receipt for a telegram. The name Elvanfoot was written in one of the spaces. But had he sent it, then? Frustration overtook him, and he wondered if he'd ever sort the mess out. The initials I.C. appeared scribbled on the bottom, but they made no more sense to him than any random letters in the alphabet. None of it did, despite the echoes of familiarity.

Then his hand reached for the final object: a collapsible knife. It wasn't the sort of thing a gentleman was apt to carry, although he supposed the weapon, like most everything else in the bedpan, must belong to him. He turned the handle over to study the staghorn grip, wondering why he'd felt the need to keep such a thing on his person. And if he wasn't a gentleman, then who was he? His breathing sped up, and a layer of sweat seeped out of the pores above his lip.

He flicked the knife open and inspected a line of rust-colored crust that had dried along the blade just as a policeman entered the hall and asked the nurse which cot belonged to the John Doe.

Chapter Four

The boy loitered in front of the shop window, waving his hands and making faces, a fresh taunt no doubt sitting ripe on his tongue. He sneered through the glass, his features as misshapen as a ghoul's from the distortion of the thick panes. Or perhaps that was merely his true self shining through, the nasty little nipper. Edwina smiled at her wicked thought as she searched beneath the counter for a proper box to display the ring in.

Mary stuck her tongue out at the boy, mimicking his hand gestures before flapping her hands behind her ears to be silly. "His name is Benjamin Abernathy." She glanced back at Edwina to see if she was listening. "Name's bigger than he is."

Edwina didn't care what the boy called himself. He was too curious and too familiar. "Impudent boy."

Mary snorted a laugh. "Like all the lads running up and down the lane. Need a little spirit in you to survive, I suspect." She took the feather duster from the nail on the wall and began the daily ritual of rearranging the dust in the shop while Edwina tucked some soft velvet inside a blue box that had once held a pot of cream for some wealthy woman shopping on the high street.

"He already thinks we're odd," Edwina said. "No need to encourage him."

"We are odd. By the boy's standards and everyone else's."

Edwina looked up from her work. There was bite in her sister's words. Too much truth in them, perhaps. Hard truth learned through the deprivation of community from most others of their kind. An even harder truth was that Mary, in particular, had always been the outcast because of her attraction to death. A fascination with whatever glittered under the moon and stars was natural enough for them both, but to see into the next realm and draw out the shiny memories of a person while they pass through the veil of death had left the mark of strangeness on the poor girl from the time they were children running in the country lanes themselves. The hedge witches occasionally showed a curiosity to know the source of the magic, but their doors were never propped open when Mary walked past alone.

Edwina glanced out the window again and saw that the boy had disappeared into the never-ending flow of people and animals traveling outside their door. Relieved, she set the ring in the box and positioned it inside the glass display so that anyone standing before the till would naturally glance down and see the value. Perhaps even inquire about its price and pedigree, and the cost of having the stone replaced. And then Edwina would suggest a beautiful garnet stone that could be had for a modest negotiable sum at the jeweler's around the corner.

The bell over the door rang, and she shut the display case. Mrs. Dower, her face like an old apple sunken from the loss of all but a handful of teeth, entered the shop with the string of her pocketbook hooked over her arm. The sisters occasionally spotted her on the fore-shore scavenging at low tide, but the mortal had no eye for treasure. No eye for husbands either, as rumor had it most of her missing front teeth were due to the fist as opposed to the rot.

"Morning, Mrs. Dower. How can we help you?"

The woman, dressed in faded plaid beneath a grimy gray apron, scanned the shop as though watchful for hidden threats in the corners. Satisfied, she said hello and made a show of browsing the more expensive items under glass. "Have you any hatpins, love? The sharper the better."

"Certainly," Mary said. She brought over a pincushion the sisters had made by stuffing horse hair and straw into an old sock and covering it over with a scrap of lilac-colored velvet. After stitching it all together, they'd secured the cushion inside the mouth of an empty blue flower vase. Edwina thought it charming the way the dozen pins they'd collected created a fanciful starburst effect when all stuck in at once.

Hatpins were easy enough to spot, whether lost and forgotten by a young woman in the grass after an impromptu picnic in the park or dropped on the street after a lady's maid had secured her mistress's hat too loosely, so that when she stepped out of her carriage, the pin slipped out and rolled into the cracks between the cobblestones. The glint of silver, matched with a shiny amethyst or teardrop of amber on the head of the pin, always caught the attention of those vigilant enough to keep their eyes pointed at the ground.

"See any you fancy?" Mary set the vase down on the counter and twisted a beautiful sterling silver pin with an elaborate enamel flower for the head between her thumb and finger.

Mrs. Dower eyed the expensive hatpin long enough to falsely suggest she could afford it if she wanted. She admired it with a nod until her hand reached for the plain brass pin with the small and practical mother-of-pearl affixed on the tip. Ten inches long from head to point, it was a serviceable and economical choice for any working woman, as were most wives who lived east and north of the shop door.

"You can see it's still in fine shape," Mary said. "Only the slight bend from light use."

"This one will do," the woman said and took a step back when Mary had approached too near for comfort. "Though I hope I'll have no need of it soon."

The sisters exchanged a look of confusion. "Whyever not?" Edwina asked.

"It's for me own protection then, innit?" Mrs. Dower's eyes dilated with the mischief of one who gets to tell something for the first time. "You'll have heard, of course? Another bloke was attacked this morning. This time below the embankment."

"Attacked?" Mary asked with eyebrows arched. She returned the display of hatpins back to the table.

"Well, he were hit on the back of the head, weren't he?" The woman pointed to her own vulnerable skull as she spoke. "Robbery, most like. Leastwise his throat weren't cut like the others."

Edwina's temples pulsed with the rush of blood and fear. "A common enough occurrence down by the docks, I should think."

The woman nodded at the truth of it. "Only my cousin Emily, not two blocks from here, had her pocketbook stolen right out of her hand last week. Broad daylight. Gangs running wild in the streets, they are. It was only last Sunday's paper that said they found a poor fella with his head bashed in and his throat cut north of the docks. Second one in a month. Mark me, 'tain't safe for man or woman to walk alone at night anymore." She jabbed the pin in the air to make her point.

Edwina shuddered at the thought. The newspapers sensationalized every transgression in the city to drive sales, but after hearing the report from Mrs. Dower, had she and Mary been near enough to a crime in progress that morning that they'd thwarted a worse attack on that poor man? Only to then steal his memories while he lay unconscious? Her hand flew involuntarily to her mouth, as if she might be ill.

"Sister, are you all right?"

She felt Mary's arm at her elbow as she leaned her hand on the front counter. "Yes," she said automatically, though she felt far from it. "It's just a shock, all this talk of people being attacked in the street."

"That's why I've come looking for this." Mrs. Dower waved the ten-inch hatpin. "I'll feel better walking home from the laundry house at night with a little protection in me pocket," she said and set her money on the counter.

"Ta," Mary said and slid the coins into the till.

Mrs. Dower left the shop still gripping her hatpin as a weapon. Mary looked left and right out the window after the woman had gone and untied her apron. "We should think of charming those pins for the women's protection," she said before walking to the back room to exchange her apron for her shawl and hat. Changed, she begged off, saying she was going to pop out to get them some milk for their tea.

"Oh," Edwina said. "I thought I might go out."

"You? Where to?" Mary asked.

There was no use in lying. "To the hospital. To check on that poor man. So we know one way or the other."

"Right. I'll stop by on my way back," she said. "A quick peek, nothing more." Mary jammed her own sharp pin through her straw hat, then left Edwina to mind the shop as she merged with the flock of city inhabitants rushing by outside the window.

Chapter Five

The ward went temporarily silent. No creaking beds, no gasps of exasperation, no curses of pain to an unforgiving god. Two patients folded their newspapers in half, pretending to read when really their eyes and ears were attuned to the policeman who'd walked to the foot of John Doe's cot. The one who'd arrived to ask how the man with the head wound and no memory had come to be on the foreshore at that time of the morning.

"Inspector Arthur Willoughby with the City Police." He held up a star-shaped badge with the number 227 embossed in the center that presumably was meant to fill the onlooker with the confidence he was who he said he was. "I'd like to ask you a few questions, if you don't mind."

Though he'd recoiled at the sight of the man's badge and occupation, there was also a sense of camaraderie at his dogged demeanor in the way he asked but really demanded. He nodded, though the motion made him dizzy. He hoped the officer was there to fill the sand back in his empty sack of a life, tell him what had happened and who had struck him, but it was more of the same rubbish questions the doctor had asked. Only this time when the question of his name came up, he didn't offer the doctor's presumption of Elvanfoot, only that he could not remember.

"Well, then can you tell me what happened?" asked the detective. "Why you were down by the river so early this morning?"

"I canna say," he said. "I took a pretty good crack on the head. Canna seem to remember much of anything yet."

The inspector remained impassive, as if he'd heard a hundred deflections from the truth before. A natural-born skeptic, judging by the pursing of his lips beneath his bushy mustache.

"Can you tell me what business you're in? Do you work in this part of the city? Generally speaking," he said, broadening the question as to encourage an answer. Any answer. Something to jot down in his handheld notebook.

At the mention of work in the city, a surge of unmet resolve asserted itself inside him, like horses ready to break for the open road. He *had* been intent on completing some task that morning. Something important. His body was yet primed for the effort. But empty of more information, the urge was left impotent, bridled by ignorance of purpose. He shook his head and felt a wave of dizziness as the surge receded. "I dinna know."

"What can you tell me about your belongings?" The inspector leaned over the opening of the bedpan, stirring them around with the end of his lead pencil. "Is there anything missing? Could you have been robbed?"

Again, he could not know, and yet *something* had been taken from him. He was sure of it. Certain in the same way he'd recognized the watch as absolutely his. He concentrated, trying to chase down more than a feeling. And then he saw them. In his mind's eye. Two figures standing over him. Two shadows. Yes, they had taken something from him. He'd come to, prying his eyes open a tiny crack until it hurt even to look at the starlight. But in that moment, he'd seen two women. In shawls. Yes, he remembered.

Spotting a change of expression, the inspector's eyes narrowed and his mustache twitched. "You've remembered something."

He ought to blurt it out. Tell the inspector about the women. About the strange blue light he'd seen rising off his body. The hollow sensation that followed in his head, arms, and chest, as if they'd taken something not from his person but from his being. But instinct held him back. Even he knew it was fantastic. Unreal. And probably a dream of the unconscious.

He shook his head. "My hat? A wallet perhaps? I have no idea if there might have been cash in it."

It did seem odd he had only a single card with a name on it. No other papers or identification. An old pipe, a pocket watch with mysterious initials, and a worthless piece of paper. And the knife. But he'd hidden that from the inspector under his blanket. He didn't know why, other than some instinct had urged him to do it.

The inspector dismissed the idea with a glance and a shrug, suggesting he was of the opinion the man he was looking at was nothing more than one of the common indigents who roamed the streets looking for work and lodging. Why else would a man voluntarily remain in a hospital if he was able to sit up and speak? And with no visitors come to check on him? "A robbery, most like. And yet this pocket watch was not taken off your person? Gold plate, at that."

The man flinched when the inspector picked up the timepiece. He had the strongest desire to swipe the watch out of the man's hands, but why would such a thing even matter? Willoughby held the gold piece in his hand and pushed the lever to open it. "Rotten luck, that. Not working. The mechanism is broken. Still, any thief would have nicked it right off, wouldn't you think?"

"Of course." *Of course!* But then what *had* the women taken? Something beyond this man's understanding and jurisdiction, of that he was certain. And yet he felt compelled now to speak the odd vision into existence, if only to testify and measure his own sanity. "There were two women. In shawls."

"Women?" Willoughby raised a curious brow. "You mean tarts?"

No, there'd been no whiff of perfume, no scent of dried sweat, no breath tainted with alcohol and sweet cachous. His brain was working fast to remember as many small details as it could before they all spilled out the wound at the back of his head with the rest of his memory. His hand reached for the reassurance of the knife beneath the blanket. "Nae," he said. "Young women, though. In black. Long fluttering shawls and dark hair coiled at the nape of the neck held with silver combs." His inner vision cast an image for the inspector to contemplate. "Like that one." He pointed to the dark figure of a shawled woman standing in the corridor, but by the time Willoughby looked, the woman had gone.

But he had seen her, hadn't he? Or had the crack on his head bruised his brain so that he could no longer tell the difference between what he saw and what he imagined? The thought sent a nauseated tremor through him.

The inspector faced him again, making a small "hmm" sound as he pursed his lips, as though already dismissing the account as frivolous. "I've got a man asking around the docks if they saw anything untoward this morning. Yours isn't the only report we've had of robbery of late. My guess is we've got a gang of street thugs who've grown overly bold. Rest assured we'll have them apprehended. In the meantime, if anything else occurs to you, please report it to a city station or one of our constables." Willoughby handed him a printed card with his contact information, not unlike the bloodstained one gracing his belongings inside the bedpan; then the inspector doffed his hat and departed. Case closed. Or at least wrapped up unless or until he could recall anything else.

After Willoughby had gone, the image of the women lingered, too real to be imagined. They'd spoken over him. Touched him. Yes, they'd felt for his pulse before taking something. *Everything.* And when they'd gone, a void of nothingness had spun in their wake.

"Sounds like our Blackwood sisters," the nurse said as she folded a set of bedsheets near enough to his cot to have overheard the conversation. Seeing him steady his eyes on her for more information, she retracted her comment. "Not saying it was them. It's just they do wear long black shawls and silver combs in their hair, the two of them. Lots of women do, of course. Only they volunteer at the hospital on occasion. Could be they were here this morning when you came in. That's why you know them. Easy to understand how that might have got in your head, love."

And yet he knew the memory—his only memory—was of the muddy bank of the stinking river, not the hospital. The smell climbed in his nostrils to remind him of how he'd lain on the ground when they'd taken *something* from him.

Whoever or whatever he was in this life, he gripped the knife with conviction. "Could you tell me how to get in touch with these sisters so I might pay my respects when I'm well?"

The nurse nodded and smiled, and he inwardly did the same when she described their shop on Old Bridge Road.

Chapter Six

Curse the stars. Why couldn't that man have done the proper thing and died in the mud where they'd found him? Edwina took that back. Wasn't wise to speak ill of the dead. Or the living. Besides, she rarely meant the terrible things that came first to her mind. It was just the flint and spark of discharging flighty emotions. It was either that or let them get bottled up inside her, waiting to explode at an inopportune moment. A trait of her father's that had taken seed in her demeanor. Something that had never served him, or her, well in the past. And yet intuition told her there was a great deal to be regretful about should the man still walk this side of the veil hanging between life and death.

Edwina stepped out from behind the counter to straighten the skeleton keys on display near the window. She liked to see them all lying straight as spines from their curled handles to their crooked teeth in a neat row, but it was merely busywork to pass the time until either a customer or her sister walked through the door. It was long past the time Mary should have returned, come to think of it. She'd been gone far longer than it took to buy a pint of milk at the nearest cowshed and walk to Saint Basil's afterward. Then again, the sun had broken through the gloom, shining blearily through the smoke and haze. Though they lived within the square mile of the city proper, the sunbeams were never anything more than a facsimile of true sunshine. Not like the country sky they'd known growing up. Still, even if Mary had taken the long way home to cut through the cathedral gardens, she should have been back by now.

With no customers and the shop to herself, Edwina returned her attention to the jewelry case where the new ring sat prominently among the other trinkets. She'd found all manner of gold and silver in her life—rings, bracelets, charms hooked on long chains. Some had been lost a week before and others three hundred or a thousand years before. How old an object was didn't matter, though she often appreciated the long journey the item had taken to find her. All she sought was the glint in the starlight and to snatch the thing and bring it home. In the same vein, she didn't mind parting with them later, selling them to strangers who would only lose them again in a few years or a decade to complete the journey back to the river. The moment of discovery was the joy that sparked the magic inside her. The same for Mary when she spotted one of her corpse lights. To snatch it out of the air at first sight, that was the thrill.

Edwina's back was to the door when the shop bell finally chimed. She spun around eager to greet a new customer, but instead of encountering a woman out shopping for a knitting needle to match the one she'd bent or a young man hoping to find a ring for his intended, she saw *him*.

The man who should be dead.

He looked for all the world as if he still stood on Death's threshold, unsure of which direction to go. His squared jaw was rough with three days' worth of beard, and his eyes, bloodshot and full of anger, stared as he held firm to the doorframe to steady himself. A white cloth had been bandaged around his head. A faint brown stain bled through near the neck.

Edwina managed an innocent enough "May I help you?" before the deception fell away and the man closed the door behind him with a slam. The panic she'd kept tethered in place at the first sight of him broke free on the path between her heart and her mind. Not knowing what to do, she backed up until she bumped into the shelving behind her.

"I saw you," he said, his eyes taking a quick inventory of her attire, the merchandise in the shop, and the shawl hanging on the peg in the back room visible beyond the curtain.

She saw no weapon on him other than the simmering anger and fear that threatened to boil over. That and the confidence he was in the right, which he wielded as deftly as a blade as he locked the door and turned the sign in the window so it read CLOSED.

Edwina retreated another three steps to the side toward the back room. "I'm sure I don't know what you're talking about."

He caught her in his gaze again, recognition so sharp in his eyes it stopped her in her tracks. He knew her. Knew she'd hovered over him that morning. Oh, she'd been a fool to give in to her sister's whim. How could her instinct have been so wrong? What had she thought? That he'd be laid out under a white sheet by now, his death absolving her and Mary of any wrongdoing? Her guilt over what they'd done to the man's mind somehow interred in the grave alongside his cold-as-winter flesh?

"I think you know well enough," he said, glancing again at her hair and clothing.

"What do you want? Money? I haven't got much." Edwina eyed the jewelry case beside her with the new gold ring as she moved to stand behind the till. She'd sacrifice it, if she must.

But her question seemed to confuse him. He leaned against the door as if thinking to himself, trying to find the answer. She waited a precious moment for the welcome sound of her sister's return or a customer attempting to enter the shop, but no one jiggled the handle.

"You and another lass," he said as he staggered slightly. "You stood over me on the riverbank." He turned his chin to indicate the back of his head, but the movement pained him and he had to close his eyes for the briefest second before training them back on her. "You did this to me."

"I most certainly did not. You were already wounded." The response had raced out of her mouth nearly involuntarily. But with the denial she'd admitted she'd been there, and so she relented. "My sister found you unconscious on the foreshore."

"Mary." He was fishing, the way he dangled the name in front of her, waiting for her to bite and confirm it. He was less certain about the situation than when he'd entered the shop, though he found his confidence again soon enough. "You both stole something from me, something . . ." His face tightened in frustration when he couldn't form his thoughts into the right words. "Something important. Something I must have back." He stared at his empty hands before squeezing them into fists, as if he could grip the thing that eluded his mind.

"What is it you think I took?" Edwina knew the shame in her eyes betrayed her as soon as she looked away to avoid his scrutiny. She never could brave her way through a lying face. But only two others—she declined to call them victims—had ever been left alive when Mary took her baubles, and so she hoped to tease out exactly how much he'd observed. How much he remembered. And how much damage Mary had done to his mind and memory.

"Aye, so you admit you were there."

"It isn't what you think."

"Nae?" He advanced and tapped his finger pointedly against the counter glass. "Whatever you and your sister nicked from me, I'll be having it back. Now."

Mary had taken all the memories he held up to that point in time on the muddy bank, but she hadn't affected the new ones he'd formed since. And though he'd appeared dead to the world then, he apparently hadn't been unconscious the entire time. He remembered them standing over him. Knew they'd taken something from him. But how much could he truly know? Or understand? Whatever he might have seen would retail as a hallucination in the telling, coming from a man recovering from a head wound. Things might still be all right.

She studied him again in the shop light. He was no dock worker, judging by the cut of his jacket and trousers and the thick leather on his boot soles. No whiff of the fisherman on him, other than the damp of having collapsed on the shore. Had she been right about him being a ruffian, then? Or a drunkard still under the influence? Perhaps she could find a way to placate him after all.

Edwina slowly reached under the counter and retrieved the gold ring. There was no way for her to explain to a mortal what they'd truly taken, so a bit of gold would have to suffice. "Here," she said and slid the ring nestled in its velvet across the glass to him. "It's yours. Take it." And she meant her offer. She was proud of the find, but if the monetary value of the ring was enough to compensate for the harm they'd caused him, she could live with the loss. All settled, she thought, and restrained herself from actually brushing her hands together in a matching gesture.

"I'm in no mood for lies," the man warned, swiping the box and ring aside so that the gold bounced off the counter and rolled across the floor to lodge against the radiator. "And I think what you stole was a little shinier than that."

Whatever this man did to earn his keep in the world, he was being deliberately brutish in an attempt to intimidate her. Did it come naturally or was it for show? Edwina's mind raced to get ahead of his accusations. She didn't like to take advantage of mortals when it could be helped, but if he was willing to turn down gold, he was on the verge of becoming too agitated to reason with. Feeling cornered, she opened her mouth and formed the beginning of a tune.

"What are you doing?" He straightened with suspicion and reached for something beneath his jacket. "Why are you humming?"

But she wasn't humming. She was singing. A spell to put him to sleep. Dulcet as a lullaby but potent as chamomile mixed with lavender and warm milk. As she sang her melody, Edwina tried to be mindful of the man's head wound. She only needed him to fall into a light state of unconsciousness so she could think what to do without him badgering her. She refrained from hitting the high notes, keeping her tune soft and subtle. Soon enough his knees wobbled and he gripped the counter. He sank to the floor, crumpling in a pile much like the one he'd been in when they'd first encountered him.

"Dozy bloke." Edwina said a quick spell to dim the lights in the shop to make it harder to view them from the street, then knelt beside the man. "Now, what to do with you."

She cradled the man's head against an upside-down wicker basket while she squeamishly turned out his pockets. She'd hoped to learn who he was, but all she found were a few coins, a cold pipe, a skeleton key, a dirty knife with a trick blade—so a criminal after all—and a curious business card with indelible green ink that glimmered as she brought it up to her face to read.

A jolt went through her, stunned by the implication. It wasn't the enchanted lettering that made her jump but the name imprinted on it: Henry Elvanfoot.

Henry Elvanfoot!

There wasn't a witch worth her salt in all the isles who didn't know the name Elvanfoot. Henry, the old man, was a wizard of renown who'd discovered the secret of smokeless propellant used in the Seven Nations War. Said to be living in infamy and regret ever since in a quiet manor house in the north beside the River Clayborn, doggedly pursuing more useful inventions. But what was this man doing with Henry Elvanfoot's bloodstained business card in his pocket?

Edwina peeled back the front of the man's jacket. He'd been reaching for the pocket watch chained to his waistcoat just before he'd succumbed to her spell. Curious, she unhooked it from the button and held it in the palm of her hand. The metal did not carry the same smooth coolness of mortal gold. Instead the thing buzzed and ticked at the particle level, connecting with the energy coursing through her aura. On a hunch she flicked the cover open. Aside from a normal clockface with two hands that purported to keep track of the hours and minutes in the day, it contained several cogs and whirring wheels that revved up when she pushed the button on the side. She suspected it could be an astrolabe of some sort to chart the position of the stars, but if so, the means didn't become immediately clear. And yet the intricacy of the parts and the manner in which they moved proved conclusively it was no mortal instrument but rather some sort of wizardry at work.

She closed the watch and turned it over, expecting some reference to Henry Elvanfoot as the owner, having been stolen by the lout asleep on her shop floor. Conversely, she was surprised to find it revealed an altogether different clue on the back, though one that shed no further light on its owner. She glanced from the engraved initials on the watch to the unshaven man snoring at her side, and a vein of sympathetic curiosity opened inside her.

"Who are you, Mr. 'I.C.,' and what are you up to?"

There was no denying the obvious. The man on the floor, the one who would not die, must be witch-born. But then why hadn't he defended himself against her rather innocuous spell? Edwina studied his face again. Beneath the scruff of new beard, he wore a stern expression, even in unconsciousness, yet the lines in his face did not bear the tolerance of boorish cruelty, despite his attempt to bully her. Given the same circumstances, she would have done no less if someone had stolen something as precious from her as her memory, which his instinct clearly understood was the case even if he didn't remember. Leaning closer, she observed no deep-set grooves from a constant frown nor a wrinkled forehead from brows constantly pinched together in anger. Instead there were opposing parentheses at each corner of his mouth, perhaps made permanent from the effort of smiling and laughing. And there, just beneath his collar, was the faint glow of a magical aura. A remarkable transformation of her opinion followed, knowing they were kindred spirits. Her mood toward him changed considerably and she found herself wishing to help the brute any way she could.

Still, the disconnect between who she thought him to be and how he'd behaved when he confronted her still irked. Was it possible to forget something as inherent as one's magical identity? Curious that his talent hadn't come naturally to him like a reflex. She didn't think forgetting one was a witch would make them any less attuned to their magic, but perhaps one could suffer from a sort of magical amnesia under the right circumstances. Of course, that begged the question of what to do about the poor man's stolen memory.

She would never have attempted to restore the remembrances of an adult mortal, knowing how flighty and righteous they turned when even a hint of the supernatural threatened their worldview. But a witch was another matter. Even if his mind doubted her because of his lapse in understanding, his body would instinctively know, wouldn't it? It must or the man risked remaining as dull-witted as a common clodhopper the rest of his days.

Edwina listened a moment to the noise and bustle outside the shop door as she contemplated the risk. Perhaps there was time to do what she must. Returning his pocket watch to his waistcoat, she left the young man resting on the floor and ran up the stairs. She rummaged through the jewelry box atop the dresser, sorting through Mary's baubles. The new orb had to be among them. It was only this morning that Mary had put the thing away. Unlike for her sister, the remembrances always appeared vaguely similar to Edwina, but she knew the newest one, the one belonging to the man downstairs, had a vein of gold and a cobalt sheen unlike the others. Yet as she stirred the baubles around with her finger, there wasn't enough distinction between them to be sure which one it was. Perhaps guilt affected her eye's judgment as much as her ignorance. The remembrances belonged to Mary. Her sister doted over them, so proud of the shine and luster she was able to preserve with her magic. It wouldn't be right to take one without permission.

Her eye landed on the pressed flower given to her by a young man three years earlier. Freddie, so handsome and industrious, had wanted to marry her until circumstances forced her family to move from the small village under cover of darkness. He'd accused Mary of bewitchment after she'd enticed him into a shaded glen. There, he claimed she'd summoned a blue light out of his mouth. He was witch-born and no stranger to spells, but he'd feared for his life and stopped her the only way he could—with a kiss. After that he would have nothing more to do with the Blackwoods, nor would anyone else in the village. The blade of regret announced itself sharply in Edwina's side for the life she'd had to say no to in exchange for defending her sister once again. It was always Mary who strayed from the confines of conformity to reveal their nature as something otherworldly to be ridiculed and feared, even among their own kind, until there was no option but to flee in the middle of the night.

Normally Edwina wouldn't allow her resentment to surface—her love for her sister was above all else—but she let those feelings well up now, enough to fuel her courage so she could do what she must for the man downstairs. She owed him that. Despite his rough behavior, he was the injured party in this unfortunate matter. And there was something she could do to make things right. At least she was moderately confident she knew the spell for how to get the memory returned to him.

With a fresh sense of purpose, Edwina sorted through her sister's orbs again, this time noticing there were at least three of them with that bright vein of gold running through the deep blue. Still, one outshone the others with the way the gold glinted from the sheen of newness, so she snatched it up and returned to the shop just as the man roused from his spell-induced sleep.

Chapter Seven

His eyes felt sticky as he struggled to open them. After a disorienting and blurry moment, his vision cleared enough for him to recognize where he was. His brain took a moment longer to make sense of how he'd ended up asleep on the floor of a secondhand-junk shop. He sat up and patted his pockets to see if he'd been robbed yet again when the woman he'd been speaking to—the thief!—walked down the back-room stairway.

"You did something to me," he said, searching his pockets for his watch with greater effort.

The woman, dressed in black as though she wore widow's weeds, stopped with her hands held in front of her. By the way she cupped them together, she carried something small, fragile. Her face, unendowed with the blush of rare beauty yet with enough color in her cheeks to arouse interest, betrayed her surprise at seeing him awake. After a quick recovery, she attempted a smile, though it was only half-hearted at best. Like the sort of expression one makes when lying bold-faced to get what they want, he thought.

"You've merely had a short rest," she said.

The man remembered her singing something odd and lilting before his head drifted away into unconsciousness. The sensation of being under her influence was one of the very few things he had any memory of. However unlikely, he suspected that she'd somehow brought on this "short rest" against his will, as if she'd dosed him with a lungful of ether.

His hand landed on the cool, smooth gold of his watch with some relief. It might be broken, but the gold was worth something. Still groggy, he attempted to stand to be on equal footing with her, but the pain at the back of his head interfered like a blow from a hammer. "You've drugged me."

"Certainly not!" After objecting, she stepped nearer. "Please, sit down. You're in no state to stand, let alone confront anyone with false accusations."

He wanted to argue with her on that point, but the pain in his head and the dizziness overtaking his body won out. The woman guided him to a chair in the storeroom in the back, where he took advantage of her hospitality despite his distrust. Still, he scooted the chair against the wall so that she could not get behind him and leave his line of sight.

"What's that you've got?" He nudged his chin toward her closed hand as he adjusted the bandage wrapped around his head.

"I should probably take a look at that first," she said, ignoring him as she slipped the thing he'd asked about in her apron pocket. If not for the dizziness, he would have resisted. Instead he gave his consent, arguing in his mind why he should have done such a thing. There was something strange yet compelling about the young woman. Certainly, she was pleasant enough for a thief. Intelligent. Thoughtful. Somewhat charming. He didn't know why he had an instinct for such things, but he was sure she was also hiding something. There was a great reservoir of mystery beyond what he'd confronted her about. Yet he could not deny she had a certain skill as she peeled the gauze away from his wound, making an almost imperceptible clucking noise as she inspected the gash.

"You're right about my sister and me," she said. "We did take something from you, but as I tried to state earlier, it isn't what you think."

"Look, Miss—"

"Blackwood." The young woman pulled away so she could look him in the eye. "Edwina Blackwood," she said, as if the full name might mean something to him. It didn't, and yet the fibers holding his muscle and bones together buzzed on alert, sending a tiny shiver skittling under his flesh.

He nodded in acknowledgment, despite the strangeness of exchanging pleasantries with one of the women who'd robbed him and likely taken part in knocking him unconscious. Possibly twice. Relying on their uneasy truce, he studied his surroundings. Though the shop up front struck him as normal enough, the back room was overrun with odd books with locks on their covers and bundles of dried herbs tacked to the beams overhead. A small desk with a cupboard held a mortar and pestle. Above was a shelf of unmarked jars filled with concoctions he'd rather not study too closely. Spiderwebs had been left untouched in the corners of the room so long they sagged from the weight of their collected dust.

Smiling in a reassuring manner, she rummaged through the small cabinet to his left. He leaned forward out of curiosity and saw the doors were decorated with indecipherable symbols painted in black and gold. From a shelf in the middle she took out a bottle containing a brownish-green botanical swimming in glossy fluid.

"Miss Blackwood, I am at a loss. First you rob me, of what I canna say, though I know it be of value enough for me to leave my hospital bed to retrieve it, and then you offer to doctor your victim?"

"Victim? Really, I hardly think that's fair, Mister . . ." She stopped herself after dabbing some of the murky liquid onto a cloth. "Are you able to remember what the *I.C.* stands for?" She nudged her chin toward his waistcoat. "Your watch. It bears your initials, does it not?"

She'd gone through his pockets. *Damn the woman.*

"I was told my name was Henry Elvanfoot." Saying the name out loud, he knew without a doubt it couldn't be true. All the same, he produced the card as proof.

"Oh, I don't think so." Miss Blackwood pressed the cloth to his head and uttered a peculiar yet soothing rhyme under her breath. In moments, the pain subsided along with his dizziness. "Sir Elvanfoot is a man held in the highest regard. You, on the other hand, present yourself as a . . ." She held her thought to herself for a moment behind tight lips before continuing. ". . . a man of no particular renown that I'm aware of. I mean no disrespect, of course. Only an observation."

Suspicious again that she'd even heard of the man whose bloodied card he carried, he stood, testing his balance, and asked, "And how do you know this Henry Elvanfoot?"

"He's quite famous. Sir Henry Elvanfoot is a master wizard who has done more for the cause of bringing the talents of magical folk out of the dark ages than just about anyone in the last two hundred and fifty years."

"What's that you're on about?" His brow twitched, and he wondered if he hadn't fallen into a hallucination from the stuff she'd dabbed against his head. "Wizards and magical folk?"

"We have more to offer the world than merely curing warts and cursing blaggards."

Responding to his basest fear, he grabbed her wrist before she could back away. "You're mad as a hare."

"I assure you I'm not." Her gaze traveled deliberately from his eyes to his grip on her arm to the calling card he held in his other hand. "I have every reason to believe you have witch blood or I wouldn't even be having this conversation with you."

"Oh, I'm a witch, am I? Not a wizard or maybe a unicorn?"

"Don't be absurd. You've got magic in you," she said with a nod. "Though what kind I cannot say. I suspect any recollection of your innate talent was drawn out alongside your other memories. Unfortunate, but I think we can work around it."

He hadn't let go, but her hand and wrist somehow shrank beneath his grip so that he held only air, while she finished spouting some nonsense rhyme with a pitying look on her face.

"Now, I don't know if it will help," she said as if nothing had happened, "but perhaps if you concentrate on using your intuition, you might recall your true name. It would make things so much easier. Is it Ivan? Idris? Or Innis perhaps?"

"Ian," he answered absentmindedly, the name coming to him out of the ether while he still stood distracted by the unnatural phenomenon of his now empty grasp. Then realizing what he'd said, he lifted his head at the sharp certainty of remembering. "Ian. My name is Ian. How did you do that?"

"Oh, thank goodness. I was afraid Mary had taken it all."

Gibberish again from this infernal woman!

"Mark me, Miss Blackwood: I am sorely tempted to drag you down to the nearest police station to explain yourself. You speak in riddles. Nae, of witchcraft. Of falsehoods. But I want the truth. Answer me plain! Or I'll make good on my threat."

"I understand you're upset. The details must all feel rather confusing in your current state." The woman took a calming breath before continuing. "Plainly speaking, Ian, I'm referring to your current state of amnesia. That is the difficult concept I wish to convey. What my sister stole from you—what *we* stole from you—was your memory." He gaped fish-mouthed, so she explained. "When a person dies and the mind has no more use for it, the vapors holding on to all those memories escape the body. My sister is able to capture those thoughts as they rise and solidify them as keepsakes. But I believe I can restore yours back to you, if you'll only give me the benefit of the doubt for a few moments."

The woman produced from her pocket a shiny blue-and-gold marble that shimmered when she opened her palm. She claimed again it was his, siphoned off his body while he'd floated in the veil that separated the living from the dead. It was impossible. Nonsense. Hysteria from a woman not in control of her faculties. And yet his blood and nerves, if they were to be believed, found truth in her words, rushing with a sort of excitement under the skin. The tension he'd been holding on to in his shoulders fell away. The crease between his brows relaxed. Curiosity took over his mind as questions he couldn't possibly know to ask positioned themselves in his mouth. Questions about charms and spells and veins of untapped energy, of which he could avow he knew nothing yet craved their comfort.

He pressed his fingers to the back of his head. No new blood came away and there was no tenderness. Whatever she'd done with her oil and words had mended him. But he was not well. No sane person put stock in the body's reaction, relying on nerves, muscle, and bone to decipher truth from fiction. The woman wasn't mad; he was.

She watched him thinking, making a plea with her eyes for him to listen and understand. Maybe he had been bewitched. Or possessed. Panicked by his reaction, he could not remain a moment longer and have either confirmed.

"I must be gone from this place. From you." He strode out of the back room until confronted by the shop's locked front door. A turn of the latch and he'd be on the street. Swallowed whole by a world in which he knew not a single soul. His fingers trembled on the doorknob, but something held him back. In the short time he'd been in her shop, she'd given him back his name. What more could she restore?

His determination to leave receded like a chill in the blood when chased away by stiff drink. He leaned his forehead against the door in a state of indecision.

"Yes, in your current state of mind, I must appear the fiend in the night. I don't mean to alarm you, Ian."

He didn't turn, yet he knew she'd come within a few feet of him. He could sense her nearness as her strange energy skittered along the hairs on his arms, his body again signaling a reaction that his mind couldn't make sense of.

"We belong to a very old bloodline, my sister and I. And you," she said. He heard the rustle of fabric, as if she'd shrugged. "Most refer to us as witches. Sorcerers. Conjurers. Wizards. And sometimes heretics."

He'd been hit on the head harder than he knew. Perhaps he was still unconscious and lying in a hospital bed. This woman and her confabulations were a mere dream he'd yet to wake from.

"I wouldn't share this with you if I didn't believe you'd understand on some instinctual level, even in your current state of not knowing who you are. As for your missing memory, I wouldn't even attempt to restore it if I thought you just another dull mortal."

He spun around. "Why not?"

"They fear us. And the things we can do. Always so certain our motives are sinister and full of bloodlust. Isn't that some of what you're feeling right now?" Miss Blackwood took a step closer and held her hand out to reveal the gemstone once more. "It will require your cooperation, both heart and mind, for the transfer, but I can give you back your memory."

The more she talked, the more it felt like his mind was reaching for a rope of understanding that was just out of grasp. Was it possible he lived in a world inhabited with magic, but the mind had lost all memory of such things? But that was absurd. Wasn't it?

"Your watch, Ian. Remove it. Study the face. That's no mortal tool. You'd know that simple truth without the benefit of remembering how the thing works."

He opened the watch and the gears spun to life. A faint whirring sound started up, and on the inside of the watch's cover, a sort of map appeared. He felt a brief tingle, light as a feather across his skin, as he held the gold. Why hadn't it worked before? He snapped it shut. Fear made him want to run again from the room, run from the city. Yet where would he go? He knew no one. Counting the doctor, the policeman, and the nurse, his longest conversation with anyone that he could remember was with the woman standing before him. The one telling him she held his memories—his life—in her palm.

"What do I do?" he asked.

She held the orb to his lips and told him to hold it in his mouth but not to swallow. Not yet. He was willing, and yet a nagging doubt persisted. "How do I know it's mine?"

Miss Blackwood pointed out the vein of gold shimmering along the orb's surface, the deep lapis lazuli blue, and flecks of black visible with the aid of the sunlight coming through the windows. "The newest ones have a certain gleam to them," she said. "Do you see how bright it shines? They tend to wear to a duller finish after a few months."

He made a brief inspection of the stone, not really knowing what to believe about its sheen. Relying on some faith he did not recognize, he took the stone in his mouth, even as he trembled from fear that he would choke. The weight of the gem made him want to spit it out as the hard stone pressed against his tongue. Miss Blackwood rested her finger against his lips, perhaps knowing how his mouth rebelled. But soon his ears filled with the sound of a soft melody that calmed the trembling. She hummed the tune first, and then the words followed.

"Feel the weight upon your tongue. Breathe air and light into your lungs. Muscle, blood, and marrow bone. Accept this memory as your own. Remember all you've ever known."

The room seemed to fade until it was just the two of them standing in a tunnel of darkness. No sound but her voice. No scent but her breath softly singing. When she finished, she nodded for him to go ahead. He swallowed the orb, feeling the hard sphere slide down his throat and graze the walls of his esophagus. It hit his stomach and he feared he'd made a deadly mistake. The thing knocked hard against his insides, and he doubled over, clutching his middle with both arms.

"Concentrate on making the memory dissolve."

Ian closed his eyes and willed the thing sitting in his gut to return his life to him. Deep in the pit of his stomach, the pain softened until he could stand straight again without feeling like he was going to be sick. Vivid dreamlike scenes sparked in his mind. Images of arched doorways, men sleeping upright behind a rope, and crooked grins on dirty faces emerged, before they slipped away again in the mist.

The witch assured him it might take some time for the magic to fully integrate, but he should be "right as rain" in no time at all. She invited him to stay, but he could not abide the confines of the witch's company another moment. He craved the sunlight and air. And so he said a weak "thank you" and prepared to leave her shop with his pocket watch, his bloodied knife, and a head full of crosshatched images that one minute made sense and the next were like looking at a stranger's photos on the mantel.

With the witch's assurances encouraging him, he buttoned his jacket and readied himself to face the street. His hand rested on the doorknob when it turned of its own accord beneath his grip. The door rattled open, despite being locked, and a young woman with dark hair and eyes that smoldered like smoky quartz entered the shop.

"Edwina, why is the door locked in the middle of the day?" the young woman asked before awkwardly acknowledging the man standing in her way. "Oh, it's you."

The woman—the sister, he believed—went white with worry before the witch reassured her all was right again.

But was it? His thoughts were a jumble and his emotions worn down to a nub after the ordeal. What he wanted, nae what he needed, was a draft of ale and smoke of his pipe in a noisy pub where he could disintegrate into the crowd and forget everything again. The sisters began to bicker about privacy and personal property. So, when the newly arrived sister ratcheted up her argument with Miss Blackwood, he recalled a corner pub, as natural as could be, not three lanes over that he'd often found camaraderie in before and left them behind without a second look back.

Chapter Eight

Hours later, with the shop closed and their supper eaten, Edwina and Mary retreated to the roof to sit under the stars, as they often did on clear evenings. With their hair loose and their shawls wrapped snugly around their nightdresses, they watched the sky and tried not to inhale too deeply the city smells of coal smoke and fried fish that drifted out of every other chimney. Though the sisters sat shoulder to shoulder as they always did, the matter between them still gnawed like mice nibbling at the woodwork.

"I wasn't sure you'd join me tonight," Edwina said at last.

"Whyever not?" Mary withdrew two cordial glasses and a half-empty bottle of sherry she'd been hiding beneath her shawl.

"I violated your privacy," Edwina said as her sister pulled the cork from the bottle. "I know how you feel about your baubles. Each one unique and special. And yours."

"You shouldn't have taken it." Mary poured the sweet wine into one of the petite glasses and offered it to Edwina. "But I understand why you did, even though I don't know how you could have known the right spell to return the man's memories." She poured herself a glass and stuffed the cork back in the bottle.

They'd been through this sort of episode before, she reminded her sister, though how she could have forgotten was beyond belief. Despite their attempts at conformity, Mary's unusual magic always seeped out into the open. Like static in the air, it raised the hairs on those who got too close. Boys were the worst. Always spying on them when their curiosity had been roused. First the boys in their home village. Then every village they'd lived in since. And now that awful nipper that kept hovering outside their shop door with his nose pressed to the glass. All she and Mary wanted was to be left alone, but to wear an air of strangeness in a crowd of sameness always found them out.

Edwina cradled her glass of sherry with two hands. "I was with Father that time you stole Billy Thisbury's memory after he'd fallen off the roof and had the breath knocked out of him. You'd run down to the river to hide when you found out he wasn't dead. I found you and convinced you to give me the orb, and then I held it for Father while he composed his spell to return the memories to the boy."

"We were only thirteen. How could you have remembered the words of his spell ten years later? We didn't even have proper grimoires yet."

Edwina grinned mischievously. "Father sang the words."

Mary nodded as if finally understanding something that had long been a mystery. "Ah, because he knew you'd have need of the spell one day. To protect some half-witted mortal from my fiendish habit. Because I'm too simple to control my impulses."

Edwina denied her sister's conclusions, though she'd often privately wondered the same, since their father knew she could remember any spell if it was sung in a tune. "You know he's in awe of your gift, Mary. We all are. It's a rare and beautiful talent."

"Then why did we have to flee our home in the middle of the night with nothing but our luggage after that boy cried about it? He should have just died like the rest of them."

"You know why," Edwina said, letting her sister's callous comment go. "And, anyway, it was a long time ago." She took Mary's hand in hers. "Am I forgiven?"

Mary made a show of thinking about it, but she'd already poured the glasses for the toast. "Forgiven," she said.

It was not their habit to drink from their father's cabinet. They rarely touched the stuff. There were times, however, when pacts were made or fences mended, that only the elixir of alcohol could provide the proper tribute required. And so they clinked their glasses and drank the sherry, feeling the alcohol settle softly in their stomachs.

With their quarrel drowned by sweet wine, they conferred with the constellations. Fixed but not rigid, the stars hung in the sky as true as any map consulted by the lost. All one needed was to know where they wanted to go, and the stars would tell them when and where to put their foot on the path. The art, though, was in the interpretation.

Mary drew her knees up and tucked her feet under the hem of her nightgown. "Do you think he'll come back?"

"Ian? I patched his head and returned his memories. I don't think he'll bother us again. He won't say anything, once the memories of his life get reabsorbed. We won't have to run this time." Edwina paused, letting a smile show in the corner of her mouth. "Though it is kind of a shame he won't be back. He was rather easy to look at, wasn't he?"

"No," Mary corrected. "I meant Father. It's been three months now."

"Oh." Edwina covered up the embarrassment of talking about Ian so plainly by sipping the last drop of her sherry and then cradling the rim of the glass against her lips as she thought. "There's still been no word about where he's gone. It's impossible to say when or if he'll return."

"But he's left." Mary rested her head on her knees. "Just like Mum."

"We don't know that yet."

But however much she wanted to disagree with her sister's assumptions, it was the most likely outcome. Their mother had disappeared in much the same manner. A kiss, a wave, a promise to return, and then they never saw her again. A year later and they still didn't know whether she was alive or dead. They hadn't given up on her, but she no longer preoccupied their hearts with the hope of return.

They tilted their faces to the constellations again. With the century coming to an end, the sisters had been studying their star charts with more vigor and knew a disturbing Saturn-Pluto conjunction in Cancer was corkscrewing nearer each day. A sign of struggle to come. Long suffering. The kind one sees in prolonged war. The perfect conditions were ticking away in the cosmos, waiting for the constellations to revolve toward each other and ignite events into motion. It would come in their lifetimes, but not today.

"Do you think Mother and Father left because of me?" Mary asked. "Because of how I am?"

It always pinched Edwina's heart to hear her sister talk about herself as somehow being damaged goods. She was rare. Different. They both were. And that sort of thing always drew unwanted scrutiny. People always wanting an explanation for why they were so odd and then running away in fear the moment they got even a slight glimpse of the truth. Moving to the city had been their father's final attempt at settling the family safely. A way to fall so deep into an anonymous stream of mortals and witches there was little chance they'd be noticed. Just another pair of stones at the bottom of the rushing river. And they'd been happy setting up the new shop. Perfectly ordinary and upstanding. But then that horrid boy showed up to stir old vulnerabilities to the surface, at least for Edwina.

She slipped her arm around her sister's. "No, of course not, my darling. Whatever drew Father away was of his own making. He'll get in touch when he has reason."

The tears had already started, but then Mary sniffled and shut them off. She shook her head to clear away any more attempts at self-pity. "Do you think he'll be okay?"

"Father? Of course. He can certainly take care of himself."

Mary grinned. "No, I meant your Ian."

"Goodness, he's not *my* Ian." Edwina blushed in what must have been a brilliant shade of pink. "But I do hope—believe—he'll recover without incident."

Mary wondered aloud if Ian had remembered anything of consequence yet or if this sort of rehabilitation spell took time to settle and show the effects. She had a point. With that awful Billy Thisbury, the family had left before either of them saw their schoolmate back to his normal bullying self. Perhaps she should have made Ian stay longer to ensure the spell had worked. But then he'd said he could feel the memories returning, filling in the blank spots in his mind. Hadn't he?

Mary pointed to a shooting star as it zipped across the sky, then fizzled. "I suppose everyone leaves in the end, don't they? But not you, sister. Promise we'll always have each other."

Edwina squeezed her sister's hand, assuring her she'd spoken a holy vow out loud. Forever and for always, they would have each other to rely on in this life, even if no one else would have them.

They each had one more nip of sherry before Edwina announced she was going to bed. Mary remained behind on the rooftop, saying she was going to stay out a little longer to stretch her limbs. The confines of the city had been hard on them both after living in the fresh air all their lives. More so for Mary, who seemed to bask in her nighttime freedom.

The instinct to reach an arm around her sister and encourage her to go back inside welled up within Edwina until she nearly sang a subtle sleeping charm to make her stay home. Instead she said good night, knowing she would lie awake on her side until her sister slipped back in through the window hours later smelling of all the wicked things the night air had to offer.

Chapter Nine

Ian, or whatever the hell his name was, stumbled out the door of the doss-house a few minutes before ten the next morning. A sharp pain stabbed his temple. He half wished his head would snap off his neck and roll down the pavement without him. He'd drunk too much ale down at the pub the night before. As punishment, his sleep had been filled with strange dreams. Nae, they'd been nightmares. The frightening details eluded him in the daylight, though a vague notion of his face being pressed nose down against wet bricks and musty straw lingered, leaving him jittery. The unsettled feeling clung to his mood like spiderwebs as he stepped into the street, his stomach full of watery gruel that threatened to erupt.

For the fifth time that morning, he checked his pockets, then buttoned his jacket against the chill. The coins, watch, knife, and pipe were still there. The key and business card, too, though what good they were to him he couldn't say. He also had no clue what had driven him to stay in such a seedy place overnight. He had a little money. Must have a home somewhere. Yet his feet had carried him to the flophouse the night before without a second thought after his head wobbled from the drink. He'd obviously trod the path before and so he'd obeyed the impulse, though a part of him rested uneasy that he was so familiar with such a disreputable house, where men and women slept in the same bed out in the open.

He was still standing on the stoop beneath the doss-house sign when a man exited behind him. The reek of ale and urine floated off the man in a cloud. He couldn't have known anyone in such an establishment, but there in the daylight he recognized the man's face. He remembered the gap in his teeth, the bloodshot streak in his eyes, the flatcap with the grease stain on the brim.

Overcome with relief at recognizing someone, anyone, he called out, "Charlie! That you?"

The man gave him the once-over. "Do I know you?"

"'Course you do. You're Charlie Dunham. We had a laugh down at the Hare and Hound 'bout a week ago." He let the memory rise without forcing it. "You had money in your pocket after pawning a pair of gentleman's boots that happened to walk their way into your lap, and I'd got me a lucky day's wage at the docks. Don't you remember?"

Charlie pulled the stub of a cigarette out from behind his ear, so Ian patted his pockets for his match safe with the mermaid decoration on the outside to give him a light but instead found a pocketful of a stranger's belongings. He feared he'd grabbed the wrong jacket from inside the doss-house.

Charlie looked both ways over his shoulders, impatient-like. "I been to the Hare and Hound regular, sure, but I don't reckon we've ever met," he said and lit his own match.

"'Course we have," Ian insisted. "It's your ol' Jake here. Jake Donovan." He could remember the night as plain as could be. They'd pooled their coins for several pints each and stayed until close before going their separate ways and sleeping rough in the public square. But his recollection was flimsy. More akin to having studied a photograph of the event until he recognized every detail yet was nowhere in the picture himself. As if he were an impostor. Same as the name that had spilled out of his mouth so quickly—false and foreign to him, while at the same time familiar enough to say without thinking.

"Nah, go on," the man said. "I know a Jake. Old fella used to hang out around these parts, but I ain't seen him in a couple of weeks now. Must be someone else you're thinking of, mate. I can't say as I ever laid eyes on you before in my life, 'cepting last night." The man in the greasy flatcap pointed his thumb at the doss-house before trotting off down the lane and offering a final wave. "Get all kinds in there."

"Maybe it was longer ago than I remember," Ian said as the man turned down a second lane and walked out of sight.

He'd sincerely thought he'd remembered the man. Believed what Miss Blackwood had said was true, that his memory had been restored. Parts of his mind did seem to recognize places and names he hadn't the day before, but it was all still a jumble. The whole thing had to be some grand joke. Or more likely a scam. He'd been hit on the head and robbed, and when he'd come demanding the thing the women had taken from him, he'd been played the chump. Conned and swept out the door with a story of witches and spells. He had half a mind to walk back to the shop and drag the police there with him and have the charlatans arrested.

Feeling himself the fool, Ian ambled in the general direction the man before him had, only turning right instead of left at the next street. He walked some ways with his hands in his pockets, avoiding eye contact with strangers he passed lest he mistakenly believe he knew them too. His mood turned foul when he remembered his odd watch and how the woman—the sister with the hazel eyes like polished agate—remarked that it was proof of his magical ability. *What a load of shite.* Humoring himself, he removed the watch from his waistcoat pocket and studied the outside. There *was* something peculiar about the way the timepiece behaved, and something even stranger about the way his body reacted to seeing it in someone else's hands. His curiosity sparked, he stepped out of the flow of human traffic to make a closer inspection.

The latch clicked open easily with a flick of his thumbnail. The gears whizzed and spun to life. He leaned against the wall behind a man selling ginger cakes from a tray strapped around his neck. He hadn't forgotten how a watch worked. This one simply defied logic. Letting the piece rest in his palm with the cover open at a ninety-degree angle, he inched his face closer to try to understand the strange mechanisms operating inside. His breath clouded against the gold, and he swore a shape began to form and hover over the maplike layout on the inside cover.

"What you got there, mister?"

A young scamp dressed in an oversize shirt and trousers watched him with greedy eyes from beside a binman's cart in the lane.

"Nothing that concerns you."

"Might be. I know a man what'll give you a good price for a watch like that. Follow me. I'll take you to him, I will."

Right, and I get jumped in some back room by a band of street kids.

"Move on," Ian said with more bravado than he knew he possessed. His nerve was paired with a threatening look, judging by the way the boy scurried off. He snapped the watch shut and kept his eye on the scamp until he was halfway down the road. After he'd gone, Ian made a sweep with his eyes left and right, checking doorways and windows for accomplices, though he didn't know why. Only that it felt like the natural thing to do after the encounter with the sharp-eyed boy.

The throbbing in his temples returned twofold. This was more than a hangover from strong drink. He feared he was becoming seriously ill. Needing to move, he staggered in the opposite direction of the overly curious boy. There was a distinct familiarity about the lane he'd gone down—the buildings, the doorways, even the smell of fried kidneys sizzling in a pan somewhere. Was this the road where he lived? Worked? But then, where? Which door? Which of these people were his kin? Why wouldn't the truth come to him so he could go home? He wished someone would stick a head out a window and wave hello and call him up, but all he heard above the din of the street was the slam of a door and the wail of an infant crying for its mother.

A stabbing pain hit his temple. He blinked until the ache subsided, then took a second glance at the dodgy lane. What had once felt familiar enough to call home now offended his senses. A dilapidated stairway on his right appeared as if the boards were barely clinging to the side of the building by two unlucky screws. A cluster of bairns squatted next to the gutter eating bread and butter as fresh rivulets of filth flowed by. Their wraithlike mothers, hovering inside narrow doorways that stood toe to toe with the road, watched over small tables of hand-knitted goods, asking mere pennies for each. The women, cradling fussy babes wrapped in brown flannel on their shoulders, eyed him suspiciously as he passed without buying.

How could he have thought these surroundings familiar? He'd never been on this street before in his life. Impossible. He'd never laid eyes on this part of the city. Confused by his own opposing thoughts, he ducked into a narrow passageway that cut between buildings. No wider than two men if they dipped their shoulders when they met, he somehow knew the alley connected the parallel-running main thoroughfares of Flint Street and Queen's Road so that the walker didn't have to circumnavigate the entire length of either to get to the other side. The deeper into the passage he traveled, the more the light dimmed, until the shadows grew so thick a man could barely see his own feet in the middle of the day.

Such a sense of dread pervaded Ian's thoughts halfway through the passage that sweat dampened his skin until his shirt clung to his back. His heartbeat sped up to a gallop. He knew he ought to stop. Go back the way he'd come. Yet he could not turn back. Again, he *knew* this place by its smell—the cool fragrance of mold that rose off the walls, the tinge of urine soaked into the stone and straw underfoot, and something saltier that hung in the air. At night, he knew, there would be braziers lit to guide the way, but they only made the darkness of the narrow space more profound as soon as you stepped outside their glow. It ought not be a long walk from one street to the other, but there were nooks and corners and short steps up and down that had been added to accommodate the bones of a medieval city whose old walls jutted out like elbows against the new.

Ian's hand instinctively reached out to feel the wall as he negotiated a blind corner. As he did, a man approached from the opposite end. There was nothing to suggest he was anything but a cobbler or leather-worker traveling from one end of the close to the other, same as him. Yet a sense of déjà vu struck Ian straight in the pocket where a man hides his most primal fear. His heart, already at a run, beat so hard he thought he might collapse where he stood. There'd been nothing about the man that threatened, not even the whiff of alcohol on his breath. But after they passed each other, Ian became so disoriented he had to hold on to the wall until he slid down on wobbly knees that could no longer hold him up.

Images swarmed in his mind like blackbirds—a man with a club in his hand; the crack of his head splitting open; his face hitting the paving stones; blades of straw poking into his cheek. Ian huddled in a corner of the passageway with his hands drawn over his head to protect himself from the scenes that would not cease. And yet they swooped at him without mercy. Memories of a razor-thin pain across his neck. The catch of breath in his windpipe. The choking reek of blood spluttering into his mouth. The life draining from his body as the blood spilled across the paving stones. A scream reduced to a drowning gurgle. And then nothing but a floating weightlessness and the absence of thought and light as his head hit the pavement, coming nose to tip with a pair of bloody brogues with stitching across the top. Then a flash of a beautiful girl with golden hair. A stranger to him, and yet he was sure she was his daughter, Molly. But he had no daughter.

Confusion caved in on Ian. He gripped his head with both hands, believing his mind was splitting in two. He had curled up on his side to ride out the wave of nausea when someone nudged his shoulder. He didn't know if a week, a day, or only a few minutes had passed when he opened his eyes again.

"What's happened to you, then?"

A boy carrying a bucket and broom stared down at him as if he were merely another grown man passed out in the alleyway. The strange images faded, taking the pain with them, but the trembling remained. He was wrung out, confused, and very afraid he was losing his mind. He pulled his hand away from his throat expecting to see it soaked in blood, but there was only the muck of the street. A final tremor ravaged his nerves. The boy, not hearing an answer, shrugged and turned to walk away.

"Wait," Ian called out, wiping his nose and eyes with the sleeve of his jacket. "Help me."

The boy was an honest-looking lad. Cautious too. He kept his distance in the passage while he waited for Ian to sit up. "What you want from me?"

What did he want? He needed help, but the police weren't the answer. Nor the hospital, which was no better than a jail. A last dark vision flew across his thoughts. A black skirt and a blue light imposed against it. He saw the scene from above, as if he were floating in the sky. The boy asked again, and he shook himself free of the vision. He dug in his pocket for his money and handed the boy a shiny coin.

"Half now and the other half when you return."

Ian explained what he wanted the boy to do, waited until he agreed, then leaned his head against the brick wall long enough to come out of the fog of a dead man's memory of being murdered.

Chapter Ten

The hired hansom cab slowed to a stop in front of a coffeehouse. Edwina had plenty of time to consider why she'd been summoned on the mile-long journey through the congested streets. The boy had described the man as being in a terrible state and having some sort of fit. She imagined any number of things that might have gone wrong for Ian. He might have been robbed or beaten, or perhaps he'd made good on his promise of visiting a pub and discovered he didn't like who he remembered himself to be when he drank. "Might be dead already," the boy had warned when he'd shown up inside her shop, eyes wide with wonder at all the shiny objects for sale.

The boy looked much less sure of his prediction as he followed Edwina out of the cab and pointed. On the other side of the street, Ian sat inside a doorway, hunched over and holding his jacket tight around him as he pressed a white-knuckled fist against his lips. He made an attempt to stand by holding on to the wall when he noticed her cross the road, but Edwina told him to stay where he was and knelt beside him.

"How bad is it? You look a fright." Edwina took out a bundle of herbs from her purse and gently crushed them with her fingers so that their aroma released under his nose.

"I dinna know what's happening to me," he began, but then the boy interrupted, asking for his payment.

"Delivered her like you asked."

"Never mind that," Edwina said. "Help me get him to the cab and I'll pay twice what he owes you."

Once the boy recovered from the promise of newfound riches, he got his shoulder under one side of Ian while Edwina lifted from the other. Between them they held his body upright long enough for him to stagger to the cab. Edwina gave the boy a gold coin she'd found in the mud a fortnight earlier, thanked him for his honesty, and then instructed the driver to return to the shop posthaste, offering him a twin of the coin she'd given the boy. As they pulled away, Ian collapsed against her shoulder, muttering about his brain splitting in two and "so much blood." She soothed him with a tune, humming a healing spell as they rolled through the city, wondering what had gone so terribly wrong.

By the time the cab returned to the shop, Ian had recovered enough strength to walk inside under his own power. Mary met them at the door. "Goodness, what happened to him?"

"Something went wrong with the spell," Edwina answered. "Quick, help me get him upstairs."

"Upstairs?" Mary locked the shop door and checked the street as if looking for nosy neighbors spying on them. "Wherever do you mean to put him?"

"Father's bed. He can rest there until I get this sorted."

Mary muttered something about propriety and regret, then begrudgingly helped get the man up the stairs and laid out on the folding bed. They managed to remove his boots and get him under a quilt, while he moaned about the blood in his throat and the pain at the back of his head. He wrestled with his covers and his brow grew damp with sweat, so Mary offered to fetch a cool cloth and some hot tea to settle him.

Edwina inspected him for any bleeding but found no new wounds—only the one that had preceded their acquaintance. Fearing his injury was internal, she held her palm to his forehead and said, "There now, Ian, you're all right." But he was far from all right. Something had gone terribly wrong. His mind and body were rejecting either the spell or the memory, yet she had no cure for either.

"Why do you keep calling me by that name? What is this place? What're you doing to me? Help!" he screamed. "Help me!"

He'd been more sober in the cab, responding to the name Ian without issue. Even then he'd slipped in and out of lucidity, sometimes eyeing her with suspicion and pulling away and other times squeezing her hand and thanking her for coming to get him. But what had gone wrong? She'd done the spell exactly right, hadn't she? *Curse Father for his selfish wandering!* He'd have known what to do, while she was left to guess, possibly destroying a man's mind in the process.

Mary returned with the cool cloth on a tray along with a small teapot, cup, and dainty pitcher of milk. "Any better?"

Edwina took the cloth and pressed it against Ian's forehead. He was merely warm to the touch, yet he writhed as if he suffered from brain fever. "No, something's not right," she said, regaining her confidence. "I'm certain I did the spell correctly, so it must be the memory itself. Perhaps too much time had elapsed to return it to him?" She turned to Mary. "What should we do? Can you remove the memory from him again?" Ian let out the strangest noise in his throat, as if he were drowning. "Oh, Mary, you must. Now!"

Her sister was hesitant. She watched Ian as she poured the tea she'd prepared. "Do you think it wise to continue interfering? With his mind, I mean. What if we make him worse? I'm not sure either of us has the skill to bring him back from that kind of damage."

Before Edwina could answer, the poor man collapsed from his fit. His face was drenched in sweat and his skin had paled to the hue of uncooked cod, but at least he'd stopped thrashing. All the fear and tension had been released with unconsciousness, and yet he remained a man in need of urgent remedy. Edwina ignored her sister and unpacked her vials and herbs. She had to do something to help him.

As Edwina set a course in her mind for which spell to use to ease his suffering, a small yet forceful voice admonished them from the corner of the room. "You must do this thing now!" it said.

Startled, the sisters twisted around to see a creature standing no taller than the brass footrail at the end of the bed. His hair was shaggy and unkempt, and he wore a dingy green wool coat with red-and-brown plaid trousers. His face was not exactly ugly. It was humanlike, only the features were more exaggerated—the lips thin but the mouth oversize, the eyes round and curious, and the nose slightly puggish. His feet, large and shaggy, were unshod and made no sound as he climbed onto the bed to better view the man lying there.

"Stars above, where did you come from?" Edwina stood to put some distance between herself and the intruder until she understood more clearly what his intentions were. "Who are you and how did you get in here?"

"Yes, explain yourself," Mary said, holding the cup and saucer with perfect poise as she studied the little imp. Mary was always the cool one when it came to confrontation, though Edwina often wondered whether the trait came from confidence or mere indifference.

The hairy thing carried a satchel across his body. He ignored their questions and removed the leather bag as he inched even closer to Ian, whose head rested at an awkward angle on the pillow. The creature squinted and reached a hand out to touch the sleeping man's arm. Edwina had never met one, but she believed him to be a hearth elf of some kind. At least he fit the description she'd read about in her spell books. Scraggly and wild, with traces of soot on his jacket, face, and hands. But what was he doing in their home in the city?

"That's quite far enough," she warned.

"As you wish, milady." The hairy being bowed his head, though he continued to stare with animated concern toward Ian. "But there isn't much time left. If the witch sister is able, she must do her magic. And then I can do mine." He rubbed his hands together, fretting. "Or what mind he has left will be lost to us both."

Mary and Edwina exchanged a quick sisterly look that expressed an entire conversation between them. Mary set the cup of tea down and bent over Ian's chest. She checked once more with Edwina, then put one palm on the man's chest and the other on his head. "I'm not sure what will come out," she said. "If he were closer to death, it would be easier, but at least he's unconscious." The creature squealed in distress. "Very well," she said and pushed.

Two small orbs of blue light rose up from the man's mouth, though the energy of one appeared to be enveloped by shadowy, cancerous-looking tendrils. Edwina was accustomed to seeing her sister's magic done at the hospital, where the elderly and infirm often succumbed to sickness. It had proved the most humane way for Mary to honor her unique magic, taking only from those who naturally crossed the threshold of death. But in all that time, Edwina had never seen anything like what arose now.

"Quickly," said the little elf. "Take the foul one. Take it out. Now!"

Mary snatched the dark orb of light in her hand. The shadowy tendrils trailed out of Ian's mouth before evaporating into gray mist. The second orb, as small as a shiny blue pearl, floated above his body, then gently settled back into his mouth once Mary clasped her hands over the damaged orb she'd trapped. She blew her spell over it, shrinking the shadowy light down to a solid sphere. This time, however, the result did not shimmer and gleam. Instead, what sat in her hand was a stone as dull as a spent cinder of coal. Used up. Dead. Useless.

"His body rejected the memory," Mary said, examining the remains. "That's the only explanation I can find. But at least it's out now."

Seized with guilt over the result of her botched magic, Edwina held a hand to her mouth. "How dreadful."

"Never mind that now, milady." The creature put himself between Mary and the unconscious Ian. "What's done is done. I will make amends."

"What are you going to do?" Edwina asked.

"I carry what he needs. You will see."

"Do you think it wise to keep meddling?" Mary retreated from the bed, pleading with her sister to stop the creature from doing any more damage. "The man will end up in an institution."

Edwina considered interfering lest the poor man's mind be harmed beyond repair, but her intuition made her hold back. She was curious about the hearth elf and what sort of magic he was capable of. "Maybe there's something he can do," she said, nodding her consent. "Go on, then."

The creature sat on his haunches atop the pillow. There, he patted his long, slender fingers against Ian's shoulder before digging in his satchel and pulling out a strip of tartan cloth. The weave was a muted green and gold with thin lines of purple and red crisscrossing through the fabric. The combination put Edwina in mind of winter fields of heather and gorse blooming in the north. The creature draped the cloth over Ian's chest, tucking it in under his chin, as if putting a child to sleep. Satisfied, he made a slight smacking noise with his mouth before crouching and resting his chin on his knees. He reached one hairy arm out, laying his hand against the man's forehead, then closed his eyes. A slight humming noise emanated from deep in the elf's chest.

At first, Edwina couldn't be sure her eyes weren't playing tricks on her as a faint golden light appeared to radiate between the creature's hand and the man's skin. Loving and tender, really, the way it circulated between them. Of course, she'd never seen it done before, but she'd lay odds the exchange was a form of tutelary magic the imp was performing. The notion calmed her, thinking of how softly the spellwork between them glowed. What creature—man, woman, or beast—didn't long for such a connection to another living soul? After all he'd been through, she hoped the light would prove a balm for the unfortunate man and ease his suffering. She would very much like to see his eyes open to the world with less anger toward her than before, though she fully admitted the act would require a double dose of forgiveness on his part.

Another two minutes passed before the little fellow came out of his trance and broke his connection with the man. "It is done," he said, opening his eyes. The cost of performing the magic reflected in his tired voice.

"What's done?" Mary asked, fidgeting with the washcloth in her hands.

"Don't you see?" Edwina said. "The little one is a guardian of some kind."

The creature nodded. "He will remember again."

Mary shook her head, not fully convinced. "He couldn't truly restore the man, could he? Certainly not without his original memories intact."

The creature cast a sharp look at Mary. "Guardian magic runs deeper than your scavenger witch magic that only knows how to take. He will recover. Memories are not only held in the mind."

Edwina took a small measure of satisfaction at her sister's rebuke and sat on the bed again beside the elf. A trail of golden light overspilled from the sprightly magic that had taken place so that her hand felt a dusting of warmth. "But how does it work?"

"Memories have memories." The little fellow rubbed his nose with his sleeve and moved to the man's side so he could better see his features. "Like a man's shadow when he walks in the sun. Only they form inside. Sometimes stored in the heart, sometimes in the bones, sometimes in the aura. And they gather inside me."

"And you were able to restore his memory from these shadows because you're a sort of guardian to him, is that it?" Edwina asked. "Yes, I think I'm beginning to get the gist of it."

"Well, I'm not sure I do," Mary said, slipping the dull memory stone into her apron pocket as she hovered near the stairs. She looked like she wanted to get as far away from their visitor as she could.

"It's a symbiotic relationship, if I'm right," Edwina explained. "There's a connection between the two. It's as if they share the same experiences and memories. You must have been devoted to him from an early age."

The elf beamed until his eyes teared and his ears poked up through his tangle of hair. "I've known my mister since he was a wee babe in swaddling cloth."

The image tickled Edwina and she beamed as well, though she half suspected the happiness she felt flowed as much from the overspill of the elf's magic as anything else. She was not a woman who readily experienced giddiness, but for whatever reason, she couldn't stop smiling at the hairy little elf and the snoring man whose life he'd presumably just saved. After straightening the strip of tartan on Ian's chest, she and the elf waited diligently for him to wake, while Mary studied the hard coal stone from her pocket, clearly regretting the loss of one of her precious orbs.

Chapter Eleven

The sunlight coming through the window sent a pain searing straight to the back of Ian's head. He shaded his eyes with his hand, blinking from one sister to the next as they stood by his bed in their dark dresses and white aprons like a pair of magpies.

"Where am I?" he asked.

"Our father's bed," said the sister on the right as she hurried to draw the shades closed halfway. "You needed a rest. You've had a trying few days."

Ian groaned and sat up, propping his head awkwardly against the pillow when he thought he might topple over if he moved that quickly again. His temples ached and his tongue furred in his mouth from dehydration. But no sooner had he taken a breath to settle himself than a jolt of fear shot through him. His hand fumbled for his throat, checking for a gash. He swallowed against his panic and quickly pulled his fingers away. No blood. Then he remembered. That part wasn't real. A dream. He shivered as if startled awake from a nightmare. Then shivered again when the threat still loomed in the shadows of lucid thought.

Aware they were staring at him, he diverted their concerned looks by asking, "How did I get here?"

"My sister brought you in a cab." The one with the smoky eyes—Moira? Mara? Mary—handed him a cup of tea that had gone tepid. "Take a sip. It will make you feel better."

The other sister, Edwina—yes, the sensible, comely witch who'd put the blue orb in his mouth—gave him a friendly, encouraging smile that set him at ease. "Do you remember being here before?" she asked. "In the shop downstairs? You've had a rather bad reaction, I'm afraid."

Bad reaction? He'd dreamed he'd had his head bashed in and his throat slit. Left to bleed out in an alley while rats sniffed at the prospect of stealing a piece of his flesh before the real scavengers turned up to peck his eyes out. But had it been a dream? His head was bruised, his teeth hurt from clenching them, and he couldn't stop swallowing to make sure his throat hadn't been slit open.

"I believe I do recall, aye," Ian said and set the tea aside without drinking. "Though I admit my mind is still a bit of a muddle." He reached once again for his throat, this time feeling around the side below his ear where he swore it still stung from the slice of the blade.

Before he could sink into melancholia over his strange and unwanted thoughts, his hand found a strip of tartan resting atop the covers. "What is this?" On the bed beside him, a weight shifted, like a cat settling down on the quilt. Expecting to find the sisters' family pet, he was met instead with a hairy yet familiar face staring up at him.

"Hob? What in blazes are you doing here?"

The little fellow peered back at him with a mixture of concern and hope. "You remember home again," the elf said, then rested his slender hand on Ian's sleeve.

Edwina Blackwood pulled up a wooden chair from the kitchen and sat across from Ian in the bed. "Your friend's magic seems to have proved vital to getting you on the road to recovery."

There was a dulcet quality to her voice when she spoke. Not quite hypnotic, and yet melodic in a way that made one want to bend their ear so as not to miss a word she said. Soothing and pleasant.

"Friend? Oh yes. Hob is . . . that is, he sort of came with the house my parents purchased decades ago."

"I am his guardian for life."

"Self-appointed," Ian clarified. "But how did you get here? You were told to wait for me at home."

Before Hob could answer, the other sister, who'd begun tidying up the room by wiping off his boots and returning his abandoned teacup to the kitchen, interrupted. "This creature claims he returned your memories, Mister . . ." But then she faltered. "I'm sorry, here you are lying in my father's bed and I still don't know what to call you."

For some reason, he hesitated. It was part of his nature to be discreet. Noncommittal. His guarded behavior was how he got away with half the things he did. But the sisters had taken him in, let him rest in their home, offered tea, and so he determined to be as forthright with them as events and his nature allowed. "It's Cameron. Ian Cameron. And you are Miss Blackwood, like your sister?"

"That's right," she answered, leaning behind her seated sister to give her a small and somewhat patronizing squeeze around the shoulders. "Neither of us is married yet."

He thought it best to ignore her odd gesture, as it clearly made Edwina uncomfortable. "As for your question, I believe I do remember for the most part, yes."

"Even yesterday morning's attack on the foreshore?" Mary prodded. She picked his jacket up off the floor and folded it over the back of Edwina's chair. "The police will be keen to discover what you know about the assailant who struck you."

"Attacked?" He reached for his throat again and then quickly pretended to scratch an itch along his stubble instead of checking for a gash wide enough to spill the life out of him. "Perhaps I spoke prematurely. While I do recall waking up in hospital with a head wound . . ." They both nodded in encouragement, so he continued, "I dinna seem to have any recollection of any attack on the foreshore. Are you sure it wasn't in an alley? Near Flint Street?" They shook their heads, but he continued anyway, overtaken by conflicting memories vying for the right to be called true. "And it couldn't have occurred yesterday," he insisted. "I only arrived in the city by train this afternoon." He stopped and pulled a face, confused again. Why could he remember a phantom attack that left him choking in his own blood but not the blow to the head that actually put him in the hospital? "Wait, that canna be right. I clearly remember speaking to you in your shop yesterday after I left the hospital. I was angry about something you took from me."

"So you remember my sister Mary and myself." Edwina glanced at her sister. "And you remember the conversation you and I had yesterday about the spell I performed? And who *you* are?"

Ah, she's prying now to know more. It was odd how his mind had filled in the gap of his understanding of magic with doubt before, yet his body and spirit had retained the truth. The essence of his being had still recognized his magical self, despite the temporary loss of memory. Curious yet reassuring.

"Aye, quite," Ian answered without wanting to give more away. Indeed, how could he forget about an encounter with two witches with such distinct eyes and manners? They unnerved and invigorated him with their mere presence. At the same time, he had to admit there was something not quite right about his recollection. "I remember," he said as a dull pain throbbed between his eyes. "But things also seem a jumble. How could I have had a conversation with you here, when I remember clearly being on a train coming from Auld Reekie yesterday?"

Hob tried to suppress a squeal, but it squeaked out anyway. He jumped onto Ian's chest and grabbed his face in his hands. The elf peered at him with wide amber eyes that had welled up with overactive concern. "You remember Hob. You remember home. Say it is so. Say you do!"

"Hob, what the devil is the matter with you? Stop that." He gripped the elf by his wrists to steady him.

"I wasn't there," Hob cried out in a shameful wail and dropped his head. "I could not put back what I did not know. Will Mister ever forgive me?"

"What's this?" A spark lit in Mary Blackwood's smoky eyes as she took a step nearer. "What's he on about?"

"I'm not sure." Ian continued to restrain the elf to keep him from thrashing about in overdramatics. "I had business in the city. I made him stay behind while I caught the train. The city is no place for his kind. Nor me, to be honest, but I'd already made up my mind to come." Ian let go of the hearth elf's wrists and wrapped the strip of tartan around his narrow shoulders in an effort to comfort him. "Now, calm ye down and tell me what happened after I got on the train. How much am I missing between then and now?"

The little elf held up his furry fingers and counted them off one at a time. "Four days since you left. I only followed you to this noisy, smelly city today when I sensed the great pain in your head and neck."

"Four days!" Ian lifted the elf off his chest and sat up with his feet on the floor.

Bloody hell.

"Mr. Cameron, are you all right?" Edwina stood and scooted her chair back to the kitchen table.

He raked his hand through his hair, scowling as though he'd just lost a bet he'd once been confident of winning. "I canna seem to remember anything between leaving the station at Everly and waking up at hospital."

Four days lost. Four days of work that had ended in an attack he couldn't remember, in part because of the women standing before him. What had happened to him? Who'd attacked him? And why? He couldn't be sure of anything from the moment he'd stepped foot in the city.

The smoky-eyed witch excused herself, saying one of them ought to keep an eye on the shop, winking at her sister before heading down the steps. Edwina remained behind, fidgeting with her hands as her cheeks flushed shell pink.

"I have to go." Ian reached for his boots and slipped them on. "My coat, Hob."

A swath of blood, presumably from his head wound, had left a stain on the collar of his tweed jacket, but the hearth elf removed a miniature whisk broom bound with golden thread from inside his jacket, then repeated, "Spot out, spot out, spot out," until the unsightly blotch was swept clean, restoring the coat to near new. When Hob had finished, Ian handed him the wee cream pitcher from the tea tray for his effort.

"Is it wise to leave now?" Edwina asked after the elf swallowed the milk with a satisfying smack. "You've only just recovered."

He shrugged his coat on and combed his hair back with his fingers. "Thank you for your care, Miss Blackwood," he said with full sincerity. "But I've lost precious time and I canna afford to lose any more."

"This is maddening. Where will you go?"

"I have four days of work I must recover. I suppose I have no choice but to begin at the beginning and start over again as if I'd just arrived." He checked his pockets for his watch and also discovered Sir Elvanfoot's business card. He took it out and flipped it over in his fingers, reminded of his promise.

"But what work is so urgent a man must risk his own health?" The witch, though tender and attentive with her womanly bedside manner, stood her ground in front of him, attempting to charm him into a change of heart with that lilting voice of hers. "Why not lie down, take a rest, until you're truly feeling your best. Let your mind be free of distress, I'm concerned for your welfare, I must confess."

He tucked the business card back in his pocket and concentrated on resisting her gentle spell by invoking the silent mantra of deflection he'd learned to perfect in his line of business. *With this charm I disarm, your magic here can do no harm.* The sweet tone of her voice dissipated in his ears, with an odd smidge of regret on his part.

"Despite the lapse, I do have my faculties back, Miss Blackwood, if that is your concern." He paused, wondering if he could confide in her. If he *should* confide in her. An ally in the city could speed things along. But could he trust her? She'd just tried to enchant him, though he supposed it was for his own good. Either she had a hand in his attack or she was someone who could possibly help him discover who did. So which was she?

"Those missing four days found you hit over the head and left for dead on the river's foreshore in the end, Mr. Cameron. Whatever it is you seek to recover led you to that violent moment. What makes you think it won't again?"

Hob jumped on Ian's back, hugging his arms around his neck the way a small child would. The contact made him swallow, reminding him of the phantom nightmare he couldn't relinquish. She was right. His investigation must have taken a dark turn. Either he'd discovered a dangerous piece of the puzzle he'd been sent to solve or merely met with bad luck in a city overrun with hooligans out to rob a man and relieve him of his possessions. Despite the events that had led him to that shore, he must retrace his steps to uncover the truth and discover what had happened over those four days. He owed it to Elvanfoot.

With Hob clinging to his neck, he turned to the witch. "Aye, it likely will, but that is exactly what I intend to find out." Something in him relented and he decided to be candid with her. "I'm a private detective, Miss Blackwood, searching for a missing person in the city." The idea of four days lost and the trail gone cold irked him to no end, knowing it was more likely than not he'd been on the verge of discovering something pivotal before he was attacked.

She gestured toward the card he'd tucked away. "Sir Elvanfoot. That's who you're working for, isn't it?"

Again, she awakened in him a vein of sincerity he'd lost touch with years ago. "He hasn't heard from his son in weeks. I'm here to find him. That, Miss Blackwood, is the work I must risk my health for."

"My family has always admired the Elvanfoots," Edwina said. "If there's any way I can help, I'd be happy to do it."

He'd taken her for a sharp-eyed, cold-as-stone southern witch—after all, who else steals a man's memories with no shame or regret?—but after her humble offer, and a prod from Hob in his ear to trust her, he reconsidered his initial reading of her. "I believe the best way to unravel this mess would be to start at the last place I was last myself in the city."

"The foreshore."

"Aye." Heeding an instinct experience had taught him not to ignore, Ian asked, "Any chance you've a moment to accompany me to the exact place you found me? We aren't so far from the river we couldn't walk over, are we?"

At his invitation Edwina paused, confessing she needed to confer with her own intuition to determine whether the tide would still be out sufficiently to allow him to view the site. She seemed to hold back a smile as her eyes lit with an amber glow once the answer came to her. "It isn't any use explaining," she said. "I hardly understand how

I know such things myself, but we have time to walk the foreshore briefly."

She agreed to escort him to the spot, and while he understood the danger of returning to the site where he was attacked, and with one of only two persons he knew to be there with him when it happened, his need for answers outweighed his apprehension. So, after explaining their intention to her sister and fetching a prim hat and unusually long black shawl, Miss Edwina Blackwood stood by the door ready to be of assistance. Meanwhile, he broke the news to Hob it was time to shoo off into the shadows. The little elf complained, but in the end, after finding a wicker basket to jump into, he was compelled to do as told. With Hob safely out of sight and Mary minding the shop, the pair took off at a businesslike pace to explore the foreshore and recapture his missing four days.

Chapter Twelve

"Who killed Cock Robin?" The boy took aim at Edwina with his pretend bow before releasing a mock arrow as the pair walked out the shop door. "I, said the sparrow, with my bow and arrow, I killed Cock Robin."

"What's that all about?" Ian asked as they headed for the river.

Edwina shook her head. "He's a local boy. Lives around here somewhere. Likes to tease. He knows my sister and I are . . . different, but can't quite figure out why, so he makes fun."

"Who saw him die?" called the boy once they passed. "I, said the fly," he answered with a grin, after making them look over their shoulders at him.

"This way," Edwina said, walking quickly to put the boy behind her. She veered them down a lane that emptied onto the embankment. From there they dodged several horse-drawn wagons, a parade of bicyclists, and a motorized cab before heading a short way east toward the pier, where a stone stairway led down to the foreshore. As she'd predicted, the river tide was rising, but there was still time to walk the distance below the embankment wall. The shore would be exceptionally muddy in places. A step in the wrong spot could land one in a sinkhole and swallow the foot and leg up to the calf, yet she'd neglected to fetch her old boots out of a concern for vanity.

Yes, she admitted it. She'd wanted to appear ladylike and attractive in her lace-up ankle boots rather than donning her work boots made for trudging through mud. Her old knockabouts were all right for traipsing about with her sister in the dark but definitely not suitable for strolling beside a gentleman—albeit a rough-around-the-edges handsome one whose prospects were yet as unknown as they were unsavory. She'd taken a good look at him while he'd lain unconscious only to discover his nose was slightly crooked from being broken, he bore a small scar that split his left eyebrow, and he required a bath and shave. Yet when he'd awoken in her father's bed with his mind and memory restored, she'd rather thought there was no man to match him once that genial gleam returned to his eyes.

Feeling a flush, Edwina turned her attention back to the river. On the opposite bank, steam shovels dug in the mud to erect a new pier. The city seemed to be in a perpetual state of repair and renovation. Burying the old and building up the new until the layers of the city resembled the sedimentary work of the river. But where generations of the past had relied on hands and shovels, coal and steam were the tools of the modern city. Coal barges in the dozens floated by to fill the constant demand, blaring their horns for fishermen and ferries to mind their passing.

"Bit treacherous down here, isn't it?" Ian descended the steps first before gallantly reaching out for her hand to steady her. "Do you and your sister often come to the river unaccompanied in the dark?"

The contact of his rough skin against her bare fingers roused her senses as she stepped onto the pebbled landing. She gripped his hand a breath longer than necessary before relinquishing it so she might raise the hem of her skirt above the mud as she walked. Though she still considered him a bit of a ruffian—she suspected the broken nose and scar were the result of brawling—she had forgiven him his outburst in the shop the day before, knowing what a state he'd been in after his ordeal. In truth, he was proving a perfect gentleman, and so she freely engaged in conversation with him.

"Mary and I search the shoreline for whatever the tide might have churned up," she said, bending to pick up a bottlecap as evidence before tossing it away. "We come day or night. But, yes, nighttime is more convenient for us. Fewer of the mud larks about."

"Mud larks?" He took a measure of the river with his eye from one vantage point to another.

"They're more like shore rats, scurrying up and down the bank, scavenging for scraps of metal. A cup. A spoon. A bit of rope. Something to trade for a meat pie or strip of dried beef. Poor mortals can't see a foot in front of them in the dark, so they flood the shore at low tide, morning and afternoon. Better than the toshers, though. Those poor souls are knee-deep in the sewers sieving for bits of treasure to sell."

Ian tilted his head to the right and pursed his lips. "But isn't mudlarking what you do?"

Edwina bent to inspect a glint of gold she'd spied in the interstices between rocks, but it proved only a broken brass buckle off a shoe. "No, it's different for my sister and me," she said, unsure how much to confide. Yes, this man was of a similar bloodline, but she still knew very little of his past or his inclinations. Not enough, she decided, to admit the entire truth. "We take what catches our eye," she explained, dropping the broken buckle on the rocks. "We're quite good at finding rings, brooches, and the occasional old coin. You'd be surprised how many turn up in the mud."

She'd never known a river to hold so many secrets. Wedding rings and lockets with declarations of love on them, though now discarded. Mirrors and combs lovingly bought for a trousseau left tarnished and forgotten. A shoe worn by a medieval child. Gold coins once spent on amphorae of wine and tribute. Bottles filled with hair and nails meant to ward off witches. The river was the keeper of the island's secrets, the guardian of time and history.

Ian watched a mother and daughter rinsing out buckets in a tide pool down shore. "But you sell your finds, too, do you not?"

"Yes, of course." She thought about the distinction she meant to convey as she scanned the rocks, as much for treasure as to avoid twisting an ankle in her improper shoes. "I suppose the difference is we only sell our findings in our shop because otherwise we'd be buried up to our necks in all the bric-a-brac other people toss away or misplace." She smiled and shrugged, hoping if she made light of it he'd get off the subject. "It's a bit of a compulsion for us, really. My father is the one who came up with the idea of opening a shop. He was tired of all the clutter in the house."

Ian walked with his hands clasped behind his back with the easy gait of a hill walker on an evening stroll, despite the rocky, uneven ground. Still, she could sense his mind whirring, somewhat like that odd watch of his, spinning his thoughts and observations into silent conclusions. He asked no more about the scavenging as he stopped to take inventory of the surroundings below the embankment. Edwina watched his face as he absorbed the view so familiar to her—the barges floating by with their heaps of coal, the clap of horse traffic on the embankment above, the whiff of fish and soot and rocks covered in algae still damp with river sludge. The tiny riverside oasis in the midst of the city had always made her yearn for home, for the mountains and rivers to the west. She wondered briefly if he felt the same, coming from the hills and dales up north.

He didn't strike her as the type to chat about his past, so she leaned forward to inspect an unusual shape poking out of the mud instead. Curious, she bent to dig the object out of the muck with a stick. A flock of seagulls, their gray wings bent like arrowheads, circled and swooped overhead. Crying wolf, she thought, until the cranium emerged bone-white against the mud.

"What is it?" he asked.

Edwina pried the thing up, and even before she rinsed it off in the tidewater of a nearby shallow, she knew it was a bad sign. Bones found in water were always bad omens, but a skull could portend serious misfortune and sometimes death. The gulls screeched above her as she rinsed the enlarged eye sockets of their mud.

"A cormorant," she said, holding the fragile skull in the palm of her hand. The hooked beak stood out against her chilled, pink skin.

"Do you often find such things?"

"Bones are common enough, but to find an intact skull is a little rarer." The fragility of the bird's remains sent a shudder of warning hollowing through her own bones, and she hugged her shawl tight around her, not knowing for whom the portent was meant.

Though she hadn't explained the ominous nature of her find, Ian checked the shoreline in a way that made her think he understood the omen well enough. "We should keep walking," he said with a hand at her elbow to move her along.

"It's this way," she said, still cradling her unlucky find in her hand, unsure what to do with it. To cast it away could bring misfortune for ignoring the message, but keeping the skull invited a connection to trouble she didn't wish to attract.

They walked another hundred yards—the length Mary had run with her skirt hiked to her knees to share what she had found and what they had both presumed moments later was a dead man. And yet here he was standing beside her, his flesh robust with life, the eyes clear, and the wounds, both physical and metaphysical, presumably on the mend.

The stranded fishing boat that marked the spot where they'd found him had disappeared. Its owner was likely out on the water in search of a decent haul of eel or skate for market. Even without the boat, she knew the shore well enough to trust this was the place, and said as much. The scent of his blood had washed away, but she was certain he'd lain in the exact spot before their feet.

"This is the place. The star of Venus was angled just there." Edwina pointed over the top of the railroad bridge above them.

Ian nudged his shoe at the rocks, but with little detectable evidence on the tide-washed ground, he turned his attention to the algae-covered embankment at their backs instead. The wall was a massive structure, faced in granite. The height of the waterline on the stone made plain the temporary nature of the ground they stood on before the tidewater filled back in to reclaim the rocks and mud. She knew from experience one had best be up the stairs by the time the water rose to meet the rocky ground at the base of the wall.

"Do you recall anything?" she asked, wondering if the musty air or the damp of the shore had the power to awaken some buried memory for him. "Any reason you might have been down on the foreshore that night?"

He pulled his watch out and took a reading before looking in the direction they'd come. "You say there was a fishing boat resting this way?" When she confirmed the hull had been tilted perpendicular to the water, he twisted around to view a weathered ladder on the wall behind them, where the vessel was presumably tethered during high tide. He took a moment, as if triangulating between the ladder, the location of the boat, and the steps they'd come down. "I might be getting a clearer picture," he said, adding the view of the top of the embankment to his calculation.

The guilt of what she and Mary had done to him festered the longer she watched him try to sort it out until she was compelled to speak. "We sent a policeman to come for you as soon as we left the embankment," she said. "But by then we thought you were already . . ."

"Dead?" he finished for her.

"The chill in your blood had diminished your aura. That's why I took you for a mortal at first. I couldn't understand how you'd survived, but, of course, if you had been mortal, I doubt you would have."

He knelt not to look at the ground at his feet but to get the vantage point of the land down shore from a man crouching. "Does she do it often?" he asked, standing again. "Remove people's memories?"

"It's part of Mary's nature." She picked up a tangle of fishing line and seaweed that had snagged on a rock. "She's drawn to the shape and color of the transition between life and death. The corpse lights." As Edwina spoke, she tied the fishing line around the skull, covering the eye sockets with the seaweed.

"She's attracted to corpse lights?"

"The outflow of one's life energy continues on, separate from the physical being after death. The floating memory forms bright-colored orbs that my sister collects. She compresses them into stonelike objects. Baubles, she calls them. Of course, you've seen how she does that already."

He'd stopped taking in the scenery and instead focused on her with that familiar unsettled look. Everyone who ever learned the truth about her sister's rare gift got the same expression on their face—fear of death, fear of someone disturbing the sanctity of their passing. As if their death were beyond corruption. As if her sister were some kind of degenerate. Ian was quicker at letting the thoughts pass like a shadow over him than most. He was a disciplined one. Well, once his restored memories had reined in the impulsive side she'd witnessed in the shop. She suspected his true nature was a cautious yet curious one, setting aside judgment long enough to learn the truth of a thing. He even offered a grudging smile in admiration of her sister's unique skill before asking the question everyone always posed: *How does she find the dead?*

Sniffing out the dead was also in the Blackwood sisters' nature, as surely as finding a prize that sparkled on the ground.

"We volunteer to sit with the old and infirm at Saint Basil's," Edwina said. "It isn't hard to find death there." She decided it was best to return her find to the river, so she found a crevice in the embankment wall where the rising tide would accept her offering later. She placed the skull wrapped in seaweed between two stones covered in slick green slime and said a quick blessing for the dead.

After, Ian absentmindedly pressed his fingers to his neck above his Adam's apple. Again. She'd seen him do it three times since he awoke in her father's bed. A quirk? A sore throat? Or something else? Though Hob had restored the man's memories with his protective magic, she couldn't be sure how complete the imp's spell would prove. Or her sister's, for that matter. Memories were malleable. Changeable. Unreliable, wispy things. Magic couldn't change that. Not until they were removed from the body and could be solidified in stone.

Ian held any further curiosity about Mary in check, letting his attention drift back to the shore, where the water had moved closer by several feet. The river had risen significantly since they'd climbed down the steps near the pier. Sometimes unpredictable, the rising water could catch the unsuspecting walker by surprise until they found themselves trudging through dangerous mud. Or worse, stranded on a small spit of high ground until it, too, eventually sank beneath the dark water.

"We should probably think about heading back," she said with a nod to the water as it lapped against the stones and shards of broken pottery.

"It's an odd location, is it not?" He scanned the treacherous terrain of the foreshore again. "For a man to be walking in the dark?" Ian was speaking more to himself than to her, as if going over some chain of events in his head that could account for his body lying on the foreshore in the wee hours of the morning. "You did say it was just before dawn."

"The water was on the rise then too."

"Aye, of course it was." Ian seemed to have got the scent of something. Something important. "And if you hadn't found me, I'd have drowned and my body would have been carried off on the tide. Perhaps I'd have washed up on some shore a half mile away, or maybe I'd have been lost to the sea, never to be heard from again."

It was a gruesome thought, one she wasn't sure served either of them well to dwell on. "It's a lucky thing we found you."

"Nae, it couldn't have been random," he said. "I obviously wasn't out here fishing or even mudlarking. So why else would I climb down to a stretch of the foreshore in the dark?"

"I wondered if you hadn't fallen off the embankment."

"Aye, but wouldn't that have broken a rib or arm?" Ian paused, as though thinking or revisiting a memory or feeling. "I was drawn here. Following someone." He paced over the rocks and rusty nails poking out of the mud. "Perhaps I discovered something someone didn't want me sharing."

"Something about Sir Elvanfoot's son? Isn't that what you were investigating?"

"Aye, and whatever I learned was apparently enough to get me killed."

Edwina thought back to that morning. There had been others on the street. There always were, day or night. The number of rough sleepers in the city could fill the ranks of an army. Any one of them could have been on the foreshore before she and Mary climbed the stairs down from the embankment. She hadn't been looking for anyone else on the shore, but it didn't mean they hadn't already come and gone. It was mere chance they'd found Ian in time to accidentally save his life.

"What now?" she asked.

He finally took his eye off the shore and turned his attention fully on her. "Thank you again, Miss Blackwood. For sending the constable to find me. I might have died otherwise, left unconscious with the tide rising. And I intend to find out why."

"You mean for the second time," she said, flushing after staring so deeply at him she'd noticed the flecks of gold in his green eyes.

"Undoubtedly. I was sent to the city to find Sir Elvanfoot's son. That was my only mission. Whatever I discovered led me to the river's edge, and I will find it again. I just have to start at the beginning. Retrace my steps." He was taking a last, lingering look at the scene when his gaze snagged on a young face at the top of the embankment staring down at them. Not the boy from the lane but a lad of seventeen or eighteen perhaps. The young man grinned beneath a mop of unruly blond hair. Even from twelve feet away, Edwina could see the discoloration of his teeth, the pockmarks on his face, and the greasy ring around the collar of his jacket. An uneasy feeling rose up in her humors.

"Tide turn up any keepers?" the lad called down when he'd been spotted. His smile faded and he gazed out at the river, ignoring the pair of them below as he sucked on the stem of a thin black pipe.

"We should probably get off the shore," Edwina said.

Ian followed her lead until they stood at the foot of the narrow stone stairs leading up to the embankment. From the ground looking up, the steps were steep and narrow, slick from slime and mud, and without any benefit of a guardrail. And now they were blocked by the boy smoking his pipe. Two other ragtag youths joined him at the top of the steps. Then two more until there were five of them crouching above, watching like birds of prey.

"Let us pass, please," Edwina said.

"Might be we should shake out your pockets first and see what the river's brought us," the lad answered, his eyes glinting hard at Ian, knowing he was in full control of the moment. "Anyways, might be one of you've got something on you that would be happier with me."

He seemed to think himself a dandy by the way he stood, confidently tucking his thumbs in the pockets of his brown-and-yellow plaid coat while he held the pipe tight in his rotten teeth, yet unaware he was still just a young street tough in hand-me-down clothes for all the world to see. The rest of the boys, one in a crushed top hat that sat lopsided on his head and the others dressed in mismatched plaids and paisleys too threadbare to hand down to even an unloved sibling, bore the scruff of first whiskers. They were a wiry and ravenous-looking lot, and hungry not only for a meal but for something more. The eagerness in their eyes as they tracked their prey from above sent a foreboding shiver through Edwina as she wondered why she hadn't thought to arm herself with a ten-inch hatpin too.

"Does he mean to rob us?" Edwina asked Ian and clutched her shawl a little tighter.

"He's a canny one, if he does," he replied. "The tide is rising and we have nae choice but to climb the stairs straight into his hands."

Edwina cast an eye up and down the shore. The strip of rocky land was abandoned. The smart ones had already climbed to high ground. It was just them and the gang of boys left to negotiate the distance between the shore and the embankment.

"Best come up now before the river swallows you for supper," the dandy said, then spit on the street as a black cab rolled past behind him.

"What do we do?" she asked. "Climb or swim?"

"Come now, surely those aren't our only options," Ian said.

Ian squinted and smiled up at the lads. He couldn't mean to reason with them, Edwina thought. Or charm them. This wasn't some quiet countryside village in the north. These were street thieves with hunters' hearts. Now that they were on the chase, they wouldn't stop until they got what they were after. But other than a few pence and the trinkets she'd found on the shore, Edwina had nothing of value they'd be satisfied with. Nothing material, anyway. Ian was fit enough, she knew, after embracing his solid body while they'd carried him up the stairs and laid him in their father's bed, but even he couldn't take on five desperate youths alone. And using magic against mortals was strictly forbidden in public. He'd be arrested.

To her surprise, Ian neither cajoled for their release nor championed for a fight. Instead he smiled and began reciting a line of poetry as he moved to stand in front of her in what she interpreted as a gallant gesture of protection. "If good, go forth and hallow thee," he called up. "If of ill, let the earth swallow thee. If thou'rt of air, let gray mist fold thee. If of earth, let the swart mine hold thee." He continued quoting his poem while the boys gawked openmouthed. "If a pixie, seek thy ring. If a nixie, seek thy spring."

When he finished, the boys' stern, unholy faces broke into laughter. One slapped his knee and pointed. "He's raving mad, this one."

Edwina had doubted Ian's ploy, but his unhinged response to their threat seemed to have thrown the boys off their predatory instinct, at least for the moment. They exchanged glances, had a good laugh, and then taunted the apparently deranged pair by flicking their spent cigarettes at them from the top of the stairs. All but the dandy with the pipe in his teeth. Straight-faced, he smacked one of the tallest boys on the cheek, and the rest sobered up, flinching in fear of receiving the same.

She had to wonder what Ian had meant to accomplish with his gibberish. They should have made a run for the stairs when the boys were distracted. Yelled for help from a passerby on the street. Or drawn the knife in Ian's pocket and fought their way off the foreshore. Instead, they remained on the bottom step while her ankles wobbled in her boots from fear, her breath catching on the stink of fish and sludge rising with the river.

The youngest of the boys, revved from taunting, started to head down the stairway to hurry the matter along when the dandy stopped him. "No need to rush in, lads. Let them come to us," he said and nodded toward the river with that ghastly, rotten grin of his. Even the fog was apparently on their side, creeping in around the boys at that very moment, thick as gauze, to hide what they were up to from the bobbies and any decent folk passing by.

River water lapped at Edwina's heels. They had no more than ten minutes before they became drenched to their calves. She tried not to think about how heavy the fabric of her skirt would become should she be forced to tread water in the freezing-cold river. She also tried not to think of having to do the inevitable. Using magic in a public space against hapless mortals—while surely a defense could be made in circumstances such as the one they found themselves in now—was the last thing she wished to do. She knew too well from experience there were consequences to revealing one's true identity in front of the wrong people. And she simply couldn't pull up stakes and move again so soon. If she and Mary couldn't find anonymity in a city of five million, then where else was there left to hide?

A wave sloshed over the tops of Edwina's ankle boots, while the gang of five squatted at the top of the steps like feral cats about to feast. "Come on up, my lovelies," taunted a boy with black hair and blue eyes that shone like ghost lights in the building fog. "Or maybe you prefer to stay in the water permanent-like." There was a quick clicking sound, and Edwina saw the sharp glint of a steel blade flick open in his hand.

The threat made her pulse course. Desperate, she cast her eye over the shore, the river, and the top of the bridge. Who would see? Who would know? Above, the boys' faces faded in and out of view as the dense mist enveloped them. The fog had crept in thick and brooding, obscuring their silhouettes though they hunkered only a dozen feet away. A ship's horn sounded on the water, but all she saw was the phantom shape of a vessel moving through clouds. The miasma of mist and foul city breath swirled along the embankment wall, swallowing up what remained of the foreshore.

Ian stood at the base of the stairs, his trousers soaking up water, and removed his pocket watch. "Now or never," he said as if reading her mind.

The boys' eyes lit up with greed at the sight of the watch, knowing the weight of that gold in their hands could fill their stomachs and their dreams of wealth for a month. Two of the boys, their boots held together with twine and tar, crept threateningly lower on the stairs. Ian merely smiled as though he were going to recite another cursed poem.

Hang the consequences. She wasn't going to stand by and be gutted like a fish. Edwina turned to the river and sang. "Haste ye help a stranded soul, wings of white and eye of coal. Come forth with claws to scratch and strike, in aid of kin and kith alike." Then she stood back as the seagulls, who'd earlier complained overhead, darted out of the sky as though loosed from longbows.

Chapter Thirteen

The attack came swiftly. A swarm of seagulls shot out of the sky, diving at the gang with wings and claws out for the strike. The unlucky lad with the pipe in his teeth ducked and covered his head with one arm, but the birds were relentless, dipping and scratching at his skin. Sharp beaks nipped at the young man as the birds squawked and chided and then slapped their wings in his face. The lad cursed and swatted, but the gulls only swooped out of reach and circled around for another attack.

Ian watched astonished. He'd expected Edwina might assist him by using that lilting voice of hers to cause the boys to run back to their lane, the consequences of using magic against mortals be damned. He'd done his best to hide their magic from view, conjuring an innocent fog by using a mortal's well-worn words of poetry, but could not have guessed she would summon a full-fledged attack.

Shaken free from his initial shock, he charged up the slick steps, knocking the black-haired lad with the knife out of the way with his shoulder. Next, he shoved the would-be thief in his ridiculous top hat onto his backside as the gang scrambled to avoid being bitten by the wild birds.

The gulls clawed and snapped at the band of young men, pecking and scratching through their threadbare clothes until the hooligans backed away with bleeding hands flapping over their heads to rid themselves of the cursed birds. Long streaks of fresh white droppings showed on the backs of the lads' coats as they ran. Ian chased after the young men for a good fifty paces until he was satisfied they were truly gone. Catching his breath, he returned to the riverside to check on Edwina.

The sound of horse hooves tramped by beside the pavement as the shape of a wagon sailed past as though floating above the road surface. A whistle blared in the distance, and Ian saw the train's headlamp shine just bright enough to form a halo. Men walked by him in black frock coats, but they were as good as ghosts in the fog. He waited, scanning the promenade while hoping to spot Edwina's shawled shadow emerge from the mist. "Aye, I may have overdone it," he admitted aloud when he couldn't see ten feet in front of him, but he didn't dare clear the air. Not yet. Not while her spell was still in flux. But where had she gone? "Miss Blackwood, are you there?" he called out.

As soon as he spoke her name, Edwina climbed up the embankment stairwell. Her skirt was soaked to her knees, and she shivered beneath her black shawl. She nodded she was fine, though she looked anything but.

"What about you?" she asked. "Are you all right?"

"Fair enough." Ian wiped his forehead with the back of his hand. "What were you thinking? I had them distracted. There was no need for theatrics."

"Theatrics? There were five of them," she balked. "The one with the"—she vaguely pointed to her eyes—"the ghost stare had a knife. Pardon me for panicking. I thought they meant to spill our blood."

"Of course they did. But the day I canna handle five mortal lads is the day I should retire and take up sheep farming for a living."

She blinked back at him, half-disgusted, before marching up the promenade, barely dodging out of the way of a man hauling a handcart full of turnips. Ian caught up to her in front of a wrought-iron park bench beneath a line of plane trees and begged her to sit so they could take a breath.

"Your skirt's soaking wet." Ian cast his eye about the hazy street until he found what he was looking for. "Stay put," he said, "while I fetch something to warm you." Across the carriageway a woman tended a coffee stall with two big copper urns mounted atop a wagon. He dashed over the road while fishing a penny from his pocket.

As he waited for the coffee, his spell faded, and the fog thinned. People's faces came into view at a reasonable distance again, yet the buildings remained partially obscured except for the odd spire or clock tower rising above the normal city miasma. Edwina waited on the bench with her shawl wrapped over her head. Ian returned and sat beside her, mindful to keep a respectable distance between them.

"I'm told one can get away with almost anything in the city and people won't bat an eye," he said, handing her the coffee in a chipped white mug. He waited to see if she'd calmed down or was the type to hold a grudge over a few scrappy words.

She let the shawl fall from her face as she accepted the cup. "That's what my father believed too. It's why he brought us to the city."

"Dinna fash yourself," he said, leaning back. "The lads won't put two and two together. They couldn't have seen anything. Besides, they're halfway back to their mothers' laps by now."

"This is your doing," she said and stretched a hand out as if she could hold the last of the mist in her palm. "That poem you recited. You called up a fog with those words."

"The boy in front of the shop isn't the only one who knows a rhyme or two." He leaned in a few inches closer and thought he felt the afterglow of magic still rising off her. "I'd thought you'd use that hypnotizing voice of yours on the lads. But then you surprised me altogether. I've never seen anyone call birds like that before."

She dipped her head to sip her coffee, as if to hide behind the edge of her shawl. He'd made her feel self-conscious, talking about the conjuring in public. He couldn't deny the spell had inflamed his curiosity about her, about her magic. In fact, he had a million questions for her. But first she asked one of him.

"How were you able to use a mortal's poem instead of an incantation?"

"Ah, that. A trick my father taught me," Ian said and brushed a speck of river mud from his trousers. "He calls it an incantation incognito. Poets' words work best. Even though the couplets are written by mortals, their words still have power. You see it in the way they're able to move hearts and minds by putting words together in the right order. If a mortal has the power to move a human's emotions with mere words, that's an alchemy all its own. And something we can use to our advantage."

"But why would you?"

He cleared his throat and, as nonchalantly as he could, checked the promenade in each direction to see if anyone was paying more attention to them than they should. "Mortal words," he explained, "they dinna raise the attention of the Witches' Constabulary. You can use them to disguise the source of your magic. For when you're left with nae other choice but don't want to be found out. You simply hide your intention behind a veil of plain but relevant words rather than use an incantation. The magic will adhere if they're crafty enough." He gestured to the fog as proof. "I was fair convinced all the city witches used that spell, living so close together as they do."

"Like a wolf in sheep's clothing," she said, as if storing the lesson for later.

"For when mortals push things too far."

"You attack the poor sods often, do you?"

"Aye, in my line of work, it's sometimes required." He knew it made him sound more hostile than he was, but he decided to leave it hanging between them as he pressed her again. "Haven't you ever used that unique voice of yours to influence a mortal? I was surprised when you didn't run those lads off with one of your songs."

"The voice doesn't work like that for me. I can't affect a group, only an individual. I think the spell gets diluted by trying to spread it too far otherwise."

"So you've tried before?"

She kept her shawl drawn over her head, even pulling it a wee bit tighter, refusing to incriminate herself with anything more than a shrug. By necessity, he'd had to become a keen observer of human nature, of behaviors and tics that gave away emotions, even when the person's words clearly indicated otherwise. Edwina, he noted, had tensed when he referred to using spells on the lads again. It could be fear or even embarrassment at having used her magic in the open, but he suspected there was more to her reaction. Her reluctance wasn't about the ethics of using magic against mortals. He rather thought it had more to do with wanting to avoid any attention on herself. *Fair enough,* he thought.

"What will you do now?" she asked. "With your investigation, I mean."

Deflection or genuine interest?

"Start over again," Ian said. "Begin where I would have on day one, when I arrived in the city. Though, actually, I'm in a bit of a spot, thanks to you and your sister." She looked him full in the face then, her hazel eyes blinking with worry. He pointed to his temple. "I canna seem to remember which hotel I was staying at. Which means I dinna have my case file, a change of clothes"—he drew a hand over his noticeably stubbled cheeks—"or even a razor."

She started to speak, but he held his hand up to stop her from apologizing. "It's all right. I'll find new lodging. I have a little coin left. Enough to rent a cot for a few nights, anyway."

"But you're quite recovered now?" she asked.

He'd lost four days, and probably more. Hob couldn't have restored everything. The old fellow had done his best, of course, but there were things he simply couldn't know. Hob seemed to think the body held on to memories as much as the mind, but that hadn't borne out by

Ian's experience. He'd tried from every angle while on the foreshore to remember what had happened, how he'd come to be there and get hit over the head, but the only thing that felt vaguely familiar was the stench of the mud and fish and brine, as if the scent had gotten in his nostrils and wouldn't leave. That and the sensation that he'd also choked on his own blood after his throat had been slit, though *he* clearly hadn't been murdered. Which meant whoever's memory she'd mistakenly given him had. Which left an altogether different taste in his mouth.

"Yes, for the most part," he answered.

"So all you need is to start at the beginning." Edwina stood and shook out the hem of her skirt, which had finally stopped dripping with river water. "We should get going, then."

"We?"

"Yes. We need to find your hotel and reunite you with your belongings."

"Miss Blackwood, that's hardly something for you to concern yourself with," he said, standing to meet her.

"Oh, but it is. If not for my sister's interference, you wouldn't currently be without your possessions. Luckily that's something I believe I can help you with."

"And how exactly do you propose to do that?"

"Where would your investigation begin, Mr. Cameron?" She straightened her back and clasped her hands together in front of her, all business. "Assuming you just arrived in the city?"

Instead of trying to remember, he answered as a matter of protocol. "My only lead was the missing man's place of employment. The Wilshire Music Hall on Concord Street in the East End. That's where I'd start. But how does that help me find my lodging place?"

He couldn't say he was sorry he'd asked, though he wasn't quite prepared for her abrupt determination to assist. After offering up that charming smile of hers, she took off walking at a brisk pace, returned the coffee mug to its grateful monger, then demanded he follow to the nearest headhouse to purchase a third-class ticket for the underground railway. He wasn't sure he'd have used the newfangled system when he'd arrived in the city from the north on the train. The idea of zooming in the dark beneath the decaying earth, with only an oil lamp to light the train's way—and where at least a small population of the dead were known to lie dormant in disturbed plague pits—raised his discomfort level to somewhere north of teeth grinding. She seemed to surmise his reluctance yet dropped the necessary coins at the ticket window for their journey.

"Are you sure about this?" Ian said as she collected the tickets.

Edwina cocked her head in the direction of the stairs leading down to the platform. "Call it witch's intuition," she whispered. "Besides, this is the quickest way." He half suspected she'd used that voice of hers to bewitch him into following along without his noticing. How else could he explain why he did as she asked?

The train tunnel went even deeper in the earth than he'd imagined. The stairs descended to a depth of a hundred feet or more by the time they reached the underground platform. The colorful posters on the opposite wall advertising milk and flour, with their rosy-cheeked cherubs, did little to ease his discomfort. Not so long as the gaping black hole of a tunnel yawned at him from either side of where he stood. It was one thing to explore a cave or burrow. Those spaces were condoned by nature and were only occasionally occupied by spirits that meant no harm. But this deliberate digging through the earth, disturbing eons-buried ground to build tunnels for human transportation, was asking for trouble.

As though mocking his concern, the arriving train rumbled to life inside the tunnel, sending a small tremor to shake the ground beneath his feet. The infernal beast hissed and sparked as it rolled forward, finally emerging in a cloud of black smoke like some medieval dragon brought to heel.

The train rattled to a stop in front of the platform. Edwina led him to a hard wooden seat in a third-class car at the back before the carriage chugged off through the dark. His hand itched to remove his pocket watch as shadows flickered in the dark outside the window. As nonchalantly as he could, he opened the timepiece and flicked the lever on the side, pretending to consult the hour as he leaned toward the window. His seatmate wasn't fooled.

"It's some sort of astrolabe, is it not?"

Ian checked the carriage to see who might be listening, but there were only three workingmen seated in the rows ahead of them, each with his nose buried in his newspaper—legs spread, heads down, postures relaxed. Behind them a young woman in a plaid shawl sat embroidering a filthy handkerchief, squinting at her stitches in the smoky carriage light. She wore fingerless gloves yet no hat atop her simple bun. None of their fellow travelers seemed to have taken any notice of anyone else but themselves.

"It does have that ability, aye." He tipped the watch so she could see the flywheel whirring around almost as if it floated above the face of the clock. "But the wheel is measuring the static electricity in the air."

"Whatever for?"

"The presence of manifestations."

Her eyes rose from the watch to meet his. "You mean ghosts?"

"Aye, it can sense those, but it's mostly attuned to pick up vibrations of auras like ours, and sometimes even the residual energy of a spell if the magic was strong enough."

He demonstrated the different settings on the instrument and how they measured for the presence of supernatural beings within fifty paces, including themselves. The arrows on the face of the watch both pointed toward Edwina with alarming insistence, as her aural spectrum overshadowed Ian's. He gave the instrument a shake to see if it would reset. When it didn't, he closed the watch up, stowed the instrument back in his pocket, and uttered a slight "humph."

"I did recently cast a spell," she said, adjusting her shawl as she tried to reassure him. The train shuddered to a stop at the next station, and two of the men departed the coach. "Do the officers of the Witches' Constabulary carry such gadgets?" she asked when the car rolled forward again.

Such a curious and clever woman.

"They wish. No, this is an Elvanfoot invention. A gift. Though I've no doubt they'll try and get their hands on the ingenious devices one of these days."

Ian felt Edwina's mind whir at the mention of Sir Elvanfoot. Naturally, she knew who he was. Every witch in the isles knew who the great wizard of the north was. Not everyone had known the man had a son, however. Sadly, the son's talents with magic had proved mediocre at best, relegating him to an unremarkable life in his father's shadow. Until later, when he'd run off to the city to become a stage magician in a music hall variety show. Oh, he'd inherited a decent amount of talent for the craft. Enough to impress an audience of dozy mortals willing to pay good money to watch a string of average tricks, but in the north, he would never have been able to fulfill the expectations one held for the son of Sir Elvanfoot. And now, of course, the unfortunate fellow was missing.

Ian checked again to see if anyone was eavesdropping and noticed the young woman in plaid had tilted her ear ever so slightly in their direction. Her eyes no longer concentrated on her stitches but rather stared down at the floor without moving. He lowered his voice and leaned in close enough to Edwina's ear to make a blush rise in her cheeks.

"He gives lectures on magic in the summer," he explained. "Sir Elvanfoot, that is. That's how I met him. He's an acquaintance of my father's, so he came to me when he suspected his son had gone missing. That and I'm the only private detective investigating the supernatural outside of the Constabulary in the whole of the isles who could locate

George without alerting the authorities and making a mess of it in the papers."

"My father spoke of meeting Sir Elvanfoot once before as well." She peered ahead as if watching for something outside the window, despite the darkness of the tunnel. "I dare say we may have more in common than we might have first imagined." The train slowed and she gripped the back of the seat in front of her. "This is where we get off."

Out of habit, he opened his pocket watch for a quick sweep of the end of the tunnel. Forewarned was forearmed. He stood to let Edwina out of the seat they'd shared so she might disembark before him. Once she was out the door, his spectrometer spun toward the young embroiderer in plaid. She looked at him and moaned, revealing a face with sunken eyes and shriveled skin. The young woman gagged and retched on the seat beside her before dissipating from the car.

"Damn cholera," he whispered and shut the timepiece again, satisfied the decades-old ghost was the only other supernatural entity lurking in the train tunnel with them.

Back at street level, Edwina led him through the crowd of passengers coming and going in ten different directions. Nothing about their surroundings struck him as familiar until they exited the station. Outside, the bustle of the East End echoed in his ear, as recognizable as it was loud. The sound of heavy-footed horses hauling wagons collided with the clamor of men going to and from work, some shouldering ladders, some carrying buckets, and others walking with parcels tucked under their arms. Newspaper hawkers competed for customers, while women and children sold posies for a penny in the street. As they walked, the call of goods for sale proved as common as a tip of the hat and a "pardon me" when passing a stranger.

At the corner of the intersection in front of the station, Edwina took a moment to get her bearings, while Ian noted the grit in the air was thick enough to taste with each inhale. Her eyes scanned the skyline—the clock tower, the gilded eaves of the Rose & Crown pub across the street, and the row of striped awnings where the smell of slaughtered animals at the butcher's shop rode on a wave from a block away.

"There," she said at last, pointing straight down the street in front of them, where a man and two boys walked by with faces caked in coal dust. "Five minutes in that direction is the Wilshire Music Hall." She then directed his attention to the right. "That way there are boarding-houses and hotels on each side of the street. No matter if you took the underground train here after your journey south or you rode an omni-bus, you would have stood at this intersection four days ago. So where would your instincts tell you to go next in search of lodging?"

He'd already deduced what she was about. By having him stand in the same place he would have made his decision four days ago, they might track down where he'd stayed. Without a doubt he would have remained close to the one main clue he had about the man's last known whereabouts. "This way," he said as recognition slipped over his body like an overcoat. Memory in the form of déjà vu guided him, letting him feel out the lay of the street rather than truly remembering. He kept his eyes on the doorways of each business they passed—a hotel and tavern, a wine and spirit emporium, a sewing machine shop, another hotel that carried the whiff of a brothel—measuring each against his body's reaction. He rejected them one by one until they came to a door flanked by weather-beaten pillars. The name above the entrance read THE THREE HARES INN.

He stopped. The image conjured up memories of his mother danc-ing on the rocky moors among the heather with the full moon shining above. His intuition spiked. "Here," he said and charged up the front steps to the hotel. He took the skeleton key from his pocket. He was certain he'd found the place he'd been staying. He knew it at once. He also knew he wouldn't have thought to find the hotel in such a manner without the help of this bewitching creature standing at his side.

"Go on, then," Edwina said, smiling and sharing in his discovery.

His heart tapped out a steady beat of anticipation as he opened the door and approached the front desk. If he'd hoped for a friendly welcome of return, though, he was harshly rebuked. The clerk, a round man in tweed who bore a black mustache that curled up at the ends, recognized him straightaway. But instead of a nod and a smile to greet him, the man snapped his fingers at a hotel porter to get his attention. "Fetch that police officer who was just here," he ordered, then grabbed a wrought-iron fire poker from behind the counter and waved it like a weapon at Ian, warning him to stay back. After a wide-eyed glance, the terrified porter ducked out the door behind them to chase down a constable.

Ian automatically shielded Edwina with one arm stretched out in front of her. With his other he tried to reason with the man with the poker and keep him from doing anything stupid. "Are you off your head, man? What's happened? Why have you called in the police?"

"My maid discovered what you're about, that's what," he answered, jabbing the poker as he spoke. "Went in to clean your room, she did, and learned what a perverted, twisted mind you've got." The clerk's face screwed up in a look of scorn reserved for the most degenerate of creatures. "You've frightened the poor woman out of her mind. To find such things after all that business in the streets a decade ago with Old Jack, and now again with that Brick Lane Slasher."

Where had his investigation led to provoke this kind of response?

"I've no idea who this Brick Lane Slasher is. Sir, I'm a private investigator searching for a young man who's been missing for weeks. If you discovered anything odd or disturbing in my room, it was likely to do with my case files. Now, I'm going to need those items back, so hand me my belongings and I'll be on my way."

"Detective, are you? You'd have ID to prove it, then, wouldn't you?" The man gestured with his free hand for Ian to produce the evidence.

Ian let out a slow breath. "I haven't . . . my wallet was stolen only yesterday. Never mind that. Just let me have my things and I'll go. You'll never see me again."

"Hand them back?" The man huffed in disbelief. "No God-fearing man should want to be in possession of such shocking things." The clerk gritted his teeth and whispered his next words as if to shield Edwina from hearing him. "Drawings of naked men with their throats cut. Their heads bashed in. And to be so blackhearted as to leave that sort of wickedness lying about where my poor Polly would find it." He shook his head and warned, "Don't you move. The police are on their way, and then they'll fix you. It'll be the gallows at Northgate for you."

Edwina tugged at Ian's sleeve. "What do we do now, recite another poem?"

He looked at her and shrugged. "Run," he said, and together they skipped out the front door and down the steps, then fled through the crowded street as a police whistle blared at their backs.

Chapter Fourteen

Edwina raised her shawl over her head and caught her breath as she and Ian crouched behind a wagon sagging under the weight of a dozen beer barrels. The city's myriad streets and landmarks flashed in her head. A living map laid out under the daylight stars. Coordinates that aligned with magnetic poles and the invisible ley lines that ran from castles and palaces to cathedrals and monuments. She'd internalized this map of the streets from dusky evenings spent wandering through the smog- and cinder-filled air. Once learned, it would never leave her.

"You should go," Ian said. "It's me they're after. There's no need for you to get dragged into this trouble."

"Trouble? It's the most excitement I've had since I was a girl," she said. "Besides, I know a place. Come on."

Ian apparently made a split decision, choosing to trust her completely by following. He could put his faith in worse places, she thought. They crossed the road, darting in front of a carriage just as a bobby spotted them from three doors down.

They zigged and zagged through the crowded streets until they slipped around the corner of a pawnbroker at the end of a crooked lane, emerging in a sooty, bricked-in alley with a doorway cut into the wall every ten feet. Bedding hung overhead on ropes tied from one side of the alley to the other to dry, even though the damp never fully went away in the shadows. The smell of old cabbage stung the nose, and a chill crept between the collar and the skin, as if the sun had been closed off by a bank of clouds. A face peeked out of a curtained window above as a whistle blared on the street behind them, calling more officers to respond.

"Wait, where are we going?" Ian asked. "There's no cover. We'll be seen."

It certainly looked like a dead end. A trap. Not a soul in the lane but a fat pigeon that flapped out of their way with a squawk. Edwina beckoned Ian forward with a wave. "This way, if you don't want to end up in Northgate Prison tonight."

She counted the doors—five on the left, four, five, six on the right. At the seventh door on the right, as plain a door as ever there was in the city, she stopped. She hesitated only a moment before knocking. A disturbingly long moment later—long enough to let panic seep under the collar alongside the cold—the door opened. An elderly woman wearing a black mourning dress trimmed in crepe squinted at them with suspicion. "Yes?"

"Merry meet," Edwina said, lowering her shawl so the woman could get a good look at her. "I was told this was a safe place to knock if ever I was in trouble." At the end of the lane, two police officers spotted Ian and Edwina, shouting at them to halt.

"I wasn't expecting you so soon." The old woman threw wide the door so they could enter, but before she shut it behind them again, she grabbed a handful of coal dust from a bucket by the door and blew it into the lane from her palm. Darkness descended at the end of the crooked lane. The bobbies' shouts went silent, and the woman closed the door and slid the bolt in place.

"The fools will mill about a few moments before they figure out they took a wrong turn." She waved at Edwina and Ian to follow her through the shabby front room with its single upholstered chair set before a cold stove, a wobbly side table with a bowl half-full of curdled mush, and plank floors covered with a moth-eaten rug that was doing a poor job of disguising the swales and warps underfoot. Indeed, the ground felt anything but stable at the moment.

"A friend of yours?" Ian whispered. He opened his jacket and reached for his pocket watch.

Edwina shook her head. "My father gave me the address. For if I ever needed help from pitchfork-wielding mortals."

The old woman looked over her shoulder at them. "I'm Abigail Featherstone. Folk around here call me Abby." She smiled reassuringly, but the effect was eerily reminiscent of a skeleton's deathly grin, offering little comfort. The woman chuckled to herself and passed through a curtain to a back room where a washtub and pile of laundry four feet high sat in the middle of the floor. There, a young girl in a filthy dress and plaid shawl stroked a rabbit she held in her arms. Her eyes brightened at the sight of Ian stepping through the curtain before her face scrunched up in confusion when she saw Edwina in her shawl.

"I'm sorry," Edwina said as doubts crept in. "I think we may have come to the wrong place."

"Show them, Charlotte. Before they change their minds and leave."

The girl waggled her finger at what appeared to be a broom closet. "In there," she said and pulled the door open. A wooden ironing board fell out and clattered to the floor. The girl made a face as though she'd made a mistake. Abigail picked up the ironing board, then quickly shut the door.

"Maybe we'd better go," Ian said, shaking his watch as if it were broken.

"Nonsense, you must stay and have some tea." The old woman briefly closed her eyes and exhaled. "Stop staring, Charlotte, and try again," she said with practiced patience.

The girl petted her rabbit three times, then again waggled her finger at the door. This time when she reached for the handle, the door opened and a warm glow shone from within. Edwina, drawn in by her curiosity, moved closer. The light was coming from dozens of candles that flickered from another room. One that had not been there a moment ago. The scent of lavender and orange petals wafted out, reminding her of a summer garden party. She stepped closer and saw that it was a drawing room with four red velvet wingback chairs and matching footstools with gold tassels. A fire blazed at the hearth, and a steaming pot of tea sat on a table aside a plate of biscuits.

"You'll be more comfortable inside," Abigail said, gesturing with an extended arm for them to enter. "Well done, Charlotte."

It took a dose of blind courage to trust the witch who was offering them sanctuary, but Edwina didn't think her father would have given her the address if he didn't mean for her to someday use it. He might yet prove himself to be the sort of person who abandoned his adult daughters, but in her eyes he was and always would be a man who'd done the best he could for his unnatural family.

Edwina felt a hand at her elbow. A caution from Ian. Yet instinct told her to trust, and so she ducked her head and walked through the closet door. The welcome warmth of the room, along with a general feeling of comfort and safety, put her at ease. The walls were delicately patterned with gold fleur-de-lis flocked wallpaper, and a crystal chandelier lit with white candles hung overhead. It had to be an illusion, but if so, the girl had done a grand job.

Edwina swung around to encourage Ian to follow when a miniature hairy creature in a tattered green jacket bowed at the waist in greeting.

"Welcome, milady."

Ian poked his head through the doorway before following her inside. "Hob? What the devil?"

"Mister! Come in, come in! All is warm and well."

"How did you get here?"

The door closed behind them, leaving Edwina and Ian alone with Hob, who jumped up on one of the footstools by the fire.

"You said stay out of sight. This is where I went." The little creature made a face like it was obvious. "This is where all find shelter."

"Ah, I think I'm beginning to see," Ian said, putting his watch away.

"Well, I'm not entirely sure I do." Edwina sat in a chair near the fire, though she did not remove her shawl. Not yet.

"It's a safe house," Ian said. "A port in a mortal storm, if you will." He sat opposite and reached for the teapot on the table between them. "A network is said to exist throughout the isles." He paused to pour them each a cup of steaming Darjeeling. "I had no idea one existed in this part of the city."

Edwina accepted her tea in a china cup and admired the black-and-gold design of astrological signs set in an intricate pattern around the rim. "I had no idea anything so broad as a network existed at all. My father merely said I would find help here."

Ian crossed the room to the bookshelf. He pulled loose a fat tome, hefting it in his hand. "*Lady Everly's Grimoire*," he said, impressed. He replaced the book and tipped the spine of another to reveal a cover made entirely of bark, entitled *Herbal Remedies of the Dryad*. "It appears to be a well-stocked library of the occult as well."

"Anything in those books that can explain what happened to make us require a safe house?"

"Ah, right." He let out a sigh and replaced the wooden book. "Hob, go fetch us a couple of local newspapers."

The little fellow stood at attention. "As you wish," he said before scrunching up his nose as if wondering where he might procure such a thing. Seemingly arriving at an answer, he snapped his fingers and dove into a decorative porcelain urn beside the fireplace.

"How does he do that?"

Ian returned to his seat and crossed his legs. "His kind has their networks too. Dinna ask me how it works. I dinna ken parallel-world theory."

Edwina set her cup down half-finished and leaned forward. "What could have provoked that hotel clerk to accuse you of those things he said?"

He leaned back in his chair and casually smiled at her. "I notice you don't seem particularly fashed by the idea of sitting in a parlor alone with an accused degenerate, sipping tea and warming your sodden feet by the fire."

"Well, I suppose I hold out hope the notion isn't true," she said, feeling a flush. It wasn't only the nearness of the fire making her cheeks warm. With the little imp gone, she and Ian had been left alone in the room without a chaperone of any kind. The tingling that arose in her bloodstream at the thought made her feel as if she could create any kind of magic she chose in that moment. He gazed at her with a hint of amusement as he pursed his lips slightly. Given her limited experience with men, she wasn't sure how to interpret such a look. Freddie's attention had always been very formal, with his mother orchestrating their every moment together. There had been furtive glances on sofas, but they always ended in giggles, as if each of them were embarrassed to sit so near the other. Not so with Ian. With her blood up, she allowed herself to wonder if such interest was based on more than mere scrutiny. She dared not look away as the firelight caught in his eyes.

"As for your question," he said, sobering, "I'd guess my investigation led me to a disturbing conclusion concerning Elvanfoot's son. If I left behind drawings and notes in my room related to a string of murders, I must have found some connection." His hand reached for his throat again and he shook his head. "Might be that's what led me to the foreshore as well. But I still have no recollection of any of it."

Edwina gave a shake of her head. She preferred to invest as little attention as possible in the mundane world of the mortals outside her shop door. Better to keep to a low profile lest trouble was on the lookout for a new perch to alight on. Still, customers were always coming in with stories of someone getting knocked on the head outside of some pub. Or someone getting cut with a knife down on the docks. The night gave cover to any number of crimes, including murder. But none of the city's dangerous side had touched her personally until she found Ian unconscious on the shore. Now it seemed to follow everywhere they went.

"A customer complained of the recent attacks the other day. I'm sorry. I should have paid more attention."

"You're not fond of residing in the city, are you?"

"No, I find the air choking and the noise unnerving. But, oddly, it has been a kinder place for us to live at times." She hesitated to reveal their father's motivation for moving the family from the countryside, though she suspected he'd already guessed their relocation had to do with Mary's attraction to corpse lights. "My sister and I are often viewed as outsiders, and always will be, but most people here are too busy merely trying to survive day to day to fixate on why we're different." *Except for that damn boy.* "Life is sometimes more difficult in smaller rural villages, though the air is cleaner."

Ian's regard noticeably shifted, as though viewing her through a different lens. She found herself slightly disappointed by the predictable turn in him, going from being a creature of interest in his eyes back to one deserving of apprehension. Curiously, he swallowed and brushed the back of his knuckles against his Adam's apple again.

"I can give you something for a sore throat, if that's what's bothering you," Edwina said, letting him know he was being watched as well.

Ian removed his hand as if he hadn't realized he'd reached for his neck. His clear-eyed gaze had been replaced by something closer to regret as he waved off her offer. "Nae, 'tisn't that." He seemed on the verge of saying more when Hob jumped out of the urn holding a bundle of newspapers in his arms. "Ah, you're back," he said to the imp, glad for the distraction.

"So many chimneys!" Hob dropped the newspapers at Ian's feet. "So dirty," he said and brushed a layer of sooty grime off the sleeves of his coat.

Ian tossed Hob a biscuit for his effort, then picked up the *Courier Times* off the pile. "Well done, Hob. Now, let's see if we can sort out what all this murder business is about."

He didn't even need to spread the newspaper open to find what he was after. There on the front page awaited the headline: BRICK LANE SLASHER STRIKES AGAIN. The report stated at least five men had been found bludgeoned over the past two weeks, all within a ten-minute walk of Brick Lane Station. Four of the five had their throats cut as well. Robbery appeared to be the main motivation in most of the attacks, as evidenced by their empty pockets, though none of the victims were considered anything more than middle-class workingmen.

Edwina opened the *Daily Gazette*, which appeared to carry a slightly different version of events. The details were salacious, describing the murders as ghastly crimes committed by a predator of the night. A creature so debased as to leave his bloodless victims lying in the road for any innocent passerby to discover. "Propped in full view, the latest mutilated bodies were as good as trophies at proclaiming the murderer's aptitude for his newfound vocation," she read aloud.

Ian looked up from his paper. "Mutilated?" He scanned ahead in his paper. "As well as having their throat cut nearly to beheading, the murdered victims each had a piece of their scalp removed just above the ear, leading some to speculate about a connection to the occult and ritual murder."

Hob swallowed his biscuit, shrank down inside his coat, and pulled his collar over his head.

"Sensationalist drivel," Edwina said and tipped the paper to show Ian the illustration accompanying the article she'd been reading, which displayed an artist's rendering of a man in a plaid suit lying in a narrow alley amid a pool of blood and what she surmised was a layer of straw to wick up the moisture in a narrow, sodden walkway. The artist had inked a bald blotch above the deceased's left ear.

Ian's expression changed from a man on the hunt for clues to one of confusion quickly dissolving into distress. He dropped the *Courier Times* and asked to see her *Gazette*. While he studied the illustration, she flipped through the morning edition of the *City Journal*, searching for any new information.

"Well, isn't that odd," she said. "This paper has Henry Elvanfoot listed as the latest victim." Beside her, Hob poked his head out of his jacket, ears twitching. "Could they mean the son, George, instead? Is that why he's gone missing? How dreadful."

Edwina covered her mouth with her hand as she read, almost afraid to continue. "But that would explain the connection of your case to the murders, wouldn't it? You were right." When Ian didn't answer, she glanced up to see he'd gone deathly pale. "Whatever's wrong?" He drew a hand over his face as if he might be sick. "Are you ill? Should I fetch some honey for a tea spell?"

Hob jumped on the arm of her chair. "I can get that for you, milady."

Ian shushed him harshly. "Never mind that, Hob. I'm not ill. I'm simply seeing shadows." He tossed the illustrated newspaper on the table between him and Edwina and pointed. "I've been there before."

She turned the paper around and read the description beneath the picture. The victim depicted had been found facedown in Wickham Lane. "A winding walkway between buildings connecting the two main streets of Flint Street and Queen's Road," she said, as her intuition began to tingle in warning. "That's near where I picked you up this morning."

"Nae, it's *exactly* where I was when I sent that boy after you." He sat back, eyeing her with what she took for suspicion. "I was there. Stumbling as though I were drunk. Hit on the head by a man I'd passed in that alley," he said, touching the back of his head as if visualizing the attack. "I fell to the ground, only to have the man lift my head up by my hair and slice my throat open in one jagged motion." He clutched at his throat again, swallowing as if it pained him to do so, then looked up. "It's where I remember being murdered."

"You know that's not possible," she said, hoping he would see the illogic of his statement. "You haven't been murdered."

"Nae, of course not."

"You did get hit on the head yesterday, but it wasn't in an alley."

"But after that. The memory you implanted, the one you thought was mine . . ." He picked up the newspaper again. "You gave me the wrong one. I think it belonged to this man," he said, pointing at the drawing. "This is what I experienced. I lived his memory of that moment all over again. I know what it felt like to have my throat cut, ye ken? I relived this victim's last breath. I remember what he suffered." He stood, too agitated to sit while he thought it through. "Your sister removed the man's memory from me this morning, aye, but first she took it from him the same way she took mine at the river." Ian paced so that he stood behind his chair, gripping the back of it. "She was there."

Edwina took a second look at the illustration. The brutal rendition of a man's demise cooled her blood but also stoked her denial. "No, she couldn't have," she said, sliding the paper back toward Ian. "There has to be some other explanation. Some corruption of the spell, some manipulation—"

"But she must have. How else could I know what this man went through?" He stood back and held up his hands. "He had a silver match safe in his pocket. With a mermaid on the cover. Does it say anything in any of the papers about what was stolen from him?"

Edwina scanned all three papers while Ian paced. She found a list of missing belongings mentioned in the *Gazette*, items family members swore the victims had on them before they died. She trailed through the mentions of rings, keys, buttons, and even a pair of reading glasses. Then her finger landed on a silver match safe described as having a mermaid on it. Could he have read ahead and seen that part already?

"What is it? Did they mention the match safe?"

She folded the newspaper closed. "There must be an explanation."

"Aye, there is. You gave me a dead man's memory; that's why my mind rejected it. Now, how and where your sister obtained the memory in the first place is another matter."

The instinct to protect Mary from incendiary accusations rose inside her yet again. "Speak plainly, Mr. Cameron. What are you saying?"

"Speak plainly? Very well. How does your sister get ahold of a man's memory who was murdered in an alley in the middle of the night?"

"There are any number of ways. At the hospital, the morgue—"

"What kind of woman does that?" Ian raked his forelock with his fingers as he paced. "Who goes to the hospital or morgue to reap a dead man's memories? What kind of lust grows inside a woman to be able to do that?"

"Her magic is complicated."

"Complicated?" Lashing out, Ian reached for the stack of papers, holding up the headlines of murder. "It's not very complicated to wonder if that gent's memories aren't the only ones she's taken."

"You don't understand."

"I think I'm beginning to ken just fine. This is the second time Mary and violence have held hands. Or do you forget I was hit on the back of the head and left for dead as well? My memories sucked out of me as if by some kind of vampire of the mind."

Edwina had witnessed her sister being accused before. She'd watched helplessly as their lives got turned upside down and inside out because of people's rush to judgment. Mortals usually. They called her unnatural, peculiar, abnormal. But this insult was too much. She would not entertain such accusations again.

Edwina set aside her tea. "I'm sorry you feel that way," she said and walked out through the broom closet door before she dared show any tears in front of Ian or any other man again.

Chapter Fifteen

A cool draft blew through the parlor at Edwina's swift departure.

Ian stared at the door. "Blast the day I ever met that woman and her sister."

"You don't mean that," Hob said, placing his hand on the chair where the witch had been sitting.

"Don't I?"

The hearth elf shook his head. "A fine lady. And she was helping you."

"Please dinna go getting sentimental on me," Ian said before giving ground. "Aye, I know. Miss Blackwood has her charms. And under different circumstances, I might give in to them. But her sister, that Mary Bewitched, is a strange one. There's an unhealthy dose of shadow lurking behind those eyes."

"You do not know everything."

"Nae, not everything. But enough. I found the truth once before, and I will again." Ian tossed the newspapers on the table. "Come, Hob, we've got work to do."

Ian stepped out of the broom closet and passed through the shabby slum house. He consulted his watch. The lane outside was quiet, empty of police and signs of the supernatural, except for the old woman and girl inside who had wished him luck and shut the door behind him. So Edwina was well and truly gone. Fair enough, he thought. By his reckoning, it was only a matter of time and dogged determination before they came full circle and met again, if his current investigation led to the same place he believed his previous one had. He snapped his pocket watch shut and flipped his collar up. "This way, Hob," he said and marched south toward the one solid lead in his missing person's case. Hob followed by diving in and out of rain barrels, bottle-washing troughs, and downspouts as he traveled his unseen network of mysterious passages.

After a five-minute walk, dodging costermongers selling jellied eel and fatty pigs' trotters and one down-on-her-luck witch pushing blister ointment made of fireplace ash and common tallow, he stood in front of the Wilshire Music Hall. Two grand wooden doors painted red loomed ten feet high flanked by ornate carvings meant to give the place a baroque sensibility, but a quick scratch with his fingernail suggested the material was a plaster veneer instead of marble. And, like the walls, the paint was beginning to peel.

He tried the front doors but they proved locked, so he scanned the venue advertisement pasted to the wall outside. As with the building's facade, the broadside displayed the same flamboyant flair, promising a show that was perhaps many times more respectable than the one that actually took place on the stage. The revue featured the usual parade of jugglers, singers, and comedy sketches. The descriptions made it sound as if entering the theater were on par with visiting the Royal Hall. In reality, most music halls he'd visited skirted indecency laws by a mere hair, which, he admitted, accounted for their wild popularity.

"There's got to be another way in," he said to Hob, cocking his head to the right, where a narrow alley cut between buildings. The imp jumped out of one of the wrought-iron urns flanking the front door, still pouting. "She'll have got home fine," Ian said, seeing his companion out of sorts.

"You shouldn't have let her leave like that."

Silently he agreed, but there was nothing to be done about it now. "We'll talk about it later. Come on, help me find a side door."

Hob reluctantly followed him around the corner of the building into the alley, where they found the stage door used by the performers. There was also a basement delivery door a few feet away at the bottom of a stairwell, but a quick glance confirmed it was occupied by a homeless man curled up at the bottom. It wasn't worth the ruckus of getting past him, so Ian returned to the stage entrance. Out of an abundance of caution, he took out his watch to take a quick reading. If Elvanfoot's son had worked the theater, then it was possible other magical folk did too. As he suspected, a spectral glow indicated the presence of—he tilted his watch to get a better view—a witch and possibly a pixie, judging by the hue and frequency displayed on the spectrometer.

"Hmm, one of yours and one of mine nearby," he stated with one brow raised.

Hob shook himself, then smoothed the hair back from his face. His eyes shone bright and curious as he pressed an ear to the door. "Do I go in with you?"

Ian's inclination was always to say no at this point. He was better off doing this sort of work alone, but as he put his watch away, he wondered what he might encounter on the other side and had second thoughts. "Stay in the shadows if you can," he said and tried the door. Finding it unlocked, they entered, only to be met by an older man sitting on a stool hunched over a tall clerk's desk with an oil lamp that emitted a curlicue of malodorous black smoke. The gentleman wore a flatcap and frizzy gray sideburns that came halfway down his cheeks, neither of which elicited any recognition whatsoever for Ian. Apparently, the ignorance was mutual.

"Auditioning for the new act, are you?" The man studied Ian over the top of a pair of spectacles. "You're late. They already started." His gaze dropped down to Hob, who hadn't quite managed to get out of sight yet. "So what are you? A ventriloquist?"

"What's a *ven trill o kissed*?" Hob asked, clasping his hands together in front of him before Ian nudged him with his knee.

The manager stared and chuckled. "Not bad. We haven't had a good dummy in the lineup for six months or more. Hope you've got some fresh material. People around here're too savvy for the same old slop. What's the puppet's name?"

"Er, Hob."

"'Course it is. All right, then. Off you go. Down the hall. Auditorium's on your right. Mind you stay clear of the liquor at the bar until after you've done your bit. Then you can buy as many spirits as you like until the crowds show up."

"Much obliged." Ian nodded at the man, then lifted Hob up in his arms to reinforce the illusion, whispering, "Quiet."

Embracing his new disguise, Ian explored the brick-lined hallway, hoping to pry loose some recognition. As he ducked around a set of wooden stairs that led to the balcony seating, he spotted the area across the lobby the doorman had mentioned. It was an okay setup with a six-stool mahogany bar and a back-wall shelf filled with enough spirits to empty the pockets of the entertainment-seeking East Enders and keep the West Enders happily drunk while out for a night of slumming. Still, his stomach lurched at the thought of a drink. It might not have been his memory dictating his actions the night before, but it most certainly was his body that was paying the price today. It agitated him that he could remember another man's thoughts yet not all his own. He must have been inside the music hall before. It would have been the first place he'd have checked for the missing son. Yet nothing felt familiar.

Behind the bar, a man in a black waistcoat and white shirt polished a whisky glass with a brown rag. Ian donned a look-of-the-lost as he casually approached the man.

"Keep moving that way," the bartender said with a nod of his head toward the auditorium door when he caught Ian eyeing the goods.

"Right, only I was wondering if I could ask you a question first."

The bartender eyed him suspiciously as he set the glass down and picked up another. "Can't run a tab for you. No buying on tick while you wait to get paid. Management will have you tossed out quicker than you can put words in that dummy's mouth."

Hob glared.

"Actually, I'm curious if you know George Elvanfoot. Supposedly does an act here as a magician."

"Who?" the man answered with a double take. "Ah, hang on, do you mean Georgie? George Fey?"

Fey? An alias? Stage name? Ian made a mental note, wishing he had his notebook.

"That's right. We did a gig together last year. Thought I'd look him up again. Heard he ran into a little trouble."

"Yeah, odd story, that. Supposedly went missing about three weeks ago. Lizzie's been broken up about it ever since."

"Lizzie?"

Lizzie. Short for Elizabeth? Elvanfoot Senior never mentioned a woman. Mental note number two.

The bartender pointed toward a poster on the opposite wall. It showed a sepia-toned photo of an attractive Black woman in a lacy dress perched on a swing embellished with gardenias. The tagline called Lizzie Stanfield "a mesmerizing chanteuse of unequal measure from across the pond."

"She's—"

"A Yank, sure enough, but sings like a right nightingale." The bartender tossed the rag over his shoulder. "She made a report with the Yard, but I don't think she's heard nothing. 'Course she's all broke up, what with all the headlines lately."

And yet Ian knew George wasn't among the listed victims.

"Any chance she's here now? I'd like to offer my sympathies after my, er, audition. Let her know Georgie's a friend." Ian jostled Hob in his arms, selling the ventriloquist angle.

"I swear that's the strangest-looking dummy anyone's ever brought in here."

"Made him myself."

"But I'm at least a hundred years older," Hob said, dutifully objecting to seal the illusion.

The man pulled a face, then nudged his head toward the auditorium. "Yeah, go on. Down to the front of the house, hook a left backstage. She's the third door on the right." He checked the clock on the wall behind him before turning his attention back to his glass polishing. "She's usually in there warming up for her routine by now."

Ian entered the auditorium with Hob still held in the crook of his arm. Inside, the grand chandelier remained dark and the empty balcony seats overhung the space like a looming apparition, but the main floor was vibrant with the noise and action of the auditions. He counted a dozen people who sat scattered among the first three rows of seats, each dressed in costume or brandishing a prop. Some rehearsed while awaiting their turn onstage, but sitting alone in the center of the fifth row was a bald man smoking a cigarette who was clearly in charge of the future of those he presided over. He called out a number, then yelled at the woman standing onstage to begin, while a piano player hammered on a few keys to check for tune.

Even from the back of the house, Ian could make out how tight the woman's formfitting gown was. The silk was a deep lavender, and she wore a matching hat with a white ostrich feather that seemed to only accentuate her already statuesque figure. The music started and she opened her fan, waving it coquettishly as she began to sing "Come Along, Johnny." The performance started out quite charming, then grew bawdier by the minute as her leers and gyrations put a different emphasis on the double entendres buried in the innocent-sounding lyrics. The sparse audience howled with laughter, though the bald man merely called out, "All right, Simon. You're in. Off you go, mate. Next!"

The commotion gave Ian the opportunity he needed to move unnoticed. He skirted the aisle on the left, hugging the shadows along the auditorium wall until he slipped through the unmarked exit leading to the hall backstage. He lingered inside the door as the woman onstage bowed. She thanked the audience with a wave of her fan and a deep-voiced "Cheers, love" before walking back to the house seats to sit beside a petite woman in a tutu. *She* must be the pixie his watch had indicated, he thought, though there was no telling from where he stood who the witch might be.

Backstage, the theater's glamorous facade had been stripped away to expose the wires, beams, and rough plank floors holding the place together. A row of costumes hung on a rack pushed up against the wall, and set pieces had been jigsaw-puzzled together and stowed at the end of the hallway. A miller moth danced around a bare electric lightbulb suspended from the ceiling as the smell of sweaty bodies and perfume lingered in the dim passage.

Ian counted three doors down. "This is where I need you to get out of sight," he said to Hob. The little fellow sprang from his arms, ready to scurry off, but then hesitated. The woman on the other side of the door had begun making nonsense noises while singing notes from low to high to low again. Ian leaned in too. The voice was smooth and practiced with an entertainer's edge, but he had to admit it was nowhere near as compelling as the lilt of Edwina's singing. An unprecedented pang of guilt interrupted Ian's focus, compounded by a disapproving shake of the head from Hob. "Never mind," he whispered, then nudged his chin at the imp, telling him to go as he knocked gently on the door.

The woman inside stopped singing. "Who is it?"

"Ian Cameron. I'm a private detective. I wondered if we could have a word, Miss Stanfield."

The door swung open and he found himself temporarily dumbstruck. A woman in a lacy white evening gown stood before him, her deep brown eyes filled with an intoxicating mix of hope and fear. A common-enough expression in his line of work, but her photo had entirely underestimated how beautiful she was in person. He'd been too slow to hide his surprise and had to close his mouth as she invited him into her dressing room.

Hand on hip, Lizzie asked, "Well, have you found him?"

He understood by the way she spoke he'd already had this conversation with her once. "Nae, Miss, I canna confirm I've found him yet. And I'm afraid there's been a complication."

No correction on the "miss," so they weren't married. Mental note number three.

She motioned for him to sit on the velvet love seat while she reached for a newspaper on the side table. "Have you seen this?" It was a copy of the *City Journal* with the headline screaming about murder.

Ian took the paper from her eager hands and read the paragraph she pointed to about the lone man who'd survived being attacked. Edwina had mentioned the name Elvanfoot was listed in the paper, but he'd been too distracted to understand the implication of what she'd said. His heart plunged into ice water at the thought of what he must tell Lizzie.

"It's him," she insisted. "It has to be. Look at the name." She bit her nail as she waited for Ian to come to the same conclusion. "That's his real name. Fey is his stage name. But why hasn't anyone from the police come by the theater to check? Or come tell me what happened or where he is?" The name in the paper listed Henry Elvanfoot as the lone victim to have survived an attack. "They got the first name mixed up, is all." She began to pace. "The papers get things wrong all the time, right? Which means he's alive."

"Nae, Lizzie, listen to me. That's what I need to tell you. The man listed in the paper is me. I'm the one they found on the foreshore. I'm the one who was hit on the head and left for dead. I had a sort of amnesia when I woke up in hospital," he said, not yet knowing how much he could confide about magic to this woman. "Couldn't remember anything. The police found Henry Elvanfoot's card in my pocket and thought that's who I was. A wee muddle. I'm sorry, lass. It isn't him."

She sank onto the stool in front of her makeup mirror. "Then where is he?"

"I'm sorry I canna tell you yet. I still dinna remember everything that's happened over the last four days. But I believe I was very close to finding him. I must have been, to earn that clout on the head."

"Four days? Didn't take you for a drinker, Mr. Cameron." Her eyes gave him the once-over, from his unshaven face to his wrinkled clothes that reeked of the foreshore and city soot. "I've seen men black out for days at a time before."

"Nae, 'tisn't that. I promise you. Just a hit on the head." He struggled with the notion of explaining the truth, but it was clear she was a mortal, and there was no way of knowing how much George Elvanfoot had confided in her. "All I know is I was sent here to find George, and I will. With your help, if you'll give it."

Ian swore she sniffed the air to see if she smelled alcohol on him, then gave a vague nod of her head. "That's what you said the other day when you were here. That you'd find him. But it's already been near three weeks since he disappeared. Why wouldn't he come home unless something terrible has happened? And with that maniac roaming the streets out there attacking people. I've checked the hospitals and the police station, but the cops don't know nothing. Or more like don't want to talk to me."

He was certain more than ever there was a connection between George's disappearance and the recent string of murders. He wouldn't have spent time drawing crime scenes in his hotel room if he hadn't thought the events were related. He didn't get distracted from a case. He charged forward, following one lead after another until he came to the end of the line, working out the details with notes, drawings, and interviews. The same way he'd worked a case when he was a detective with the Witches' Constabulary. Whatever happened to George Elvanfoot, or George Fey, was inexplicably tied up in the city's latest drama.

"I'm sorry to do this to you, Lizzie, but can we start over again? Can you tell me everything you told me before? When was the last time you saw George? Did anything unusual happen that day? His father gave me the name of this music hall as a contact point, but he wasn't sure if it was still true, so maybe start with why he might have said that."

Lizzie had been lost in her own thoughts as he spoke, obviously listening with only one ear. But at the mention of the father, she seemed to find a steady point to hold on to. "George didn't think his father approved of his work in the city. I've never met his father, but I know he's never made the effort to visit us. Shame, really. George has made a real name for himself recently."

"He works as a magician, doesn't he?" Ian casually opened his watch to get another reading, wondering if Lizzie knew of George's magical heredity. He was reasonably certain she was pure mortal, but it never hurt to check, especially for those attracted to the stage.

"He was still doing his magic act when we first met. We got hired on at the Wilshire at the same time two years ago. He had a natural gift for doing tricks, you know? Never even rehearsed. But it wasn't what he wanted to do. Not long term."

"What did he want?"

Lizzie picked up a stick of lip color and turned toward the vanity mirror. "Like I told you last time, he's an actor now," she said, as if George had achieved the highest rung one could reach. She drew a layer of rose pink on her lips that accentuated her flawless skin and brown eyes. "He got the lead in a new play by Jacques Dubois. Not in one of those West End house productions but very up and coming. In the city proper at the Belfry Theater." She stopped and pressed her lips together. "Only it's an odd play. About man's duality and inner demons. Half-man, half-beast storyline. Don't get me wrong, he was perfect for the role, but the burden of taking on such a disturbed character changed him."

"Oh? How so?" Ian asked.

Lizzie hesitated, as though unsure how much she should share, then apparently erred on the side of more was better if it meant finding George and bringing him home. "He got real philosophical, you know? Asking questions about the meaning of life. The inequality of power. He was always a serious man, but he knew how to have a good laugh too. It's why I fell in love with him. But after performing the role for a couple of weeks, he began sulking during the day. I'd catch him staring out the window in the middle of the afternoon. Just watching the crowds and carriages going by for an hour or more, and all the time talking about how depraved people really were on the inside. And how if only there were windows on people's brains, you could see what despicable thoughts they were truly having."

Ian didn't think it out of the ordinary for someone working in the arts to be moody, but if the behavior was unusual for George, the development could be significant. "Tell me again about the day he disappeared."

Lizzie's shoulders fell as she put the cap back on her lipstick. "He was supposed to meet me here to escort me home. His play ends about eleven. I don't finish here until well after one in the morning, so he walks over and waits in the back of the house until my final song."

"Does he ever stop off for a pint at a pub on his way over? Meet friends? Regularly stop anywhere else in between?"

"You really don't remember anything I told you before, do you?" She shifted on her seat to look him in the eye. "Must have been some serious knock on the head." When he didn't offer any more explanation, she turned back to her mirror and fastened a white gardenia in her hair. "He doesn't drink. Claims it interferes with his concentration. Only he does sometimes wander the back lanes. Says it helps him clear his mind to walk the quiet streets at night when everyone's gone to bed."

Though not thoroughly familiar with the distance on foot from one part of the city to the other, Ian tried to do the math in his head and figured it might take a man about thirty minutes to walk from what he judged to be the city center. "But since he goes to the back of the house to wait, you wouldn't really know what time he arrives, isn't that right?"

"Well, isn't that funny; that's exactly what you said a few days ago."

"Suppose it's how my mind works when it isn't all a jumble." Ian felt a slight tingle creep up the back of his neck. His intuition was whispering in his mind's ear that he was close to discovering something. "Remind me again where the Belfry Theater's at."

"On Finley Street near the embankment at Old Bridge Road."

"Old Bridge Road?" His intuition's voice went from a whisper to a scream, stopping him cold. A mere two-minute walk from the very spot he'd climbed down from the embankment only that morning to see where he'd been hit on the back of the head. He swallowed, feeling his Adam's apple rise and fall, resisting the urge to clutch his throat and check for a bloody gash.

"Just one more question," Ian said. "Did George ever mention a woman named Mary Blackwood?"

Chapter Sixteen

Edwina ducked inside the shop just as that horrid boy spotted her and grinned in that disconcerting, bullying way of his. Why was he always watching the shop? Why couldn't he harass some malcontent toff on the high road for a change?

"Where've you been?" Mary asked.

Edwina shut the shop door behind her. "Sorry I've been gone so long," she said, swinging her shawl off and hanging it on the hook behind the counter. "I lost track of time."

Mary, who'd been polishing the silver pieces, placed a spoon on a front table, arranging it beside its twin. "Best be careful with that one," she said. "He's handsome enough, but there's something suspicious about a man's intentions when he asks a woman to escort him to the foreshore unchaperoned."

"Don't be absurd." Edwina tried to cover up her discomfort at the mention of Ian, but she could never hide anything from her sister.

"Are you saying he was a complete gentleman?"

"In the ways that count." Edwina looked at the tally book to see if they'd had any sales while she was out.

"Oh, do tell."

"You sold that handsome set of mother-of-pearl buttons." Ignoring the demand for more information, Edwina tried to read the amount, but the numbers blurred in her teary vision. What was happening to her?

Mary swooped in and put her arm around her sister. "There, there, what's the matter? It's not like you to cry like this." The combined scent of vinegar and baking soda clung to her sister's hands and sleeves from the polishing, making Edwina pull away.

"Oh, it's everything. Mother leaving. Then Father. Both without a word of explanation. As if we were a burden they grew tired of carrying around. Us never fitting in anywhere no matter how hard we try." Edwina sniffled and gestured to the window, where the nipper with the name too big for him leaned his back against the glass. "And why is that wretched boy always hanging around our front door with that smirk on his face?"

"Oh dear. And perhaps a certain man has proved all too human?" Mary said. Edwina dabbed at her eyes as her sister turned them both away from the window so they wouldn't have to see the boy anymore. "Let's close the shop early. I made some very good sales today. The women on the street can't buy enough hatpins lately. We should have our rent money by now. Come upstairs. I'll put a kettle on and you can tell me all about your day's adventures."

It was far too early to close the shop, but Edwina agreed to the tea. The events of the past two days had been emotionally exhausting, further reminding her of her limitations and her limited life. Her sister was mildly teasing her. Mary knew adventure wasn't a word or deed that naturally bonded itself to Edwina. Duty and responsibility, that's what steeled her blood. Oh, but she had enjoyed the morning hunting on the foreshore for clues, fighting off a gang of thieves (even if they were mere teens), flying underground in search of forgotten lodgings, and even drinking tea in a witch's safe house while reading the ghastly details of the city's latest murder spree to try and piece together Ian's lost few days. Until he turned horrid with his accusations. Like everyone always did in the end.

Mary went upstairs to make the tea, so Edwina remained behind to watch the shop. While she waited for her sister, she returned to the ledger to check whether Mary was right about the rent. Since their father left, they'd managed to pay on time each month, though every now and then Mary had to magic up a tiny gem—nothing too extravagant, just an opal or teardrop of amber—that they then affixed to a hatpin or letter opener. While not strictly legal, according to the city bylaws for witches, selling such things to the occasional well-to-do customer browsing the shop for a bargain afforded them the money needed for food and maybe even a new pair of shoes and stockings. She ticked off the sales they'd made in her head and found Mary was correct. The mother-of-pearl buttons, along with a pewter mug and three hatpins, had put them over the top of what they needed to earn a profit for the day.

Outside, the boy paced in front of the shop until something stole his attention. His head snapped up and he trotted off, as if answering a summons. Drawn to the window to satisfy a nagging curiosity, she barely caught sight of the boy as he rounded the corner and disappeared. One of these days she'd follow him home and speak to his mother. If he had one. The thought spiraled into a plan in the back of her mind as Mary descended the stairs with a tray laden with blessed relief in the form of tea.

Edwina joined her sister behind the curtain in the back room, where Mary poured a steaming blend of chamomile tea from their mother's pot into two chipped china cups that bore similar yet different patterns. Cherry blossoms ran around the outside rim on one, rose tendrils on the other. While the patterns were complementary, Edwina had always been embarrassed by the obvious mismatch when set side by side. But then other days she was grateful to have a china cup at all to drink from, when half the time it seemed they had to practically steal from the Fates to afford anything new. And how thoughtful of Mary to set out two slices of brown bread for them to share as well, each with a smear of butter across the top.

"Better?" Mary asked before blowing on her tea.

"Very nearly." Edwina sipped, knowing there was no remedy like hot tea to be found in any tincture bottle or spell book. It worked for fatigue, body ache, headache, and, she supposed, mild heartache as well.

"We'll have a nip of Father's sherry later on the roof." Mary lifted her brows, smiling as she drank. When she set her cup down, she got that playful look of dare in her eye. "So what did you do all day?" she asked, leaning forward conspiratorially. "Did he try to kiss you?"

The tea was helping, but Edwina was in no mood to be teased. Not with so many unfinished thoughts still swirling in her head. What was she to make of Ian and his claims of experiencing another man's memory of murder?

"Don't be daft," she said. "Mr. Cameron simply wanted to see the spot where he'd been clouted, as he put it."

"It doesn't take four hours to walk a man down to the river and back."

Four hours? Had it really been that long? Time had passed as though she'd fallen down the rabbit hole. But she wasn't so thick as to believe it had anything to do with where the day had taken her. It was Ian and the way he made her feel that made time disappear. Handsome enough, Mary had called him. Yet his attractiveness was bolstered by something beyond his physical features. He was active. Bold. The sort who went after life with a club. No waiting for adventure to come to him. He hunted it down, skinned it, and wore it like a trophy. She envied and admired his freedom, which made what she and Mary had done to him all the more grotesque. It was bad enough her life had been stifled by her sister's dysfunction, but to think they'd nearly ruined such a man—

"Edwina?"

"Yes, we walked quite a bit," she answered distractedly before changing the subject. "Mary, dear, you must realize by now I returned the wrong memory to Mr. Cameron. That's what caused his terrible fit. Do you recall where you collected the orb I so dreadfully gave him?"

Mary took a bite of buttered bread and slowly wiped a crumb from the corner of her mouth. "I can't really be sure whose memory he received. The remembrance was ruined by the time I removed it again. Nothing but chalk left."

Edwina looked down at her hands, still smudged with ink from thumbing through the city's newspapers. She'd left in haste. Perhaps too hastily. She'd seen her sister accused of ghastly things before. Sometimes the accusations were borne in a grain of truth, though they were always exaggerated to make her out to be a deviant worthy of scorn. But on reflection, she knew Ian hadn't inflated the truth with rumor or innuendo. It was a poor choice of words on his part, certainly, but after what Mary had put him through with her magic, she supposed he had every right to say what he had. Especially given the current terror overtaking the city.

"And yet I know that's not true," Edwina said, pushing back. "You know every bauble by its unique properties. You'd know exactly which one was missing."

"What's happened? Why are you, of all people, asking me this?" Mary tossed the rest of her bread on the plate. "It's him. He's trying to turn you against me, isn't he?"

"It's all right," Edwina said. "You're not in any trouble. Not with me. Not ever." She reached out to hold her sister's hand, surprised to find her skin so cold to the touch. "You're sensitive to these things, I know. But events have taken a serious turn again."

Mary took a shuddering breath. Edwina knew what was coming next. They'd talked about their natural-born eccentricities all their lives, pulling at threads of common sense to figure out how and why the magic in them worked as it did. They yearned to understand the odd compulsions that made them aberrations in a world full of mortals, yet they were also desperate to learn how to live among their own kind as the beings they were born to be.

Most witches discovered a vocation they excelled at. Their magic bent toward a certain talent that they cultivated into a profession or way of life. Their mother had worked a loom, weaving strands of magic into the fabrics she made. Sometimes the threads wove together to provide protection, or sometimes the weft and weave interlocked to create an aura of glamour, depending on what the wearer required. Their father earned a decent living as a scribe, writing legal documents with an enchanted fountain pen that responded to him and no one else. His handwritten letters were often remarked upon as being as uniform and neat as if they'd been done on a printing press. Many a city witch, they'd discovered, used their talents to cook or distill or brew, or even take up private detecting, but the sisters had yet to find another witch who could spot a dropped coin in a gutter from twenty feet away or remove a man's memories and turn the glowing light into an orb to adorn a jewelry box. In so many respects, she and Mary were congenital anomalies, even among witches.

"It's the lights," Mary confessed. "I can't help but notice them in the dark."

"I know." Edwina patted her sister's cold fingers, noticing the nail beds had a ghostly pale cast to them like crescent moons.

"The lights glow so bright sometimes. They leave a trail as they float away from the body. And if there's been rain during the night, they're as tempting as chasing fairy lights."

Edwina nodded, knowing the attraction her sister felt for such things. Even so, she had to ask the difficult question. "That man, the one who owned the memory I gave to Mr. Cameron, that man died very recently, didn't he? Did you follow his corpse lights at night?"

Mary pulled her hand away and folded it in her lap with the other. "The police took him to the morgue."

"And you followed?"

Mary paused, then shook her head. "I found him before they did. His eyes were still open, but they'd gone flat. He was a rumpot, that one, but his memories were crisp and sharp, rising like blue flames." She pressed a finger under her nose as if she could still smell the alcohol on the man.

"Do you know how he died?"

"Murdered, I expect. There was a lot of blood."

The attraction to death was always the same. For Mary, certainly, but for those who accused her as well. Death was the ultimate fascination. The finality of a person's life confounded the ego. How could a body and mind that walked, talked, and had brilliant, witty thoughts suddenly cease to be? How could a body shrug off its mortal coil and become common carrion simply because the blood stopped pumping through the veins? How could the mind and all its memories become mere wisps of nothingness floating in the ether because the spark of thought no longer flared bright inside the cranium? The mystery of human death was too grand to be regarded as anything less than sacred by those facing their own mortality. Which put Mary Blackwood's ill-born nature at direct odds with most of humanity and their regard for the sanctity of death. She, who was attracted to the very essence of death, had an unhealthy and suspicious relationship with the unholy. Look such a creature in the eye too long and one invited ruin.

"Have I got myself into a pickle again?"

"Yes, dear, I'm afraid you might have."

A more piercing question begged to be asked about what else she might have seen, but Edwina held her tongue. Never ask a question you don't want to know the answer to; that's what their mother had always said. Though she sometimes wondered if their mother hadn't disappeared because the dam of unasked questions had grown too heavy to hold back any longer. There were days the weight felt like a storm surge against a beaten wall, even for a sister who understood almost everything about her twin.

Mary pressed her finger into the crumbs the bread had left on the table. "We're alike in so many ways, yet I'm the one who's always making a mess of things." She put the crumbs in her mouth, then brushed her hands together, fiddling away the rest before reaching for her shawl. With a flourish, she swung the wrap around her shoulders so that the hues of indigo, copper, lavender, and iridescent green woven into the threads showed in the black wool. "Could we go to the tower tonight?" she asked. "Visit the castle on the river?"

"If you like," Edwina answered.

"Wouldn't it be jolly to pretend we're overlooking our bay of pirates once more?"

"I think we could both use a pleasant reminder of home."

Sitting among the crenellations to scan the water seemed the loveliest of ideas to Edwina. There were so few places in the city that could truly transport their hearts back to their carefree childhood. A simpler time before compulsion became their tyrant.

A customer entered the shop, interrupting their tea. A toff browser, by the look of him, on the prowl for a bargain in his ostentatious-looking gray homburg. Edwina kissed her sister's forehead, then went up front to see if she could talk the man out of a penny or two in exchange for a brass buckle, aware that despite the broken heart she'd dragged in with her through the front door after her confrontation with Ian, it was Mary who had once again devoured all the sympathy in the room.

Chapter Seventeen

Think!

Ian had found evidence leading to George Elvanfoot once before; he could do so again. He must. Lives depended on it.

Standing in the alley outside the stage door, Ian dug in his breast pocket for the photo Lizzie had given him of George Fey, the actor. A slightly different pose, she'd pointed out, than the one she'd provided before. This one showed George in costume for the play he was starring in, and *this* picture she wanted returned in one piece, along with her fiancé. Her demands were made clear, as was her denial he knew any "floozy" by the name of Mary Blackwood.

Unfortunately, the first photo must have been confiscated along with his other belongings from the hotel room. The thought of all that investigative work already done and of absolutely no use to him any longer made him want to cast a spell to plunge the city into fog permanently.

And maybe that's just what the moment called for, Ian thought, getting an idea.

He couldn't go to the Metropolitan Police to make inquiries about one of the city's missing citizens. They'd arrest him on the spot, thanks to the hotel clerk and his nosy maid. They likely didn't give a toss about a missing actor anyway. But there was another place he could go for information. This was witch business, after all. The only problem was the whereabouts of the headquarters. The location was always changing.

"Hob, you there?"

The hearth elf popped his head out of the broken pane of the nearest streetlight. "Sir?"

"We need to get into a little mischief." Before the elf got too excited, he cautioned, "Just enough to attract attention. I dinna have time to spend the night behind bars."

Hob's grin fell slightly, but he still rubbed his hairy hands together before shimmying down the lamppost. "We could snuff all the city lights out," he suggested, eyeing the place he'd jumped from.

"Won't be dark enough to cause a scene for a few more hours," Ian said, conferring with the stars. "Afraid we haven't got time to wait."

Hob drummed his fingers against his chin, thinking. As he did, a rat wandered down the alley, twitching his nose as he sniffed a suspicious trail of black goo that oozed toward the street. Ian and Hob watched the rat waddle in front of them, then exchanged a mischievous glance.

"Aye, that'll do." Ian checked the stairwell quickly to see if the homeless man was still there sleeping, but he'd already stumbled off somewhere. "Give me a little space," he said to Hob, who backed away from the rat. "Let's hope he has a few friends nearby."

Ian shook out his arms to warm up while he waited for a couple to pass by the opening to the alley. You couldn't walk thirty seconds in the city without bumping into someone, but for the moment the alley was clear. Ian concentrated on the rat, who shuffled along unaware, or unimpressed, by the two other creatures he shared the space with. All the better. Ian cleared his throat.

"Carriers of plague, vain and vile, scourge of this industrial isle. Vermin gather single file, off you go for, er, the course of a mile." Ian finished his incantation and pointed to the street as the gathering rats emptied out of gutters and crevices in the bricks to form a line. More scampered from farther down the alley to catch up to the others until there were a hundred or more walking nose to tail along the main road. The stunned hush from witnesses on the street was audible as the rats formed their march.

"Your wording was a little harsh," Hob said as he watched the last rat's tail slither around the corner.

"Never did learn to appreciate the little buggers." Ian checked his pocket watch, then snapped it shut. "I'd say we've got twenty minutes before the proper authorities come to investigate. Fancy a meat pie? My treat."

The pair remained in the alley while they ate their meal. Luckily the rats had vacated, so their crumbs didn't attract any unwanted guests. A few of the singers who'd been auditioning exited the stage door but didn't give a second look to a man sharing a pie crust with a hairy dummy.

"A glass of ale wouldn't have gone amiss," said Hob, wiping his mouth with the back of his hand.

"Aye, but you've got a full belly for the night, have ye not?" Ian brushed more crumbs off the front of his jacket as the clatter of well-shod horse hooves on the road attracted his attention. "Ah, here's our man, and early too," he said as a hansom cab pulled up in front of the alley entrance. "Time for you to go."

A man of middling authority in a black frock coat and silk hat and carrying a walking stick stepped out of the cab. Ian didn't recognize him, but he did note the lack of credentials pinned to his lapel. Dressed like a physician or a gentleman out on business, he drew little attention to himself other than from the mildly curious wishing to see why a hansom would stop in front of a narrow alleyway beside an East End music hall. They'd sent a rookie, right enough, pulling up to the spell's epicenter. It was a boy's magic trick he'd done, so they couldn't have expected the constable would find anything more than a rowdy youth practicing magic in a public street as a prank. Which made the man's mustachioed face appear all the more hilarious, once it scrunched up in realization that the culprit he'd come to chastise was actually a grown man in a tweed jacket.

"You there, what's the meaning of this?"

Ian stood and approached the constable with his hands held open before him. "A bit of harmless fun, is all. Wanted to eat a meal without having to share with the rats."

The officer looked left and right, then signaled him forward with his walking stick. With a gloved hand he removed a leather wallet from his breast pocket, displaying identification that bore the official insignia of the Witches' Constabulary. It was accompanied by a grainy black-and-white photo of himself without his mustache.

"Constable James Bottomfield," Ian read out loud. "A pleasure."

"What's next, a parade of pixies down the queen's high street?" Bottomfield flipped the ID closed and returned it to his pocket, then gave Ian a sniff as though checking to see if he was drunk. "You ought to know better than to perform a spell on a city street. Your rats have marched straight past the tower, down the embankment, and on to the public square. Made three circles around the monument, then ran like their tails were on fire." He twitched his mustache at Ian. "That'll make the papers, it will."

Ian shrugged. "The area seemed overdue for a good purge."

"Right." Bottomfield jerked his thumb toward the carriage. "Come on, you'll need to take a ride with me to explain yourself to the chief inspector. And hurry up about it. We don't want anyone seeing *him*," he said, pointing up at Hob, who clung to the top of the lamppost.

Ian waved at Hob to get out of sight, then stepped into the cab. The constable jumped in beside him and tapped the roof three times with his walking stick, and the carriage took off. It was a comfortable cab, lined with velvet and leather and smelling of boot polish.

Elegant enough, considering the seat was most often occupied by those who defied the laws of the three kingdoms.

Half a mile later it was clear Bottomfield was taking him back to the city center. The carriage driver veered them into the path of one of the city's busiest commercial thoroughfares, where they joined the throng of foot and wagon traffic. There, a dismal bank of clouds sank over the tops of the buildings, smothering the street in gray fog and the threat of rain. Their carriage, one of a hundred black coaches jockeying for space on the grim thoroughfare, pulled to the left and stopped astride a statue of a dragon that had been planted atop a plinth in the middle of the road. The officer hopped out on the left in front of a black door. Above it was a plaster relief of a lion, a dragon, and a unicorn standing over what, to most mortals, might appear as swords but to the witch's eye were actually crossed wands symbolic of the Constabulary. Bottomfield advised Ian to follow him inside without incident as he stamped his walking stick on the pavement. Not being a fool, Ian complied as the coachman, amid calls for the daft bastard to get off the road by the other carriage drivers around him, drove away.

Inside, the constable led Ian down a short corridor lit by candles suspended in a wrought-iron chandelier. He noted the beige paint on the walls was as clean as freshly churned butter and the wooden wainscoting polished to a rich mahogany gleam. He almost felt ashamed when the nails on the soles of his tackety boots broadcast his every step on the white marble floor underfoot.

"This way," Bottomfield said as his smooth leather soles made barely a sound on the polished floor. Once they reached the end of the hall, the constable escorted Ian up a set of stairs to where a burly desk sergeant, dressed in a similar long black coat and silk top hat, stood behind a massive wooden desk. Its corners were embellished with rowan, ivy, and oak leaves carved into a winding trellis pattern.

Ian nodded and said, "Afternoon," to the sergeant, who merely looked at him over the top of his tea mug and shook his head in disgust.

The constable directed Ian up the next flight of stairs to where a corner office hummed with activity. "Have a seat," he said, pointing to a chair beside a fern where a great arched window embellished with black mullions in a spiderweb pattern overlooked the busy street below. "The CI will want to have a word soon."

Ian unbuttoned his jacket and sat, hoping he hadn't pushed his luck too far by deliberately breaking the law to gain entry. But the Constabulary wasn't like the mortal police force, with station houses situated conveniently around the city. The Constabulary had a single central command center that never seemed to stay in the same place for very long. Last time he'd been in the city on a case, he'd had to navigate the underground vaults below the city's namesake bridge to get to their headquarters. Tucked away beneath the southern abutment, he thought the secret tunnels were an ideal location until the Constabulary suddenly picked up stakes and moved again. The rumors blamed poor ventilation for the relocation after a mere ten months, but Ian was able to later suss out the truth about too many ghosts interfering in the hallways for anyone to get their work done. Even when one knows apparitions are present, the heart shows a tendency to fright in dark, claustrophobic spaces.

"Cameron!"

His name had been spoken as if it were about to be snapped in two. The source of the threat came from a woman wearing a long white jacket over a white skirt and carrying a file folder. He knew nothing of women's fashions, but the lace bodice of her blouse was spellbinding for the way it climbed up her neck in a delicate pattern that eerily matched the mullions on the windows. The silver buttons on the sleeves, each slightly different from the next, were a nice touch to indicate her rank.

"Chief Inspector Singh," he said, standing. "Good to see you again."

Riya Singh, first sorceress to be named inspector in the Isle Division, and ten years later the first woman promoted to chief, folded her arms, which only showed off her impressive silver button insignias to greater effect. "What are you doing back here breaking the law in my jurisdiction again so soon?"

"So soon?" Of course. He'd already attempted to find Elvanfoot's son by getting arrested and making contact with the Constabulary. He was nothing if not consistent. "Tell me again, how long ago was that?"

Singh turned to Constable Bottomfield in disbelief, then back to Ian. "I haven't seen you in three years and now I get the honor of arresting you twice in one week. Are you saying you don't remember you were in here three days ago?"

When he explained the reason he had no recollection of the events of the past few days, while keeping somewhat vague about the specifics of Edwina and her sister, Singh's eyebrow quirked as if her instinct and curiosity had been equally piqued, and so she invited him into her office. "We'll take tea, Bottomfield," she called to the constable before shutting the door.

If he had been in her office before, he found it difficult to believe he could have ever forgotten such a place. At least two dozen glass terrarium domes sat atop a pair of file credenzas, each with a fat orb-weaver spider sitting in the middle of a delicate web. Singh caught him looking.

"They're part of the latest advancements in enforcement techniques. We've enlisted twenty-five of them, one for each ward in the city. They're enchanted to react whenever a filament in their web is disturbed."

"Isn't that what all spiders do?" Ian asked.

"Naturally," she said, swiveling in her chair to take a closer look. "But these are trained to react when people like you choose to conduct unwarranted magic in public. Their webs are enchanted to intricately entwine with the streets they watch over. When a thread gets triggered by illegal magic, they glow." She pointed to one of the domes on the far right and leaned in. "This is the one that caught you today. Two days ago, it was that one," she said, nudging her head at one nearer the middle.

So that's how they keep track these days. When he was with the Northern Constabulary, they'd still used scrying stones. Examining the spiders closer, Ian observed that beneath each web sat a map of a city section. Like newspaper spread at the bottom of a birdcage, he mused.

"Every jurisdiction outside of the square mile has their own setup," Singh said, swiveling back to place herself in front of her desk. "So walk me through this again, Cameron. You say a witch stole your memories?"

"I'm still missing the last four days."

"And yet you're able to remember where this occurred?"

"Aye, just here," he said, using one of the spiders for a point of reference to show the strip of foreshore he'd been attacked on. He further explained that it was only because of his hearth elf that he was able to reclaim the majority of his memories outside of the questionable four days.

"Hob is still with you? Elves these days are usually so fickle."

"He's a wee bit older than most," he said. "Still carries old-fashioned notions of loyalty."

Singh's eyes traveled to the spider he'd pointed to and back before checking a chalkboard on the wall behind her that logged individual incidents. "As you can see, we've had no reports of any spells of that nature in any of the wards." She folded her hands together and gave him a solemn look. "Though I do tend to believe you may have taken a blow to the back of your head."

"There are ways to fool the system," he said knowingly. She had to understand that as well, though Ian imagined it was nearly impossible to admit after boasting your department had only recently installed the latest advancements in detective work. Besides, not all magic relied on spells. Some magic was inherent.

"Do you want me to arrest the witch?"

Two hours ago, he would have screamed yes. His instinct had been tempered since then, instructing him to wait and watch. Mary's magic was peculiar and macabre, but if Edwina was right and he was being hasty by jumping to conclusions about her connection to one of the victims—the one whose death he'd relived—she may yet hold the key to identifying the killer. And how he would love to be the one who figured that out first.

Singh drummed her fingers on the desk before reaching into the credenza. She thumbed through a number of files before plucking an anemically thin folder out. "Three days ago, you had yourself arrested so you could ask about George Elvanfoot. Apparently, he's been missing for approximately three weeks now." She looked up. "Any luck finding him?"

This was where it got tricky.

"I believe so," he began. "It's possible some piece of information you provided me with three days ago led me to his whereabouts."

"But if you found him, where is he? You haven't lost him, have you?"

"Aye, that's the question." He pressed his palms against his trousers, as much for the sweat building on them as to brace himself. "I suspect I found him, or at least had a strong lead on where to find him, a few days after arriving in the city. Whatever I discovered took me to the foreshore at low tide two nights ago, where I was hit on the back of the head."

"And that's where you claim a witch stole your memories once you were barely conscious."

"It sounds daft, aye, but I'd be grateful if you could enlighten me about what we talked about last time I was here."

"You really have lost your memory." Singh shook her head as though it was easier to just accept what he said, then studied the brief report tucked in the folder. "Very well. We talked about his father, as I recall. We speculated about whether the son was missing or simply didn't wish to be found, though I believe you ruled that out after talking to his acquaintances." When Ian nodded, she leaned back in her chair as if to evaluate the situation from a different perspective. Then she dangled the bait. "You know, there are other men who've notably disappeared from the streets of late. Mortals, that is. Any thoughts on that?"

"I read they've all turned up in the morgue with their throats slit."

Bottomfield knocked, then entered the office carrying a tray with a pot of tea, two cups, and a plate of chocolate biscuits. Singh thanked the constable, handed him a report for him to pass on to one of her detectives, then waited with her hands propped under her chin until he left to speak again. "The men were robbed too. First a blow to the back of the head," she said pointedly. "Supposedly to stun but not kill, rendering the men incapable of fighting back. Then the knife across the neck, two of them to near decapitation."

Ian swallowed uncomfortably at the familiar shadow memory. She noticed.

"Getting squeamish in your new job?" Singh asked as she poured the tea. "That's not the detective I remember."

He hadn't yet shared the second part of his ordeal, of being given another man's memory, of being the victim of the very things she'd just described. He wasn't yet certain how the sisters had come by the memory. Was Mary involved in the murders? Was Edwina? Was there an exceptional explanation that exonerated them both? Was such a thing even possible? There was something odd about them, or about Mary, at least. Something about her magic unsettled the heart. The business of taking memories put him in mind of a snake his best friend had kept when they were bairns. Interesting enough to observe the animal's daily nature, but once a month one had to offer up live prey for the snake to devour. And even though they were naught but mice, Ian couldn't help seeing them as victims in a brutal cycle, daft as that was. But aside from his misgivings, and despite his denials, he did seem to care about Edwina Blackwood's good opinion of him. He didn't wish to upset her by rushing to judgment too soon about the sister.

"Aye, I've gone soft working missing persons cases."

Singh smiled politely, but he knew what she was thinking: Why had he quit a job with the Constabulary only to take up private detective work? He often asked himself the same question when he found himself on surveillance in the middle of the night with the rain pouring down and him out looking for a lost sprite or nixie in some dark fen, freezing his arse off. But he'd never have to work another child's murder case as long as he was the one who dictated what job he accepted or not. For that alone, he'd made the right choice.

"Privately, the City Police are under the impression robbery was an afterthought," she said after sipping her tea. "Murder was the real endgame."

"In more ways than one." Ian considered the drawings he'd left behind in his hotel room and pushed for an answer. "Any evidence the rumors about the murders being part of an occult ritual are true? Some kind of blood magic or curse at work?"

The chief inspector's eyebrow twitched again as she reached back in the credenza for a second file. This one was as fat as *Lady Everly's Grimoire*. Singh dropped it on the desk so it landed with a resounding thud.

"What's this?"

"*Your* file." She smiled, enjoying the brief moment of discomfort she'd caused him before opening the folder. On top were what appeared to be drawings and a black-and-white photograph of George Elvanfoot. He didn't recognize them as his, yet he knew what they were.

"How did you—" he began to ask, but he already knew. The Witches' Constabulary monitored everything both the City and Metropolitan Police did, in case of potential crossover, by infiltrating the ranks of the mortal police with a few of their own. Naturally, they had an interest in controlling access to information about certain incriminating incidents, if they happened to involve the use of magic. "Nice grab. Saves me the effort of sending Hob over to the local nick to steal them," he said, grinning like an imp himself as he tilted his head to see the sketches better.

On examination, they were as graphic and disturbing as the hotel clerk had avowed. He was no great artist, but he could enchant a stick of graphite as well as the next. The drawings proved to be detailed depictions of the recent murders, but closer scrutiny—once Chief Inspector Singh gave permission—revealed they were based on more than the actual crime scene photos. As Ian shuffled through the drawings, he noted the angles of the bodies and the settings where they were found all matched what he'd read in the newspaper accounts, but there was one big difference.

He pulled free a drawing of a scene at once familiar and sickening. Days before he'd been given the memory of a dead man, he'd sketched the scene of the victim's murder in the narrow alley. The drawing conformed with his shadow memory, as the illustration in the newspaper had. Yet in his sketch he'd depicted the man without clothes, which gave the drawing an even more lurid tone. He understood better why the clerk had contacted the police over what the maid had found. Poor lass. Looking closer, he began to work out what he'd been up to. He'd drawn a short spiral on the left side of the man's head above the ear. Beside it he wrote "occultatum." On the spots above the kidneys, the heart, and the lungs, he'd drawn different symbols with question marks beside them. The sigils, when bonded with the right words, were associated with certain blood-magic rituals of transformation—a star, a crescent moon, a cross-roads. He looked up at Singh, hoping for more details.

"You were apparently working on a theory that the killings were ritualistic in nature. Biscuit?" She slid the plate of treats his way. "That's where the newspapers picked up on it. From the hotel clerk. He'd sent for the police, but one of our officers got there first and confiscated your notes. The clerk still talked to reporters, though."

"And was I right? *Are* the murders ritualistic?" He slid the plate of biscuits back, wondering how his missing persons case had morphed into one about possible ritual murder.

"We don't have any reason to believe they are. Autopsies showed each of the victims had an unusual bruise above the ear on the left where you've drawn it. I'm assuming you got that piece of insider information through a bribe or other shenanigans."

"Likely enough."

"But despite the newspapers' appetite for the grotesque, there were no missing organs, no burn marks, no other mutilation besides the slash across the neck," Singh said, shaking her head. "So why did you speculate there might be witchcraft behind the marks? And why were you even looking into the murders when you were supposed to be here looking for a missing person who clearly is not one of the victims?" She held up a hand to stop him from answering. "I know, you don't remember. Humor me with your thoughts. Opinions. Educated guesses."

Ian reached for his tea as he tried to reconcile the jumbled memories of his past two days. "I've spent the day retracing what steps I would have taken in the investigation. Before I came here, I spoke with the girlfriend."

"Lizzie Stanfield."

So they knew about her, which meant they were following up on suspicions, same as him. Officially, it was a mortal-jurisdiction case. But if the Constabulary shared the same suspicions he did, then it was a crossover crime. Singh lowered her eyes, knowing she'd let slip they were more interested in George's whereabouts than she'd admitted.

"Aye, that's right. She was convinced George was the latest victim. Because of a mix-up with the name in the paper." He explained about Sir Elvanfoot's card being in his pocket when they took him to the hospital, then waited a beat to see if the inspector would volunteer anything new.

"What else did she have to say?" she asked.

Hmm, stonewalled.

"Lizzie claimed George had been acting different lately. In a brooding sort of way. Questioning life and man's dual nature because of some play he was starring in. Good versus evil and all that shite." He decided to try one more time to get Singh to show her hand. "If I had to guess, knowing how my mind works, I was probably intrigued by the coincidence of George going missing at the same time the bodies started turning up. Like you say, I must have got wind of some detail the general public dinna know about. Something suggesting the crime could have something to do with magic. And since I was looking for a missing witch, I must have got curious."

Singh shuffled the drawings back into a neat stack, including the photo of George Elvanfoot. "I'm willing to drop the charge of using magic in public. Again," she added as she placed the papers back in his file. "But you have to promise to come to me first if you find anything incriminating about this man."

"Wait, that's it?"

"You know I'm not at liberty to share more."

"Hold on," he said before she closed the folder. He knew she'd confiscated the sketches and wouldn't give them back, but there was something else in the folder of interest. "May I?" He slid the photo of George out and gave it a proper look. The face was the same, but he realized just how much the picture he had in his pocket, the one Lizzie had given him, was of a man in character. In costume. The one he looked at now was of the man without pretense, not hiding behind an act or persona. Eyes bright, hair combed back, a silver pin stuck through his lapel, shining even in the dull patina of a grainy photo. There was something achingly familiar about him, about the way he stood, his build, even his clothes. Ian couldn't put his finger on it, but his intuition was flaring like one of those newfangled electric torches.

"Just one more thing," he said, peeling his eyes away from the photo. "Ever had one of your spiders jump because of a pair of sisters by the name of Blackwood?" He tapped a finger outside the terrarium of the spider hovering over the ward where he'd been attacked, the question forced to the surface by a combination of intuition and experience telling him everything was related. Like the interconnected threads of the spider's web, the photo, the murders, the sketches, and the sister with the uncanny ability to snatch a man's memories out of his mind were somehow connected.

"No, not that I recall." She tracked the positions of each spider with a quick glance. There was no twitch, no quirk of her brow, no attempt to evade. "Should I have?"

"Nae, I was only curious, is all."

He glanced again at the photo, committing as much information to memory as he could. Their conversation ended, and Chief Inspector Singh had Constable Bottomfield escort Ian back to street level. The constable lingered on the pavement with him a moment. "The boys inside said you used to be one of us. That true?" he asked.

"Aye, up north. Seems a very long time ago."

After a grunt of—what? Disapproval? Grudging respect? Ambivalence?—Bottomfield went back inside and shut the door as a heavy drizzle descended from the clouds, freezing the skin on the back of Ian's neck.

He didn't know why he hadn't just come out and said what Mary Blackwood had done to one of the victims. To him. To who knew how many countless others who'd died in hospitals. Maybe he believed Edwina. Maybe he thought he was wrong to say what he had. He'd been inside the dead man's head, experienced his memories, watched the outline of the murderer approach, and it was not Mary Blackwood. Nae, she came later, after the deed was done, like her sister said. In the alley, in the morgue, or somewhere in between. What a god-awful thing to have to live with, he thought. To chase the dead, and occasionally the living, to satisfy some unnatural craving or compulsion to possess what's in their head.

He flipped his collar up with the idea of walking toward the nearest pub to have a proper think when he was stopped at the next corner by a man with gray muttonchops, a tweed suit, and a battered brown bowler leaning one shoulder against the wall. "I trust you didn't tell the CI about our agreement," the man said, blowing out a stream of cigarette smoke to mingle with the gray city air.

Chapter Eighteen

Agreement?

As Ian was becoming accustomed to, he had no recollection of the man. Caught on his back foot, he played along, if only to clarify what the man meant. "Not a word."

"I'm going to need the rest of the money, though."

"Remind me again how much we agreed on?"

"Ha, cheeky. A pair of queen's heads'll do, mate, and I get you that second look at the other autopsy photo like you wanted."

Ian stared at the man full in the face. Red veins swollen from years of drinking trailed over the man's nose and cheeks. Rheumy eyes stared back as the stranger offered him his cigarette case with a conspiratorial smile, shaking the tin for good measure. Presumably he meant for Ian to slip the coin inside under the innocent pretense of sharing a smoke in the drizzle. He fished in his pocket discreetly for the money, pulling his pocket watch out at the same time as if to check the hour. He didn't know the man in the least, but he knew his type. Exactly the sort of dead-end copper he'd approach with the clink of money in exchange for information only someone on the inside could get. A sergeant who'd topped out in his career, if he had to guess. He glanced down at the spectrometer on his watch, verifying the man was witch-born.

He returned the tin of cigarettes, and the sergeant jerked his head, instructing him to follow. They crossed the street in front of the dragon statue, though Ian kept a good distance between them as the man lumbered east. A few paces on the sergeant veered left, disappearing down a narrow opening between buildings. Ian stopped flat. He'd grown leery of narrow passageways after recent events, so he tossed the unsmoked cigarette in the street and watched where the man went first. The arched opening led to a small brick-lined courtyard with a garden enclosed by a wrought-iron fence. On the right hung a sign advertising a pub. Not just any pub, though. A witches' pub tucked away in a small alcove. Ian walked forward, then craned his neck to look back at the bustling street of venders, omnibuses, and carriages full of people all rushing by oblivious to what remained hidden to them behind the facade of a dead-end passage. Another quirk of an old city, he thought, and entered the pub.

Inside, the main room was half filled with patrons nursing mugs of dark ale and reading newspapers. Ribbons of spiced vanilla swirled from the tonka-bean cured tobacco smoldering inside their pipes. One or two looked over the rims of their glasses when he entered but went back to their reading when he proved harmless enough. The wide plank floors creaked underfoot as Ian nodded at them and searched for the sergeant. He soon discovered there was more to the pub than the main room. The place was a maze of small alcoves that went three levels deep, each arrived at via a narrow set of wonky wooden steps. Portraits of notable witches, draped in cobwebs, hung on the walls of the upper stairway. Lower down, it was the skulls of the infamous that filled the nooks and niches. The three-hundred-year-old cranium of an Alistair Ainsworth had been worn brown and smooth from a thousand hands touching it for luck as they passed. Ian did the same, tapping his fingers against the skull as he spotted the man with the muttonchops. He'd found a table on the bottom level inside a cavern-like space, where low-hanging beams on the ceiling threatened the head of any man of average height. By the time Ian caught up to the sergeant, he'd already procured two pints of brown ale. Fortunately, he slid one of the mugs across the table when Ian sat opposite.

"Apologies for taking the long way down, but it's best if we have a little privacy," he said and slid two photos across the table next to the beer.

"You have them on you?" Ian was stunned.

The man wrinkled his brow as if confused by Ian's surprise. "Same as last time. I leave the police an illusion of the photos, while I nick the real ones temporarily. No harm done. Just haven't turned them in to Singh yet."

Of course. He knew the Constabulary copied everything, if it was pertinent to an investigation they were interested in. Ian resisted shaking his head at how efficient he could be when targeting sources for his own benefit.

Ian studied the first of the pictures in the greasy lamplight. It was a crime scene photo of a man lying on his right side at the base of a step in what appeared to be an enclosed brick-lined space, like the kind found in front of a block of terrace flats. The head rested at an odd angle, as if the man had slumped over in sleep. A black pool of what he assumed was blood had spread out in a full moon beneath the victim's head, the apparent source being the gash in the man's throat.

"Right or left handed?" he asked.

Muttonchops shrugged. "Right." He nodded at the autopsy photo, which showed a clear, thin tail to the right side of the slash left by the swiping of the blade against the skin from left to right. "Assuming the assailant stood over the victim's back and lifted the head by the hair." He mimed a slashing move with his hand to demonstrate.

"After the victim was already incapacitated from the blow to the back of the head."

"Right," said the sergeant. "So, if robbery is our motive, why cut the throat too?"

Spilling the victims' blood afterward would support the theory of ritual murder as motive. The blood or some other part of the body used in conjunction with a forbidden incantation could boost the intent and power of the spell. He'd investigated the serial killing of cats and foxes in the countryside under the same assumption, their bodies drained of blood until they were nothing but desiccated corpses. An earl had turned up dead at the same time, as empty of his blood as the cats. They'd suspected the wife, but he could never link the two incidents together despite his misgivings. And yet Singh had said they held no such suspicion in this case. Why? Because one of their spiders didn't jump? But then why had he focused on the occult angle in his drawings?

Ian shifted his attention to the autopsy photo. The same victim was positioned on his back, eyes shut, skin ghastly pale. Even in the black-and-white photo, the body had the lifeless hue of a block of ice cut from a pond. The man's hair had been shaved off, and the body bore the typical stitch marks on the forehead and chest from where he'd been sewn up after the coroner's inquest had pried back the flesh for an examination of the bone and gore beneath.

The sergeant pointed his tobacco-stained finger at the victim's head, where a dark smudge was visible above the left ear. "Same mark as the others."

Singh had described the mark as a mere bruise, but the photo clearly showed a bluish spiral about as big as the queen's head coins he'd just paid for the view. The same symbol he'd drawn in his sketch of the other victim.

"Drawn on?"

The sergeant shook his head. "Doc insists it's bruising. Called it a . . ." He stopped to open a notebook he kept in his breast pocket, then read, "A trauma-induced hematoma."

"What kind of trauma leaves a bruise like that?" But, of course, there were very few real options. A spell was the most likely answer, though if the spiral shape was the result of an incantation, he wasn't familiar enough with the form of magic to say so definitively. He supposed a stamp with that design struck against the side of the head would do it, but to what end? A maker's mark for a murderer? Ridiculous.

"All the victims were mortals?" Ian asked.

"Something happen to your head, mate? You keep asking the same questions I already answered last time. Get yourself one of these," he said, waving his palm-size leather journal before tucking it back in his pocket. "Write it down."

"Just being thorough," Ian bluffed.

"Did you figure out how your bloke fits in with any of this?" The sergeant sipped his beer while his rheumy eyes watched Ian's face closely over the rim of his mug. "Still got him stashed over at that boarding-house on Cedric Lane? Or maybe you moved him somewheres else?"

Ah, so that's what this is really about. Ian had to work to keep from telegraphing the epiphany igniting in his brain like a high-voltage arc lamp from one ear to the other. This old copper wasn't just his bribed informant; he must be Singh's too. Which only confirmed the Constabulary was more interested in the missing George Elvanfoot than she'd let on. They knew he'd found him once and were hoping he could still lead them to him. So did that make George an official suspect in the murders? The report she'd passed to that constable while he was in her office probably alerted this old geezer to wait for him out in front of the station, tempting him with these photos so he could feel him out for information on George's whereabouts.

Ian took another gander at the photos. "I've lost track of him," he said with a small shake of the head. "But if this witchwork does turn out to be his," he continued, pointing to the marks on the side of the head, "he's a better sorcerer than I gave him credit for."

"How's that?"

"You ever seen a mark like that from a spell anywhere else?"

The sergeant mopped foam from his mustache with a swipe from the back of his hand. "I seen it on some old standing stones once. Pagan nonsense. Up north."

The implied pejorative of "up north" struck home. An insinuation about the way witches cleaved hard to the old magic in the north as practiced by men like his father and even Henry Elvanfoot. The sergeant was a fool if he thought his kin up north were backward cunning folk leaping over bonfires and peddling sleeping potions to ailing mortal tourists for profit. Respect for the deep roots where their magic was born had kept the tender sprig of isle enchantment alive, not only in the people but in the land as well. But he took the man's point: a northerner was missing, and a northern symbol was the common supernatural link between the murders.

"Aye," Ian said amiably. "We're fond of our ancestors in the northern vales."

The two men clasped their hands around their mugs and sipped in silence for a moment, while the clatter of laughter and the creak of the timbers above suggested the place was filling up. Soon punters would be spilling into the basement as well.

"Right, well, I'd best be off," said the sergeant. "The missus'll be steaming like a kettle if I don't get home soon." The man winked before downing the last three inches in his mug. He swept up the two photos and tucked them away in his jacket alongside his tin of cigarettes and left.

With the bulk of his lodgings money gone, Ian was left with little option for the evening. Luckily, the good sergeant had given him the location of a nearby boardinghouse. One that might offer a valuable clue.

Chapter Nineteen

The steady clop of horses pulling carriages over the bridge from one tower to the next played like a drumbeat in the distance. Dark and silent, the moving water below made smears of the streetlight reflections illuminated on its surface. The sisters, clothed in their lace-trimmed nightgowns and black shawls, stood behind the upper parapet of the white castle, where the air, heavy with mist and the scent of coal smoke, rippled through Edwina's hair. Grateful for her sister's insistence they go out, she leaned her head against Mary's shoulder.

"I don't know what I'd do without you," Edwina said.

"You would live in a whitewashed house on Cricket Lane with two children running in the courtyard most like, if not for me."

She didn't like it when Mary made herself the martyr. Though their life was unconventional, there were times their unprecedented independence made up for every slight affixed to the wing of an arrow aimed their way. Gazing at stars in the middle of the night atop an eight-hundred-year-old castle, as the river below flowed out to sea, was a worthy-enough trade-off for a life that would likely only ever exist in a daydream.

Edwina moved to sit atop a stone crenellation, letting her bare feet dangle over the side. Mary joined her, leaning against the edge to view the tower green below.

"They died right there," Mary said, pointing. "The pretty ladies who lost their heads." Her eyes flitted from spot to spot, tracing the shadows of the women's spirits as if they were fireflies. Too long dead for Edwina's eyes, the ladies remained invisible to her, but she knew they were there, glowing like dull candlelight for her sister.

While Mary watched the dancing ladies, Edwina reached into her pocket. She couldn't see corpse lights like her sister, but she could spot the glint of metal in the grass brighter than Venus at its zenith. She'd found a brass button, three coins, and a young lady's locket after only one pass over the grounds. Only a night like this one, of following her nature's true course, could have eased her heart of the bruise it had suffered from the day's earlier disappointment.

Such lunacy to hold on to so much aching and want, only to have it answered with repulsion and rejection. Being in Ian's company, she'd felt as if she were under a spell. Love, she'd once been warned, worked in much the same circuitous way as magic, with its enigmatic energy concentrating in the eyes of some but not others. Love was a potion as potent as hemlock or wolfsbane in the right proportion. But was it love she felt? How could it be, when she'd known the man for only two days? Rationally, the encounter was more inclined to be a matter of chemistry, the humors of one body attracted to another through some invisible mist breathed between them. A sort of temporary madness manifesting from nearness.

"Does he make your insides quiver low in the belly?" Mary glanced at her out of the side of her eye. "Is that why you can't stop thinking about him?"

Edwina turned her head away, embarrassed that her thoughts were so plain on her face. She shook the trinkets in her palm, sifting them to test their weight and value, as if she hadn't been thinking of Ian at all. "None of that matters anymore." To prove she had more pressing things on her mind, she held up the locket. "I might have the perfect chain for this back at the shop."

Mary retreated from the edge and caught Edwina's eye. "Lie to the rest of the world if you like, but not to me." Not waiting for a rejoinder, Mary climbed on top of the crenellations. Slanted like a roof, the capstones were slick with mist. Anyone else would slip from the stone and fall to the earth below, where the queenly ladies pranced in deathly shadows. Yet Mary skipped along the ancient battlements like a girl playing at hopscotch. "He lopped their heads off as if they were dandelions," she said, speaking of the old king with the sharp ax. "Out with the old wife, in with the new. Men can be fickle fiends."

"I need to get back," Edwina said. "The tide's receding, and I'd like to skim over the shore once before the shop opens."

Mary looked over her shoulder at her. "Suit yourself. I'm going to stretch a little more."

There had been a time they'd done everything in twin-esque syncopation, but ever since the move to the city, the tiniest of fissures had begun fragmenting between them into verifiable cracks. Perhaps it was a matter of course for two young women forced to find their wings in the world. They couldn't cling to their childhood inclinations forever. Even so, the tiny places where their differences had found space to splinter apart had worried Edwina of late. The freedom they felt in the middle of the night above the rest of the world was one thing, but too much independence in a young woman on the ground could lead to unspeakable trouble. She hoped Mary had enough sense to recognize her limits as she waved and said she would meet Edwina back home.

Two hours later, Edwina stood alone on the foreshore. The river, as ever, slithered by on its stomach in search of more shoreline to consume. The constant flow of water churned up pieces of the past as easily as it swallowed down chunks of the present, burying everything in layers of mud and sludge. Everything eventually fell to the river in the end.

Edwina half-heartedly dug a finger in the mud where a sharp point stuck out at an interesting angle, but it was only an old door hinge rusted through in the middle. Beside it were several bent nails and a watery strip of leather that may have once been a belt or apron. She could barely find anything worth the effort of picking up. Her vision was off. Blurred by the distraction of the growing yet inevitable rift between she and Mary and of falling out with Ian until nothing would shine for her.

She decided to pace the shore nearer to the bridge, exploring the sand and rocks that pushed up against the buttress. The low clouds and leftover chill in the air from the night's mist made for a morning sky heavy with the portent of ill luck. Knowing she stood in the same place she had the day before with Ian, she scanned the wall for the nook where she'd wedged the skull between stones. It was gone, of course. Taken by the river. But if the water swallowed her offering, it had also swallowed her blessing. She hoped it might fend off the oppressive mood that lingered inside her from some vague yet persistent warning.

The fishing boat was back, lying on its side awaiting the rising water. Low tide had come an hour later than the morning two days ago when they'd found Ian unconscious on the shore. Two days ago, in the last twinkling hour before the dawn, the sky had still been a cloak of midnight blue. If the sky had been lighter, as it was now, she wondered if they'd have left him be. Without the darkness to keep their secret hidden, they might have simply alerted a policeman to the body and been done with the whole affair. No stolen memory, no pulsating guilt, no exposure to the frailty of human emotions burnished by hope. But even she was beginning to suspect life would not have gone on as normal no matter whether the sun or moon had ruled the sky that morning.

"You're a Gloomy Gus when left on your own." Mary had crept up beside her as silent as morning fog.

Edwina lifted her head and nearly laughed at her sister's oblique observation. Hadn't her whole life been spent in the gloom? What had changed now to cause Mary to notice such a thing? But, of course, she knew. The hairline cracks that had formed between them had also let a sliver of light in, if only for a brief afternoon. Falling out with Ian must have doused the brief spark of light from her aura once again.

"Not having much luck today," Edwina said and nudged the rusted hinge deeper into the mud with the toe of her boot.

Mary, perhaps sensing she trod on tender ground, changed her tune. "Well, I've already found some things you overlooked," she said, holding up a silver-plated hip flask and a small folding pocketknife, the sort men sometimes used to clean their fingernails and teeth. Both had a glaze of mud on them, but neither appeared particularly water or weather beaten. The brandy flask had scratches on it, but they were the sort easily accounted for by the effort of slipping the container in and out of one's pocket. She doubted it had ever been pressed hard beneath the weight of water for even a day of its life.

"Might have been flung off the bridge," Mary said, reading her doubt.

Edwina agreed the items would be nice additions for the shop. Ones that would sell quickly. She tipped her face up to the bridge, trying to imagine the rattle of a train crossing over while some passenger tossed a perfectly good flask out the window after the last drop of brandy was gone. While she dwelled on the improbability, a familiar shape crossed into the halo of lamplight on the bridge. The boy. He stood at the end near the embankment, watching her and Mary through the dawn mist and fading moonlight. This lurking of his had become something more than curiosity. More than mere petulance too. She turned her attention back to the mud at her feet as if she hadn't noticed him, then stole a glimpse at Mary. Her sister merely smiled, proud of her finds, as she rinsed the flask and knife off in a pool of backwater.

"I'm ready to call it a morning," Edwina said, lifting the hem of her skirt to trudge over the mud and algae.

"So soon? There are fifty-three minutes yet until we open."

"Your marvelous finds have more than made up for my bad luck this morning," she said. She narrowed her eyes at Mary. "Coming?"

But no. Mary stood and pulled her shawl around her, saying she'd best go and fetch the milk fresh from the udder for their tea. She handed off the flask and pocketknife so Edwina could take them back to the shop and clean them up for sale. Together they ascended the moss-slick stairs to the top of the embankment, where they parted ways. By then the boy was nowhere to be seen, though Edwina suspected he wouldn't be far from wherever Mary went.

Back at their aerie top-floor bedroom, Edwina tossed off her muddy knockabouts. As she laced up her ankle boots for shop work, the rarity of her sister not sitting on the bed opposite to show off her finds plucked a melancholy chord inside her. Alone, she picked up the flask and turned it over in her hands under the light. Not a speck of mud inside, and the whiff of alcohol still wafted out with the cap removed. The knife, too, though still wet with river slime, showed no sign of rust. Edwina's chest fluttered with doubt as her intuition pushed up against her ribs.

She walked to the dresser and opened the jewelry box on top. It was the same as before, with Mary's baubles taking up the majority of the space, though a few now seemed to be missing. She moved them around with her finger, wondering how something as morbid as her sister's talent came to be in the world. There were creatures like moth larvae and carrion beetles whose unpleasant work did the task of breaking down skin and hair and bone in a perpetual cycle, but what purpose in the natural order of life unto death was served by stripping memories from cold flesh? The person's thoughts weren't preserved in any measurable way. The memories, sitting as idle orbs in a secondhand jewelry box, died as surely as if they'd stayed with the body. And yet the compulsion ruled her sister's life. And hers, too, in ways too painful to recount some days.

Edwina shut the lid to the jewelry box but hadn't quite quelled the nagging caution flapping about inside her. Kneeling at the foot of her bed, she opened the lid on the cedar hope chest she and Mary shared to search for anything new she didn't recognize. Instead she found her lavender blouse with the pearl buttons buried near the bottom wrapped in butcher's paper. The shirt, with its straight front bodice and mutton-leg puff at the shoulder, along with a matching skirt, had been put away for a special day, one she knew all too well might never come.

She lifted the blouse out of its burial place and held it up to her face. As she stood before the looking glass, the color made her pale cheeks pinken so that she almost looked like the carefree girl she used to be, running beside the stream in the snowy hills and collecting leeks to be cooked with cream and thyme. In her odd mood she considered wearing the blouse, but she found the memory of a childhood home she could no longer revisit had drained the blush from her skin again, so she wrapped the blouse in its paper and smothered it again deep in the chest beside her sister's similarly stored outfit of midnight blue.

The clock struck the hour, so she shut the chest, finished with looking through the past. Feeling the tug of obligation, Edwina let suspicions about her sister fall into the familiar groove of forgive-and-forget and swung her shawl over her shoulders. Taking Mary's finds with her, she headed downstairs to open the shop. She turned the OPEN sign around in the window and noted the clouds had cracked apart, letting spindly legs of sunlight seep out around their silvered edges. Good weather made for slow business, but the human traffic lumbered by as usual outside, with one notable exception. The boy hadn't come to take his normal place in front of the glass.

Mary was also still missing, but she was often late when she claimed to be fetching the milk. Edwina had calculated the distance from the shop to the milk cows in Saint Jonathon's Square weeks ago and knew it to be an hour round trip, but Mary was often gone twice as long. Those were the days she came home smelling of tobacco and sweat, though she always had the pint bottle tucked under her arm as expected. Still, Edwina knew her sister had been wandering off somewhere else, *with* someone else, but had never questioned her for fear of, what? Breaching her sister's privacy and upsetting her? Perhaps today she would confront her about the long absences, and hang the consequences.

While she waited for Mary to return, she spread a cloth out on the counter. With only a little spellwork she thought she could smooth the scratches off the flask so it looked near new again. Besides, busywork usually proved the best cure for an unsteady heart.

Edwina had just taken out her rag and polish, forming a metallurgy spell on her tongue, when an elderly gentleman with a white beard and tan bowler hat entered the shop. A private carriage with a golden dragon coat of arms emblazoned on the door waited across the road. He wasn't the normal sort who usually popped in to browse their secondhand goods. Aside from the carriage, the cut of his plaid suit and the shine on his shoes marked him as a toff. The second that week. Perhaps the shop was finally gaining a reputation for its odd and unique finds, some of which were quite valuable. There were never bigger bargain hunters than those with money.

The gentleman closed the door behind him, then looked at her with eyes so bright and blue they could have been backlit by starshine.

"Oh," she said before she could stop herself. The gleam in his eyes wasn't merely a quirk of heredity; it was the force of his aura sparkling through. "Merry meet," she said with a nod of recognition.

The gentleman said a quick, "Good tidings, miss," in a broad northern accent and removed his hat.

"Anything I can help you find today?"

"I'm hoping I've found it already." For a moment the gentleman appeared confused as he looked from the door to the counter. "I've been up and down this street three times. Your sign reads Mercier and Sons, though if I'm not mistaken the Mercier family left a year ago to open an *apothicaire toxique* on the continent." He stopped and took a moment to appreciate the wares on display under glass and those hung on the walls, nodding as if satisfied he was not standing inside an apothecary shop.

"My apologies for the confusion. Father never bothered to change the sign. He didn't think 'Blackwood and Daughters' would bring in as many customers."

"Ah, Blackwood, you say? Then I have indeed arrived at the correct place." The man withdrew a pair of reading glasses and a telegram from his jacket pocket. He slipped the glasses on and unfolded the paper, glancing quickly at the contents to verify the message once again. "Curiosity shop run by the Blackwood sisters," he read. He nodded and made eye contact with Edwina over the top of his eyeglasses. The stunning starlight quality of blue in his eyes did not fail to shock her anew.

"Someone sent you here to my shop?" The notion struck Edwina as unlikely, unless he was a collector of the odd piece of mismatched silverware or perhaps a pair of secondhand opera glasses. "Was there something specific you were looking for?"

"As a matter of fact," he said, exposing the palms of his hands upward in an unguarded gesture, "I am looking for my son."

Edwina fumbled the flask so it slipped from her fingers and clanged against the counter. "You're Sir Elvanfoot," she exclaimed. She righted the flask, apologizing for her clumsiness, though she remained baffled as to how or why the great witch of the north had come to be standing inside her shop, and deliberately so.

He extended his hand. "I am indeed, miss. And may I presume by your reaction you have an inkling as to why I might have been instructed to seek out your shop? Or where I might find either my son or Ian Cameron, the man I hired to find him? I'm told there is a key in your shop that I am to obtain."

After introducing herself, Edwina confessed her confusion. "I am acquainted with both Mr. Cameron and your mission to find your missing son, but I can't for the life of me understand why you were directed here. Or what this key is you mentioned. Who was it who sent you?"

"Why, Mr. Cameron himself." Elvanfoot opened the telegram again. "I received this update from him three days ago and came as soon as I could." He read the telegram aloud for her benefit: "Found George. If convenient, come to the city. Am at the Three Hares Inn. Curiosity shop run by Blackwood sisters holds key."

"Three days ago?" she asked. He tipped the telegram so she might see the date, which confirmed what he said. The fluttering warning in her chest earlier had found its way to the spot behind her right eye, making itself an unwelcome guest with its dull, throbbing insistence that she see what stood before her. "I don't understand. I only met Mr. Cameron for the first time two days ago. There was never any mention of a key, although . . ."

"What is it?"

Her skin flushed hot knowing what she must confess. "He did come to the shop, but the situation is complicated. Compounded by unusual circumstances."

"Involving magic?"

Edwina nodded, and Sir Elvanfoot rested his hands on the glass display case while she explained about Ian's missing memory and how it had come to pass. The gentleman witch listened with eyes gleaming, as if collecting every word she said and evaluating them against his own pool of knowledge and skill. Twice he interrupted to hear again the details of how Mary had extracted the memory, seemingly impressed by her rare gift. But when Edwina had finished the tale, Elvanfoot was no more enlightened than she as to what Ian Cameron might have meant about finding a key at the sisters' shop.

"By your account, Cameron sent this telegram while still in full possession of his faculties," he said. "He wouldn't have wasted words in a telegram, my dear. There must be a reason he deliberately mentioned your little shop and this mysterious key."

Edwina was stymied. She'd checked Ian's pockets while he was under her sleeping spell. There had been a key, but it was for his hotel room. "We do have a large collection of keys, but I don't think he could have meant one of them has anything to do with your son's case."

"Hmm, possibly." The white-haired witch cast his eyes about the shop, unconvinced. "With your permission, might I have a look around to see if any of your offerings spark a connection for me?"

"Of course. Feel free to browse the items. Our keys are over here," she said, leading him to a round table near the front window, where the display of skeleton keys remained as straight as when she'd last fidgeted with them.

Naturally inquisitive, Edwina shadowed the famous witch, offering to remove any of the other items out of their display cases should he care to make closer inspection. While he browsed the keys on the table, laying a finger aside a silvery one with elegant scrollwork she'd spotted behind a rain barrel on Broad Street a fortnight ago, she watched how he used his intuition to guide him. She could have told him where and when she'd found each and every piece of metal he explored, but it would not help him find what he was looking for.

It was only after she'd watched Elvanfoot make his way around the entire table that the question of what the alleged key might unlock finally occurred to her. She fumbled with the conundrum—a door, a chest, a padlock?—until he gave up on the mismatched assembly of discarded keys and set his interest on the table where the women's hatpins were displayed. He touched an amber stone embedded at the end of one of the pins with the tip of his finger but found no joy. He shrugged and turned his attention to the knickknack shelf in the corner behind him instead. The look in his bright eyes suddenly changed, gone from blinking and uncertain to as alert as a fox after discovering a mouse under the snow.

"What is it? Have you found something?" she asked.

"There is a slight flux in the energy here." He spun around with his hand outstretched, searching, feeling, sensing. A shimmer of luminosity glowed around him, enhancing his aura. He was calling his power to him, using every instinct to find the thing calling to him. Edwina checked the street to see if anyone spied through the glass to witness his magic, but blessedly the flow of people continued on as usual, as if she and her shop were nothing more than a muddy bank at high tide.

"Somewhere here," he said, eyes searching the array of items on display. He nudged aside a pewter spoon and a green bottle and retrieved a long silver pin with a thistle head for a decoration. A small amethyst stone had been inlaid to serve as the bur's purple flower. "Good heavens," he said and held it up for her to see.

Edwina had never laid eyes on the object before. "What is it? Where did it come from?"

"A pin for weighing down the plaid when a gandaguster catches hold of your kilt. It belongs to my lad." Elvanfoot turned the pin over in his hands, confirming his suspicion. The wrinkles in his forehead deepened. "He vowed never to take it off when he left for the city." The old witch cast a wary eye at her and asked, "How is it you came by this?"

Edwina had no answer. If he'd asked where the pewter spoon came from, she would tell him she'd found it three months ago on the south side of the bridge under an inch of gravel. If he'd inquired about the silver bell, she could have said she'd picked it up along the bend in the river where the tide lapped its tongue against the foot of the quay below the Red Fox Inn. He'd have looked at her with a degree of skepticism, but it would have been the truth. She could retrace her steps for a year and never recall seeing the kilt pin before. "I have no idea how it arrived in this shop, sir."

The look of skepticism presented itself on his face anyway. "You have a sister who works in the shop with you, do you not? Perhaps she could shed some light on the matter. My lad's been missing for three weeks now."

Oh, Mary. Where have you gone to?

Despite Sir Elvanfoot's excitement, it was not a key he'd found, and yet it must have been the very thing he'd been meant to find. He took the telegram out once more. "Curiosity shop run by Blackwood sisters holds key," he read, and then read again. At last he let the message drop. "How could I be so damnably stupid?"

"He doesn't mean an actual key," Edwina said, seeing it for herself. "He meant to express the shop held the key to finding George."

"There isn't magic enough in the world to explain such a coincidence," he said, holding the pin up to the light coming through the window and affirming yet again it was a family heirloom. "But what connection does my son have to your shop?"

As he asked, a newsboy hawking papers on the corner called out with an all-too-familiar refrain: "Murder! Murder in the streets! Brick Lane Slasher claims another victim!"

Edwina stepped to the window. At the sound of the newsboy's calls, the warning that had flustered and clawed inside her all morning begging to be heard finally broke free. She feared the answer to Elvanfoot's question. Feared it lived in the street with the call of murder. Elvanfoot, a father with a son missing for weeks, blanched at the spectacle on the street of citizens rushing to purchase news of the grisly event. Fear. Doubt. Bargaining with the All Knowing for release from any connection to the events unfolding outside—the range of reactions she and Elvanfoot shared at the window created a sort of bridge of understanding between them.

"I don't know beyond the discovery of that pin within the shop what the connection to your son is," Edwina said. "We are not pawnbrokers and we do not accept merchandise on consignment, so it was not sold to us by him or any other." Her intuition swelled unpleasantly beneath her ribs again. "Likely it was found by my sister, and we'll ask her about that when she returns. Until then, I will try to reunite you with Mr. Cameron." There was only a momentary pang of added discomfort when she committed herself to the task of finding Ian. "I can't say for certain where he is at the moment, but he has a little fellow devoted to him who might be able to help us."

"Old Tom Hob? Good heavens, the little imp is here in the city?" Elvanfoot pocketed the pin. "I had no idea. We must summon him at once." The witch paused and scrutinized the shop goods for an entirely different purpose than before. "Have you a washbasin about? Or a good-sized vase? Even a commode will do, come to think of it."

"Yes, of course." Edwina spun around, searching. "Will this do?" she asked, removing an umbrella from a brass stand by the door and presenting the empty container.

Elvanfoot looked it over, tapping the solid bottom with the flat of his hand. "Aye, that'll do. Bolt the door. We'll fetch him here quick as we can."

The pair went into the back room, where Elvanfoot set the canister on the floor and took two steps back. Edwina, meanwhile, looked to her jars and elixirs to see if anything might aid in the magic. She held up a bundle of grapevine with a questioning look. The elderly witch approved of her innovation, so she set the coil of woody vine inside the canister.

"It might be a good idea if we also add a drop or two of alcohol, if ye have it, to sweeten the spell," Elvanfoot said.

She went to get her father's sherry; then together they lit a candle for good measure. "T'would be ideal to lure him with song, but I'm afraid my voice would only scare the unfortunate creature," he added, suggesting she do the honors. "Mind, you must lean into the container so that your voice does not disperse in all directions. You do not wish to call in any strays lurking about." He twitched a finger at her in admonition born of experience.

Edwina, though nervous about performing magic in front of such a renowned witch as Sir Elvanfoot, agreed to do the summoning. After pouring a drop of sherry into the umbrella stand, she began to sing. "Pixie, fairy, goblin, sprite, 'tis mischief in which you delight. Hither, thither on your flight, we call you stand before our sight. Hallo, hallo, old Tom Hob. Hallo, hallo, old Tom Hob."

The grapevine coiled inside the umbrella stand lit up with a shimmering glow of copper light, whizzing her request, and presumably a nip of sherry, through the mysterious otherworld where the hobgoblins roamed.

"Splendid voice, Miss Blackwood. Truly mesmerizing."

Elvanfoot's blazing blue eyes rested on her in a most curious way, as if he gleaned in the halo of her aura something that both intrigued and frightened him. He made a slight nod to himself before crossing his arms and leaning against the wall to wait.

"How long do you think it will take for him to hear the call?" Edwina asked.

"Oh, I think he's heard word already, but it would never do to appear to be at any witch's beck and call, saving for the one he serves. They're a proud lot, elves. Diminutive in size, but their bloodlines are some of the most ancient in the New World, and they never let you forget it. He'll be here by and by."

"I'd never encountered one before, but he's very loyal to Mr. Cameron, is he not?"

"Indeed. We should all be so lucky to have lived in a house set on such an important crossroads."

"Important crossroads?"

"The lad grew up on Hare Hill. Famously occupied by the fair folk in the last age. They still pass by there on ceremony days on account of the lake and river nearby. Hob, as I understand it, became attached to the house and stayed after the original owner showed him a kindness. If I'm not mistaken, Ian's family is the seventh generation to occupy the home."

"How perfectly enchanting," Edwina said. She felt a shiver, as if a sprinkle of Hob's golden magic had settled on her skin.

"You say that now, but were you to meet any of the fair folk while they're in a foul mood, you'd bolt the door and cross yourself. Trust me, I was married to one for nearly twenty years."

Edwina smiled politely, while inside she was dying to ask every impertinent question darting through her mind about such a relationship.

"But perhaps you've more of an acquaintance with the fair folk than you give yourself credit for," Elvanfoot said, sobering. The intensity of his startling blue eyes unsettled her casual mood and she straightened, on guard again. His gaze did not falter when he said, "I should be curious to hear more about your relations."

Edwina wasn't sure she was up to such scrutiny, but then the gentleman witch got a lesson in her family anyway as Mary returned to the shop. Her sister's face was red, and the cheek under her left eye was beginning to darken into a bruise.

"Stars above! What happened to you?" Edwina asked, but her sister, looking as if she were drenched in shame, would not say. At the sight of Elvanfoot in the back of the shop, Mary covered her face with her hand and ran up two flights of stairs, where she slammed the door.

Edwina, caught between propriety and duty to her sister, excused herself with a bow of her head. "I really should go check on her."

"Anything I can do?"

No doubt there was considerable magic he could do to attend Mary, but he'd already shown enough curiosity about them. "No, I'm sure she'll be fine. I'll make her a pot of tea and a calming potion and she'll be right as rain. Please, make yourself comfortable," she said and started to make her way upstairs to see after her whirlwind of a sister.

Elvanfoot sat on the chair with a hard glint in his eye and simply stated he'd wait.

Chapter Twenty

Ian finished his breakfast of tea and a scone, while disappointment settled beside it in his stomach. The boardinghouse on Cedric Lane in which he sat had proved the source of his indigestion. Not only was George no longer there, but the innkeeper relayed that he'd left in a rage three days earlier, the same night Ian had gone to the shore and been hit over the head and robbed of his memories. The innkeeper, an easy-mannered witch gent by the name of Mr. Wallaby who was fond of bright red waistcoats and plaid trousers, insisted George had been fine when they'd first arrived. It was only after Ian left to prowl the riverbank that the gentleman became angry. George had been left alone in the sitting room to browse the books, while Wallaby prepared his tea, when his agitation grew. Wallaby had returned to find several irreplaceable spell books burning in the fireplace. He'd bent to save them when he felt a shove from behind that knocked him to the floor. By the time he'd returned to his feet with an incantation sharp on his tongue, George had vanished over the threshold and into the night.

Wallaby entered the breakfast room still drying his hands after washing up the dishes. "Will you be off to look for that fella, then?"

"I wouldn't know where to begin at this point." Ian threw his napkin on the table. "Is there anything else you can tell me about George Elvanfoot? Anything at all?"

"I've told you all I remember. It were just the one hour he were here."

"How did he appear to you that night?"

"Well, you saw the state of him. 'Twas a right mess he was in."

It was too much to try and explain why he had no memory of the events. Instead, Ian slid the photo of George in his costume across the table. "Perhaps you could recall how he was dressed when he was here?"

"To be honest, I nearly didn't let you in," Wallaby said. "Your mate smelled like he'd been rolling around in the gutter. Imagine he'd been sleeping rough and drinking. We're a boardinghouse catering to witches, sure, but we're no home for feral dogs wandering in off the street."

"His outfit?" Ian pressed.

Wallaby peered closer. "No, he weren't in no top hat or cape. I believe he were wearing a long gray coat, though 'twere dirty as a coal porter's. And he weren't wearing nothing as fine as that sparkly pin in his lapel."

Ian looked closer at the pin. It struck him for the first time that George was wearing the thistle pin in both photos. An item like that must have some significance for a man to wear it in two separate photos, one in costume and one as himself. He reasoned such a thing could easily have been lost on the street. Or pawned. Actors made little enough money, and yet its absence nagged at his intuition. "Thank you," he said and took a last swallow of tea.

He was still pondering the missing pin when Hob popped up out of a coal scuttle near the fireplace. The little fellow shook off, creating a cloud of black dust.

"Hob? What the devil are you about now?"

"They are looking for you," Hob said. "Miss Blackwood and Sir Elvanfoot."

The peculiar pairing of names unsettled him. "What? Where? Henry Elvanfoot has arrived in the city? They're together?"

Hob twirled his finger and the dust lifted off him, swirling into a funnel that emptied back into the scuttle the moment he hopped out. "So many questions." The little imp grabbed a scone off the table and broke off the corner to eat. "He is at the shop with milady. They await you there, but it is set to be a sorry affair."

"But how? Never mind. Come, we must go."

"Not I," Hob said, unbothered by the crumbs falling out of his mouth. "I'm to go north and fetch Sir his books first."

"His books? Whatever for?"

"What does one ever need books for? To read what is not already in the head. 'Tis the other Miss Blackwood who has roused him to it, methinks."

"Very well, I'll meet you there." Both had turned to go their separate ways when Ian stopped, baffled by what he'd heard yet again. "By the way, why do you call Miss Blackwood 'milady'?"

Hob jumped in the coal bin and shrugged. "It would be rude not to."

While he suspected there was more to it, the elf's logic could not be argued with, so Ian bid his mate safe travels. After consulting with his pocket watch to check the street, it took a mere five minutes for Ian to walk to the shop. Curiously, the boy with the dirty face and head full of nursery rhymes was propped against the window again. Ian approached the shop front and peered through the glass as if window-shopping for a new spoon, pretending to ignore the boy.

After a few moments standing side by side, the boy was the first to comment. "You back again?" He grinned and shook his head as if to imply Ian was some kind of nutter.

"Do you make it your business to keep track of who comes and goes in this shop?" Ian asked, still paying the boy little noticeable attention.

"It's my street then, innit?"

"So it appears," Ian said somewhat more amiably, finally glancing down at the boy. "All right, Mr. Clever Clogs, how many times do you reckon you've seen me enter this shop?"

Before the boy could answer, a cry of "Murder!" was shouted in the street. The call came from the paperboy on the corner as he cut the twine on a bundle of newly delivered papers. "Murder on Dorset Street!" he shouted again to drum up business. "Brick Lane Slasher strikes again. Read about it in the *Daily Gazette*. Renegade rats run rampant in the public square. Read about it in the *Daily* here!"

"There's been another?" Ian's breakfast churned in his stomach at the news.

The boy's smile dropped, too, replaced by a scowl. The expression was too old and pained for a child of his age. It was the sort of look shaped from rough years spent living on the pavement day and night, wary of strangers, yet seeing them as a necessary means to an end—a meal, a smoke, a tossed coin. At least that's how Ian imagined his young life had gone. The boy's attention shifted to shadows across the street. "My mistake, mister. I ain't never seen you around here afore." He folded his arms over his fragile bird-bone chest. "And sure enough you ain't seen me afore either."

The change was remarkable. His pity was likely misplaced, but Ian fished in his pocket and set his last few small coins on the window ledge. The impish smile returned as the boy eyed the coins. But instead of scooping them up and running off to the nearest costermonger for a bowl of jellied eel, the boy crossed his arms and sang through his gap-toothed grin. "Three blind mice. See how they run. They all went after the farmer's wife, who cut off their tails with a carving knife. Have you ever seen such a sight in your life as three blind mice?"

The words of the nursery rhyme followed Ian inside the shop, leaving him to wonder if the boy had somehow been affected. The thought quickly dissipated once he caught sight of Edwina standing in the rear of the store, backlit by golden lamplight. How had he ever deemed the blush of her cheek merely interesting? Her brand of beauty had an ethereal, immeasurable quality, arresting the observer in his tracks.

"Ah, arrived at last." Sir Elvanfoot somberly stepped forward with his hand outstretched. "I knew the elf wouldn't let me down."

Behind Sir Elvanfoot, Edwina dipped her head in brief acknowledgment, not looking him in the eye or even bending a lip in a polite smile. The rebuff stung more than he cared to admit. He was accustomed to people being angry with him. It came with the job. But he'd not anticipated, upon seeing her again, how her withdrawal of friendship would unsettle him so.

"Sir," Ian said, shaking the elderly witch's hand. To Edwina he returned her nod, daring to hold his gaze on her until she chanced to lift her eyes. "Miss Blackwood." He then gestured to the street and the ongoing clamor of murder. "More dreadful news this morning."

"Grisly business," Elvanfoot said. "But come. We have much to talk about. I want to hear about your investigation."

"I admit my surprise at seeing you here. I thought we agreed you would remain in the north until I had something to report."

"Ah, yes." Elvanfoot exchanged a glance with Edwina. "I understand you've suffered a gap in your memory." He produced the telegram from Ian to explain his appearance in the city. "As you can see, my presence was requested."

"I summoned you here?" Ian shook his head before removing the telegram receipt in his pocket. "I admit I haven't any recollection of this. Or why I thought to alert you to the Blackwoods' shop."

"You claimed you'd found George," Elvanfoot said. "But now I'm to understand he is missing once again."

"Aye, and I'm sorry I dinna have better news." Ian explained about the boardinghouse and George's growing agitation while there. "What I canna explain is why I went out that night, leaving George behind. Or why he pushed a man down to escape a place where he was perfectly safe. I'm sorry to say no one has seen him since."

"And this was the same night you were struck and your memories taken from you?"

"It dragged on until morning but, yes, the very same."

Both men went quiet. The feeling of helplessness Ian experienced could only be a fraction of what his esteemed friend suffered. To have a loved one missing without a word or hint of why or where while the call of fresh murder rang out on the streets must have been turmoil.

"So," said Elvanfoot. "The solution to the dilemma seems simple enough. If you were to have your missing memories returned, you could no doubt tell us what compelled you to go out that night. And what transpired with my son and where I might find the lad now. Therefore, I submit we find this bauble, as Miss Blackwood calls them, and have the memories replaced in your head, where they may do some good."

"I'm afraid it's not that simple," Edwina said. "There is a spell for such a thing, but—"

"My dear, there is a spell for everything."

"Yes, of course, but as Mr. Cameron will attest, the results are not always worth the risk."

In truth, the specter of having received another man's memories and the ill effects that followed had rendered Ian spell-shy of ever hoping to retrieve his true memories again. The thought of suffering through another man's final moments left him queasy and unmoored, as though his legs might wobble beneath him. And yet how much of his own life was he missing? Hob had done his best, but there were thoughts, deeds, regrets that could never be fully known by anyone but himself, but even that was not enough to douse his misgivings about having his memories reinstalled by spellwork. "It's not as straightforward as one might believe when dealing with the mind," Ian said. "Gets a bit twitchy if you get it wrong."

The old witch waited for an explanation, but even upon learning from Edwina about the mismatched memory, he would not be put off.

"I believe there may yet be a way to ensure all is well." A can rattled in the back room. "Ah, yes, here he is. Right on time."

Hob climbed out of the umbrella stand with a clatter. Arriving with him were two books: one black with a silver clasp and the other a dusty tome that was nearly as big as Hob himself, about which he complained bitterly as he hoisted the thing out of the metal bin. "I had to climb three shelves to get this one. Dinna yell at me if the blue vase on your desk is in several more pieces when you get home than when you left."

Elvanfoot rolled his eyes and took the heavy book from the over-wrought imp and placed it on the shop counter. The black book, small enough to sit comfortably inside a breast pocket, he tucked away as if keeping it for later. "Miss Blackwood, do you mind if I take the liberty?"

Before she could ask him what he meant, Elvanfoot narrowed his eyes and swept his arm out as if parting a curtain. The bolt slid in the lock on the shop door, the sign turned itself to Closed, and a veil of darkness surrounded the shop's interior. And all without speaking a word of incantation.

Edwina stared somewhat openmouthed. "How did you do that?"

"My dear, I've been studying and practicing magic so long the incantations have worn a rut in my brain so deep I need not utter them aloud any longer."

"That's brilliant," she said. "But if I keep closing my shop during the day, I'll not see a penny for my rent come the end of the week." She shrugged in defeat, admitting the moment was greater than the paltry sales she'd have on a quiet morning when talk of murder was the prevailing business on the street.

"Now," said Elvanfoot, rubbing his hands together. "I may have exaggerated my skill a wee bit a moment ago, for there are a few spells in which I need to confer with my grimoire. The uncommon, often once-in-a-lifetime predicaments that one can never anticipate. Naturally, those spells are not committed to memory. And that, Miss Blackwood, is where we find ourselves." He opened the heavy tome resting on top of the glass countertop and thumbed through several pages before stopping and stabbing the open book with his finger. "Ah, this section here," he said. "These writings on crystal scrying may lead us in the right direction." He bent his head forward to read the tiny cursive inscriptions as he held his glasses steady. "Or not. It's all a matter of finding the right magic."

Ian leaned over the witch's shoulder to get a better look at his grimoire. The handwriting was rendered in an ornate calligraphy style, as though each word was meant as a dedication to the craft. He shrank back knowing his own scribbled Book of Shadows was often hastily written as an afterthought, and only after he'd relied on absolute instinct to guide his sometimes reckless magic. He'd no aptitude for herbal charms or potions. His primary skill lay in the quick reflex that relied not on incantations but on instinct. By comparison, the pages of his Book of Shadows could easily be folded over and stuffed inside his boot, while the great witch of the north couldn't lift that damn grimoire of his without using two hands. He left him to it.

While Elvanfoot searched through his spells, Ian asked Edwina for the opportunity to speak to her, gently prodding her by the elbow to step a few feet away. "Is your sister here?" he asked.

"You mean my sister the vampire?"

Hob, overhearing, eyed him with curiosity. Ian regretted his choice of words with Edwina and for raising his voice the day before. Of course he did. "I deserve your scorn for that," he said, bowing his head in contrition. "There's something unique and rare about your magic and hers. I know you've had to keep it hidden from others for most of your lives. But I also dinna believe what happened to me was the first time she's taken memories from the living." Edwina was visibly uncomfortable at such talk, but he continued. "Still, it canna be easy being uncommon even among your own kind. Please accept my apology."

"Thank you. And I apologize for my sister and I putting you through such agony. You had every right to be angry with me. With her. But you have to understand, I'm very protective of her. She may be all the family I have left. And she's been so different all her life. Always the one to draw the worst attention from those who would judge."

"Of course. She's lucky to have you," Ian said. Edwina gave him a genuine smile then, one with the power to buff the edge of cynicism off him.

"She's upstairs resting," she said. "She had a fright earlier. A man attacked her on the street. Struck her in the face." She looked away again, uneasy. "She claimed it was random, but I'm not sure I believe her. I've privately wondered if she's been seeing someone unsuitable. Leastwise, she never mentions him."

"Attacked? Have you notified the police? A man like that ought to be horsewhipped."

Edwina shook her head. She appeared to want to share something more, gazing up as she listened for sounds of her sister's presence on the floor above. Instead she presented a carry-on-with-it smile. "She'll be all right. I gave her tea and applied a calming spell so she can rest."

How her eyes did sparkle when she allowed herself to be free of care, he thought. Ian nodded his endorsement of the sister's treatment, while hoping the discord between he and Edwina had been mended. Hob, too, smiled with approval from where he sat on the counter beside the spell book.

"Here we are." Elvanfoot straightened and removed his glasses, giving them a wipe with a handkerchief. "I believe, if we follow these instructions on electromagnetic attraction, we may achieve a more accurate result in returning the correct bauble to the correct body."

The memory of the man's lifeblood draining out of him, the contraction of light in the pupil as his consciousness faded, and the flash of a beloved child's face never to be seen again in this life—the risk of experiencing another's pain, or even bitter joy, at the end of life was an emotional bridge Ian wasn't ready to cross again so soon.

Elvanfoot slid his glasses back on, peering at Ian through what felt like a more powerful lens than that afforded by curved glass housed in wire frames. The scrutiny was almost unbearable until the wizard relented, lowering his gaze back to the book. "Your resistance is understandable," he said. "Something went terribly wrong last time. You repelled the implanted memory. But I am not the witch Miss Blackwood is."

Ian thought to protest, but the truth of it was plain enough.

"You've had portions of your memory returned," Elvanfoot said with a glance at Hob. "And it may feel as though you are whole, apart from those four days, but I would caution you against such thinking. While your guardian here has done his best to give back all he contained of your life, in your heart you know he could not know all. If the witch's bauble is still intact, we can give those remaining parts back to you. If you're willing to trust. And then perhaps we might also find my son again."

Seeing his reluctance, Elvanfoot made a proposal. "A test," he said. "Describe for me, if you can, the first time we met. Your imp, I can attest, was not there, so how much do you recall in detail?"

Hob shrank inside his coat, a move that did not fill Ian with confidence. As he thought back on the first memory he had of the infamous witch, an image of the white-haired man speaking behind a podium rose up. "Three years ago, you gave a speech on the influence of magic on modern thought in science and medicine," Ian said, triumphant. "You wore a gray jacket with a waistcoat. And a kilt of red tartan. I went up to you afterward to shake your hand." He closed his fist as if grabbing another thought, but all he came up with was empty air. What he remembered next was the familiarity that already existed between them. Neither had felt the need to introduce himself. They spoke as if they were well acquainted. "You asked after my parents. But how would you know their names, if we'd just met?"

Elvanfoot was circumspect. "I recall the night you describe. We did shake hands, certainly. But in truth we had met for the first time perhaps two years earlier." Ian shook his head in doubt. "You were still working for the Constabulary then. A young investigator who'd been called on to handle a domestic dispute." He leaned toward Edwina to fill her in. "My wife tried to have me dispatched by feeding me a potion made from bark and fungus. Fly agaric, to be precise."

"How terrible," she said.

"Regrettably, not as uncommon as you might think, and yet still against the laws of our Order of Witches." He returned his attention to Ian. "You did not catch her, by the way. She slipped away in the middle of the night, back to her people. However, you did save my life by applying the correct antidote in the form of a purging spell. I smelled of codfish oil and rosemary for a week."

"You're mistaken. It must have been somebody else. I dinna remember any of that."

"Your imp was not there," Elvanfoot reminded him. "You explained to me you routinely ordered him to stay away while working cases, after that dreadful incident with the parents murdering their child because they believed she was a changeling. I assume you told him to stay away when you came to the city to look for my son as well, which is why you can't remember."

Perspiration dampened Ian's skin. There was a fair amount of empathy in Elvanfoot's demeanor, yet his tale was a dream from another life. There was naught but denial in Ian's mind that he'd been involved in a case of a wife trying to poison Sir Elvanfoot. Yet the echo of truth in the case involving the child confused him. He knew that to be true. Knew that he'd quit the Constabulary because of it. He could still feel the sting in his heart at what he'd witnessed, yet he could not bring up the details.

Elvanfoot reached in his pocket for the small black book. He opened the silver clasp, and a slip of newspaper slid out from between the book's pages. He unfolded it and held the article up for Ian to read the first paragraph, where he was named as having saved the life of Sir Elvanfoot, inventor of a smokeless propellant used in the Seven Nations War.

Hob slunk away and crawled into a wicker basket.

The implication was clear. Four days of missing memories in a city he wasn't from was a manageable setback, but he couldn't possibly know how much else he'd lost—intimate moments that might earn him a wink on the street, a life-changing handshake with a superior, or the fallout of a past assignment with the Constabulary he could no longer recall. The consequences of what else might have been lost sobered him, stripping him of his nonchalance. Was living with those gaps a forfeiture he could abide? If there was a way to restore what had been lost to the mist, shouldn't he take it? If those missing four days could be returned to him, what mystery might they solve? For him? For Elvanfoot? For a city at the mercy of a ruthless killer?

"Show me the spell that can assure me the memory is mine and I'll do it," he said.

Edwina rested her hand on his arm as she begged him with her eyes. "Ian, are you sure?"

Before he lost his nerve, he patted her hand and said that he must be. For his sake. And George's.

"Miss Blackwood, if you could retrieve the baubles your sister has collected," Elvanfoot said as he cleared a space on the shop counter, "we can then begin."

"Of course," Edwina said and excused herself. A moment later she came down the stairs holding a wooden jewelry box. "She's still sleeping. I'm almost certain she could identify the source of each and every one of these if prodded. They are that dear to her." She glanced back at the stairs as though ashamed at the deception of taking her sister's things without asking. "But perhaps it's best to do this while she's asleep. Goodness knows we owe you your restored peace of mind," she said to Ian, setting the box down on the counter.

Elvanfoot opened the lid. He did not touch anything, but he clearly took inventory. "I hadn't expected so many," he said. "So many lives. So many memories."

Ian leaned in for a look. To think one of those small blue orbs, each like a tiny world unto itself, held everything he could ever remember inside it. There had to be a dozen or more, each one representing a person's life like his own, though presumably their owners were all dead now. Philosophers might ask if a capsulized memory removed from the body could survive past a soul's demise, but he knew already that it could, having briefly lived in the mind of another man's recollections.

Elvanfoot looked sidelong at Edwina as the wrinkles in his brow deepened in probing curiosity. "How long has your sister had this ability?"

She hesitated at first before admitting it began at age twelve. At her maturity. She and Mary had both experienced changes in their abilities then.

"Both?" The old witch grew thoughtful as he scratched his beard. "Yes, I believe I'm beginning to appreciate the rarity of your situation."

"Then you may be the first to do so in a very long time," Edwina said, dipping her head in deference, a gesture that he returned.

Something unspoken had been conveyed, something bewitched between the two of them. Ian understood nothing of the accord they'd negotiated, yet it seemed to settle Elvanfoot on the matter.

"Come," Elvanfoot said. "We must make haste." After conferring with his spell book one more time, he asked for a lock of Ian's hair, something of solid gold, which Edwina provided, and a jar of ginseng, which she did not.

"I have no such herb," she said in alarm as she handed over the gold ring she'd found on the foreshore to use in the spell.

Elvanfoot tapped his finger on an apparent substitute listed in his spell book. "Root of ashwagandha will do," he said, looking up in expectation.

His request was met with not one but two faces reflecting ignorance of such a substance.

The old witch read his third choice. "Surely, you must have leaf of lemon balm in stock."

To everyone's great relief, Edwina fetched a packet of the dried leaves, proclaiming them to be as potent as newly picked.

Ian reached for the knife in his pocket so he might cut off an inch of the required hair, but the weapon wasn't there. "The knife," he said, patting his pockets. "It's gone." He quickly thought back to the last time he'd seen it for certain and landed on an image of himself standing outside the doss-house before he ended up lying in bed upstairs in a fever dream of someone else's mind. Perhaps it had fallen out of his pocket, lost in the cab or in the crease of a blanket.

Edwina approached him with a pair of scissors from her cupboard. "May I?" Her hand swept the side of his face as she collected a twist of his hair in her fingers. Her face came close enough to his for him to smell the flowery pomade she massaged in her own hair. The nearness of her skin, mouth, and eyes to his kindled his desire. He swallowed, wondering which forgotten memory of the flesh had been resurrected. Whatever the source, he could no longer deny the pleasantness of her body next to his.

Edwina snipped the lock of hair, letting it curl around her finger until she dropped it beside the gold ring. Elvanfoot crushed the dried leaves of lemon balm and sprinkled the flakes into a small porcelain bowl he'd snatched off a shelf.

"A candle, if you please."

Edwina lit a beeswax candle in a brass holder with the snap of her fingers. Her attention briefly flitted to the front of the store, where the odd boy cupped his hands around his eyes and pressed his face to the window.

"Never mind the mortals outside," Elvanfoot said. "They can see nothing of our business here. Only shadows of an empty shop." The witch cleared a space on the counter for the baubles, cleansed the air above with the smoke from the candle, then put the ring, hair, and crushed leaves in a pile together. "It's a variant of a common attraction spell. The leaf will help boost the power of memory. The hair will attract like to like, meaning you," he said to Ian. "And, with a wee bit of luck, the gold will enable the energy to flow between the two. If all goes as planned, the rightful memory will make itself known so that we may restore it."

The detailed preparation settled Ian. He no longer blamed Edwina for her part in the false memory he'd been given. Looking at the collection of stolen memories, he understood the challenge she'd faced and reasoned she'd tried to restore his mind in good faith, choosing the one she felt most confident about. It was plain, both then and now, how she'd defied her sister's nature to see the right thing done. He stepped up to the counter ready to risk the process of recovering what he'd lost all over again, despite the sliver of doubt reminding him of the feel of the phantom knife sliding across his throat.

Elvanfoot had been brushing his beard absentmindedly as he peered one last time at his book. Seemingly ready, he nodded and looked up. "Let us begin."

"Begin what?" Mary stood on the third stair from the bottom. Her hair was a tangled mess from sleeping. A bruise on her left cheek had blossomed into a purple rose. Edwina went to her, hoping to offer comfort, but those eyes full of smoke tracked to the old witch and the items arranged on the counter. "What's going on? Why do you have my things?"

"We need to return Ian's memory to him," Edwina said. "The correct one."

Mary ran down the last few steps, agitation and disbelief flaring in her eyes. "Those are mine. You can't just take them."

Edwina put her arm around her sister's shoulder. "Mary, we need you to help us."

"You took my baubles from me? Without asking my permission?"

"It's very important we return the correct memory to Ian so he can remember how he found Sir Elvanfoot's missing son." Edwina smoothed a loose strand of Mary's hair behind her ear, but her sister shrugged her off. "We're going to use a spell—"

"Why are you all conspiring against me?" The distress in Mary's eyes turned to fury. "Get away from me!"

A plate that had hung on the wall for six months shattered and fell to the floor. A mirror cracked.

"Mary, stop it! This is unseemly. Please, we need you to cooperate." Edwina tried to maintain her composure, but her ire was building as well. "A man's life may be at stake. Surely that's more important than a few shiny baubles collecting dust in an old jewelry box."

Mary's fury combusted into fire. "You're no better than all the others. You betrayed my trust again. And for what? Him?" She pointed at Ian in disgust. "He doesn't even notice you, you dried-up old spinster."

Elvanfoot attempted a gentlemanly intercession. "Miss, if you'll allow—"

But she cut him off, charging forward and swiping her arm across the counter, scattering the ring, hair, and leaves of lemon balm before grabbing the jewelry box. Observing the outburst in his distracted, studious way, Sir Elvanfoot backed away and raised his hands, apparently not intent on interfering with her rampage.

Ian caught the toppled candle in its brass holder by reflex before it fell on the wicker basket where Hob crouched. Enough was enough. Mary's reaction was too reckless, too vicious. She wasn't in her right mind. Still gripping the candlestick, he slipped his spell inside a poem, the words falsely gentle. "O rose, thou art sick. The invisible worm, that flies in the night, in the howling storm . . ."

"No, Ian, wait." Edwina gripped the arm bearing the candlestick, begging him to hold his tongue before casting a spell against her sister. "She's overwrought. She doesn't know what she's doing."

With his incantation incognito left hanging in the air, Mary bolted up the stairs with the jewelry box under her arm. Ian set the candlestick aside and followed, taking the stairs two at a time, but still she eluded him as though she'd turned to vapor as she fled to her room. The door shut in his face and the lock bolted before he could catch her. Edwina joined him at the top of the stairs and pounded on the door, demanding to be let in as the sound of something heavy crashed against the hardwood floor.

"I don't know what's got into her," she said to Ian. "Mary, open this door at once!"

Ian put his ear to the door and shook his head, unable to hear even the sound of heavy breathing after running up the stairs. He made a silent motion with his hand to indicate a key.

Edwina stood back, the urgency gone from her. "It's too late. She's gone."

"Gone? How?" Ian didn't wait for an explanation. "Hob! Undo this lock."

They heard the scatter of small feet inside the room and then the door opened. The imp swung from the doorknob, then jumped aside. "She isn't here," he said, shrugging his tiny shoulders. Behind him, the curtain flapped in the breeze of the open window. On the floor were a dozen scattered baubles and the overturned jewelry box. Ian went to the window and looked down, expecting to find a tragic scene of death or injury, but there was no body. And no sign of Mary high or low.

She'd simply disappeared.

Chapter Twenty-One

Edwina bent to pick up the scattered orbs and return them to the box, avoiding Ian's gaze.

"How?" Ian was incredulous as he inspected the window frame, the eave above, and the ground below. "How does a woman, even if she is a witch, vanish into thin air?" He turned from the window, posturing in predictable male aggression when the answer evaded him.

Hob helped Edwina scoop up the baubles, collecting those that had rolled under the bed. The little fellow emerged covered in dust, blowing on the orbs to clean them. "I did not pass her," he said to Ian, referring to his uniquely elvish means of transporting himself from one location to another unseen.

"Of course not," Ian said. The man was completely confounded. He bent down to search under the bed, apparently unaware of the invasion of privacy of having entered a woman's bedroom without leave. The thought made Edwina flush even in the midst of all the confusion. "But then how the devil did she get away?"

Ian searched the room, pulling back the curtain on a small closet and lifting the lid of the cedar hope chest at the foot of Edwina's bed. The second smaller trunk in the corner, the one Mary used to store old clothes in need of mending, was no exception as he bent to unstrap the buckles holding it closed.

It was one thing to invade the room in search of Mary, but Edwina had to object to him riffling through her sister's things. "Not even I search through her personal belongings without permission," she said, though she could not deny her resolve had been weakened by curiosity. The flask, the pocketknife, the thistle pin—too many unanswered questions had begun to stack up on the scale against her sister.

Ian tested that resolve by prying the lid open anyway. Edwina did not object a second time; instead she bent down to see what might be contained within. "At least allow me to do it," she said. Having already crossed the threshold of violating her sister's privacy and trust, she convinced herself to lean in to the greater good of discovering the truth. Or at least that's what she told herself as she peeled back the old nightdress with the torn hem folded neatly on top. Beneath, she found what she expected: a pair of stockings needing mending, a sewing kit that was their mother's, and some embroidery work left undone. But then she spied a red-and-gold decorated tea tin she'd not seen in the trunk before, and beside it a cloth bag with a drawstring top.

Her hand shook as though a premonition of ill fate had sent a tremor through her body. She removed the tin's lid and drew in a breath. Inside were six blue orbs nestled in a square of velvet. Each with the sheen of newness, each containing a person's memory she had no recollection of.

"I can't explain it." She looked up at Ian, confused. "Where did these come from?"

He tore into the bag beside the tin, spilling the contents onto the nightdress. There were brass buttons, two gold rings, a set of keys, a pair of wire-rimmed spectacles splotched with what appeared to be dried blood, and a silver vesta match safe with a mermaid imprinted on its face. The items were of little monetary value, yet their weight sank Edwina to her knees.

Ian pressed his knuckles solemnly against his lips as he studied the contents. "There may yet be a good explanation for how she came by these things," he said, though with little conviction, as he glowered at the match safe.

"I read the newspaper accounts as closely as you did," Edwina said. He tried to interrupt, but she shook her head. "There's more. A flask she said she found on the shore this morning. And a pocketknife. But neither had been in the water, I'd swear it." She paused as Elvanfoot entered the room, pressing a hand over her stomach to quell the growing nausea.

"And there is this as well," Elvanfoot said, holding up the thistle pin that belonged to his son.

Edwina bent toward Ian. "We discovered George's pin hidden in the shop earlier."

Ian slipped the items back in the bag gently, as if each were a sacred found object. Evidence. Proof of a crime. Though not the one they were both thinking of. It simply couldn't be true. Robbing the dead, surely, but not murder.

"May I?" Ian asked to see the pin.

Elvanfoot handed off the silver thistle in exchange for the tea tin. "And she had these baubles hidden with the stolen items?" he asked.

Edwina's stomach lurched at the implication. "She didn't. She couldn't have," she pleaded.

"But she has fled, has she not?" Elvanfoot's face was a puzzle of conflicting scowls and begrudging awe as he, too, looked out the window to see for himself the impossibility of her escape. And yet there was no other explanation but that Mary Blackwood had gone out the window. And with it the hope that he might learn what had happened to his son.

He tipped the tin to let one of the orbs fall into his hand. Pinching it between finger and thumb, he held up the gemlike ball to the light of the window. "Did she take anything with her?" he asked, staring in almost mesmerized wonder at the bauble's translucency.

Edwina made a sweep of the room and shook her head until Hob dumped the recovered orbs from the floor into her hands, saying that was all he could find scattered. She sorted through the memories, at least the ones she'd known about, closing her eyes briefly in disappointment. "An orb is missing. There was a second one with a brilliant vein of gold running through the blue, but it's not here."

Elvanfoot nodded. "I think it fair to assume she's taken Ian's memory with her, judging by her actions downstairs. There's something she does not wish him to remember. Undoubtedly, some revelation about my son and the others," he said, taking back the thistle pin.

Ian rubbed his temples. "There's something about the pin, but trying to remember is like grasping at shadows. He's wearing that thistle in his coat lapel in the two photos I've seen of George. But the witch running the boardinghouse I took him to swears he didn't have any such thing on him when he arrived. Which means somewhere between his disappearance and me finding him again he lost that pin."

"At least that suggests he's still alive, does it not?" Elvanfoot made a quick glance at the other items in comparison. "Presumably these other items were taken after the victims were killed, so the possibility still exists that the pin's presence in the shop is a mere coincidence unrelated to . . ." He gestured to the array of jewelry and other personal items.

"Aye, it would seem so," Ian said, though he sounded somewhat less relieved about the conclusion than Elvanfoot did.

Edwina had no choice but to add up the evidence of the hidden baubles and the collection of items missing from the victims. The seriousness of her sister's predicament prodded her to act. "I need to go find her, talk to her. Make her see reason."

"Can you?" Ian asked. "You saw how erratic she was." He shut the lid on the trunk. "Never mind, I'm going with you," he said and ran down the stairs before she could argue.

After he left the room, Edwina felt the weight of Elvanfoot's scrutiny. Certain he could see right through her, she suggested Mary wasn't in her right mind. That she believed her sister had recently suffered the misfortune of a wounded heart, as well as a bruised cheek, from a suspected secret lover. All would be well if Edwina could just find her and bring her home for a proper heart-to-heart.

"And yet I suspect that's not the entirety of it," he said, fishing for a more complete explanation from her as he gazed again at the bauble in the window's light, but he let the matter go when she said she mustn't waste any more time.

Elvanfoot asked permission to remain behind in the shop so he might read further on the subject of memories being taken from the body. On the off chance Mary returned before she did, Edwina invited him to make himself comfortable downstairs in their father's old chair, though perhaps with a defensive spell at the ready. He bowed his head, then followed her down the steps.

After securing her black straw hat with the green silk ribbon around its band, Edwina shook out her shawl to straighten the fringe, then swung it over her shoulders. "Ready," she said.

Ian held the front door open for her. "So where do we start?"

"You might try that gadget of yours," she said, nudging her chin at his pocket watch. "If there are any indications nearby, we might yet catch up."

Edwina took pleasure in his reaction as he belatedly came to the same conclusion. He drew the timepiece out and aimed it toward the street, while she took note of the boy's thankful absence. Blessedly, that was one less distraction to have to deal with. After all the whirligigs and wheels finished spinning on his watch, Ian got a reading. Besides the three witches and singular imp within the shop, there were two other possible figures. One was moving at a high rate of speed, the other stationary and situated somewhere at the far end of the street. They followed the moving target.

"That way," Ian said as they rounded the corner and followed the lane east for perhaps a quarter mile.

The city street quickly narrowed, casting a pall over the couple the farther they ventured from the commercial lane. In this part of the city, middle class and poor were stitched together in a mismatched patchwork of varying extremes. Stationers and milliners occupied streets once removed from tobacconists and butcher shops, doss-houses and gaslight pubs. Middle-class terrace flats stood back-to-back with tenements built with uneven bricks and wooden slats held together with rusted rose-head nails.

Ian stopped and checked his watch again. "She's stopped moving," he said after turning in each of the four directions while conferring with his device. "Possibly there." He pointed to a corner pub with windows trimmed in black paint where piano music spilled into the street every time the door opened. Above the windows, a banner of faded gold lettering read THE STOLEN DOVE.

Edwina's intuition rebelled. "Why would my sister come here? It doesn't make any sense." Left to her own instincts, she would have searched for Mary by the river, or along the battlements of the old castle, or even atop the parliament clock tower.

"She's run from us, and until we know her motivation, I wouldn't dare to speculate. And yet I think it's safe to say she won't be happy to see us again when we find her." Ian had been glancing up as he spoke, taking in the neighborhood with a suspicious eye. He lowered his chin and looked Edwina full in the face then. "Would you rather return home? I can continue to look for her myself, if you'd prefer not to confront her this way."

"And endure her wrath alone?" His kind offer steeled her courage. "No, we're in this together," she said. "It's clear that whatever path my sister has taken, it has converged with your investigation. Besides, she may not talk to you. Of course, she may not talk to me either, but perhaps together we can try and make her see reason. Or at the very least explain herself."

The urge to enter the pub and call out to Mary to see if she truly was inside was held back only by the prospect of drawing the attention of everyone in the vicinity—friend, foe, or merely the curious. Edwina exhaled in frustration. Mary's behavior had left her disoriented before, but this time she truly was adrift on a sea of confusion. What was her sister up to?

"Miss Blackwood?" A woman with a face like a dried apple approached on the pavement from the other direction. "Now there's a fine hello. I was only saying how pleased I was with myself for buying one of your hatpins, what with another murder last night, and speak of the devil, there you are. I'd recognize that shawl anywhere."

"Mrs. Dower, hello."

"What brings you this way, love?" The woman looked around to see what might have induced a young lady with a man at her side to venture onto her street.

"I'm looking for my sister, actually." Edwina's eye went to the corner pub. "You haven't run into her, have you?"

Mrs. Dower ran her tongue over her mostly toothless gums while thinking about it. "Can't say as I have today, love." She thought about it some more and offered, "But I saw her yesterday one lane over that way. She was with that tall young man of hers. Thinks he's the cock of the walk, that one. Passes by my window some mornings, though by the look of him, he's on his way home when the rest of the world's just waking up."

Ian took a photo from his pocket and held it out to the woman. "Would this be the young man she was with?"

Mrs. Dower leaned in, squinting at the photo from a few inches away. "My eyes aren't what they used to be," she said, angling the photo to better catch the light before shaking her head. "Sorry, I can't make out his face that well, but it could be, though certainly not with a top hat." She laughed at the notion. "Sorry I couldn't be more help, but so many of these young men have the same look with their long coats and high-and-mighty manners."

Ian retracted the photo and put it away in his pocket. "Thank you," he said. Though the woman didn't seem to notice the disappointment in his voice, Edwina did.

"Thank you, Mrs. Dower. You've been most helpful. Please come by the shop if I can ever be of service."

They said goodbye, and after the woman went on her way, Edwina asked, "Is that a photo of George? Why did you show it to her of all people?"

He exhaled, avoiding her eye. "Just a hunch."

"You think George is involved with my sister?" Edwina looked at the corner pub again, wondering if it could be true. She'd suspected for weeks her sister was seeing an inappropriate young man, but George?

"They've obviously crossed paths." He crooked his finger to lure her into a darkened doorway to get out of view of the pub. "You said yourself you dinna know how his pin came to be in your shop, so it had to be Mary. The only question is, how did she acquire the damn thing?" He leaned in close, the heat of his breath on her cheek making her light-headed with want. "How did she acquire *any* of those things we found?"

"This can't be happening." Edwina leaned her back against the door as if to steel herself. "If those items belonged to the murder victims . . ." She shook her head when it didn't make sense. "But George wasn't one of the victims listed in the papers."

"No, but there's a connection. She must know George." He leaned his shoulder against the door, losing any pretense of formality with her. "Listen, I couldn't say this earlier with Sir Elvanfoot standing there, but you remember those drawings I left in the hotel?"

"The ones that nearly got you arrested?"

"I've done some digging, and apparently I'd been working on a theory that the murders were ritualistic. There was a mark found on each of the victims' bodies during the autopsies. A sort of spiral shape. I thought it might be a symbol used in a forbidden spell or curse."

"A death spell?"

"Or a form of blood magic," he said. "I've seen something similar before when I worked for the Northern Constabulary, but I could never prove the intent or the motive. The victims there were all animals."

"You don't think Sir Elvanfoot's son is involved in something so heinous, surely?"

"His initial disappearance roughly coincides with the date of the first murder. And then I learned he ran from me after I got him to the boardinghouse." He shook his head, defeated, and kicked at a weed growing up between the cobbles. "Then again, you could be right. The timing might be nothing more than a coincidence and George has other problems I know nothing about."

Edwina hugged her arms as cool air seeped in under her wrap. Alongside the chill crept an unpleasant truth. Mary had apparently fled to meet a man in a pub, one whom she'd been keeping a secret. "But if it's George she's meeting, shouldn't there be two indications on your watch? If there's another witch inside with her?"

"Bloody hell, you're right." Ian dug the watch out again, letting the cogs and levers whir until the single aural spectrum showed up in the direction of the pub. "I'll be damned." He was about to close the watch when the cogs spun again and a second glowing dot revealed another presence.

Edwina's face fell in disappointment. "So she really is in there with him?"

"Seems as likely as not."

The obvious question of whether they should simply barge in through the front door of the pub and find out for certain was preempted when the boy from the shop wandered around the corner, stopping to loiter in front of the pub. The coincidence of seeing him lean against the building made gooseflesh of Edwina's skin.

"What's he doing here?" she wondered aloud, feeling that familiar pressure in her throat when she swallowed that told her Mary was about to ruin everything of what was left of their family again. "There's something not right here."

"Aye, that there is." Ian watched the boy before catching Edwina's eye. "If you dinna mind doing a little detective work with me, I think we ought to stay and find out exactly what it is."

Her first instinct was to turn away. Go home and forget she'd ever followed her sister to this unfamiliar street or this seedy pub on a dodgy lane. Go home and prepare for a quick and anonymous departure once again. For where, she couldn't fathom. Father had always taken care of that part. But even without knowing the full and complete truth, and despite whatever promises she'd made to Mary about unconditional forgiveness, this time she feared the transgressions had gone too far to be remedied by a mere change of address.

Edwina breathed in the nearness of Ian's skin, his clothes, and the light perspiration rising from the collar of his shirt. Flight had always been their fancy, she and Mary. To escape, to flee, to stay one step ahead of scrutiny. But in fact, she'd never truly been free. Not when she held firm to the limited vision of what she imagined her life was destined to be. "Oh yes," she said, daring to relinquish the fear holding her back. "I think I would like that very much." And she did not blush when he returned her eager smile.

Chapter Twenty-Two

"We need to find a better location where we can keep an eye on the place," Ian said as he and Edwina stood huddled in the doorway. "We'll be seen if we stay in the street too long."

"Where can we go?" Edwina asked.

He looked up and down the lane before settling on an idea. "Wait here," he said and darted across the street to where a pile of empty crates leaned against the alley wall. "Hob," he called out. "Are you there?" A man passing by just as he called hello inside a turnip crate offered him a suspicious look. "Lost my dog," Ian lied, trusting Hob would wait until the man had left to show his face. But no—the elf jumped up from the box with a wilted leaf on top of his head. Ian flung his coat open at his waist as if searching for something in the pocket until the man walked on.

"I was helping Sir with magic," Hob complained.

"Aye, and a great help you were, I've no doubt." Ian signaled for Hob to lower his head. "I need a wee favor from you and then you can head back." After a sigh from Hob, Ian explained how he needed him to find an empty room across the street. Main floor would be best. A sitting room, a bedroom, a storage room. Something with a window facing the corner pub. "The usual conditions apply. No one home to raise a fuss."

Hob flicked the leaf off his head, then dropped back down inside the crate. Ian stuck his hands in his pockets while he waited and nodded at Edwina across the street. He knew few women outside of the Constabulary willing to stand in the damp on the forsaken end of the street without complaint. In truth, he thought she was made for better things than traipsing over the city in search of a sister who'd likely breached the wrong side of the law—be it witch or mortal—and yet, seeing the glint of anticipation in her eye, she seemed to flourish at the notion of risk.

The crates rattled behind him before the top one tumbled to the pavement. "Have a care," he said, righting the empty container.

"There's a storage room next door to the tobacco shop." Hob pulled a clay pipe out of his jacket and winked, proud of his mischief. "I took the liberty of topping off," he said and put the pipe in his teeth, which were worn and brown as an old dog's.

"You left it unlocked?"

Hob feigned offense. "Och aye."

"Good lad. Tell Sir Elvanfoot we're following a lead and may be late."

Hob lit his pipe with the point of his finger and dropped out of sight in a cloud of cherry-scented smoke. That sorted, Ian crossed the road to break the news to Edwina about the truth of surveillance work.

"The boy kept watch on the street a few minutes, then went inside the pub," she said, drawing her shawl up over her head. "I don't understand. What is that boy doing here with Mary?"

"We'll find out soon enough, if you're still willing to see this through to whatever end it brings us to."

She said she was, even as she shivered from the cold, so they walked a quick clip to the tobacconist. The door to the storage room proved a solid arched wooden thing left over from another age, with thick wrought-iron hinges holding it in place, if slightly askew in the frame. Ian pulled on the handle and it creaked open. "Hurry," he said, slipping through the opening. Edwina pressed in behind him and shut the heavy oak door, which had the effect of blocking out half the light. The other half came from a small window situated four feet above the top of the door.

Ian cursed the damnable elf under his breath. Not only was the window out of reach, the space was little more than a long, narrow closet, as if an alley between buildings had been bricked up. It was cool and dark and smelled of tobacco.

"Can't we stack some of these boxes and climb up to reach the window?" But even as Edwina suggested it, she saw the challenge. The boxes would block the door and a quick exit should the need arise.

"We're going to need a modification," Ian said. "Nothing too fancy. A wee spell should do."

"Won't that draw the wrong sort of attention on the street?"

"Nae, the Constabulary only responds if you make a right nuisance of yourself in public. We just need a window at eye level so we can keep a watch on the pub yonder." He stood back and tilted his head to the right as he eyed the door. "I think the owner might agree a nice viewing slot would be an improvement."

"You're a regular outlaw, aren't you?" Edwina said.

"Aye, sometimes it's necessary to put one foot on each side of the law to walk a straight line." He grinned, then marked the outline of a rectangle on the door with his finger as he recited his incantation. "Make a cut against the grain. Make no noise within the lane. Carve a window in the door. One the owner will ignore." He continued tracing his finger over the wood in a rectangle shape until the scent of charred wood lifted from the door and a chunk of oak the size of a brick fell in his hand. "Might not be fancy like Sir Elvanfoot's work, but it'll do," he said, peeking through the opening.

Once settled in the space among the crates and loose straw, they took turns standing in front of the small window overlooking the street.

There was no new sign of the boy, but occasionally they saw a silhouetted figure that resembled Mary walk past the window.

"So this is what you do?" Edwina asked. "Wait and watch and hope your suspect will show himself?"

"More often than I like, though I'm well pleased not to be sitting in the rain this time." Ian stepped aside to give her an opportunity to look through the slot. "And I'm not usually in such fair company." He startled himself by saying that last part out loud. He'd thought it, certainly, but Edwina Blackwood wasn't the sort of woman you dangled innocuous flattery in front of. He imagined her being more like a placid dark lake that one had to give their soul over to for the privilege of knowing how deep her waters ran. "I'm usually on my own," he added.

She smiled, but then grew pensive, leaning her head against the door as she watched the people come and go in front of the darkened pub. "I don't want it to be Mary," she said. "But after what we discovered in her trunk . . . there was still blood on the spectacles." Edwina closed her eyes, as if the thought of what they'd found sickened her.

Ian gripped her by the shoulder, making her face him in the confined space. "You remember what I told you about me reliving the memory of being murdered?" He glanced out the slot in the door, then back at Edwina. "Your sister isn't a murderer. It wasn't her hand that took that man's life. But I do worry she's an accessory. Possibly in grave danger. Because she was there in the alley at some point. She had to be to steal that man's memories after he died."

"Mary said she found the body before they carried it to the morgue. That she took the memory after seeing the corpse lights on the ground."

"And you believe her?"

"I've given my sister every benefit of the doubt. Defended her against all those who misjudged, and believe me, there have been plenty." She relented in his grip. "But the sight of those spectacles among my sister's things . . . I'll never get the image of them out of my mind. I don't know if I can ever forgive her."

Ian had to fight the impulse to pull Edwina into his arms. He wanted to stroke her hair, shush her and let her know everything would be okay, but he would not lie to her. And he would not take advantage while they were secreted away in a dank storage room in the back end of a dodgy lane speaking of murder, even if he sensed it's what they both wanted. Instead he let her go and leaned his back against the brick wall to put as much space between them as possible in the narrow corridor.

"The dead man had a mermaid match safe on him," he said. "I remember every detail of the piece. And then there it was among your sister's things. So maybe it's time you tell me exactly what Mary is capable of." He half worried she'd flee at the challenge as she had before, that he'd have two sisters to chase after, but she made no move for the door. "There's a curious undercurrent to your magic. It's stronger than mere witchcraft." He struggled to find the right words to describe what he'd experienced in the wake of her spells. "Something strange but beautiful in the way it manifests. Like it's drawing from a deeper, older source. Only in a way I canna quite put my finger on."

Edwina peeked out the slot in the door. The sun had set behind the buildings, but her eyes gleamed in the glow of dusk from the street. She was about to answer him with the truth this time, he could swear it, when she startled. "It's her. She's walked out. She's leaving."

Ian looked through the slot. Mary was walking east as if she didn't have a care in the world.

"I have to go after her," Edwina said. "I have to speak to her."

Before Ian could stop her, Edwina pulled the door open and shot outside. Cursing under his breath, he made a quick check of the pub, making sure no one from inside had caught up to Mary, then followed. "Keep your pace natural, like we're out for a stroll," he said, catching up to her. "Let's see where she's going first before we let her know we're here."

"She's my sister, not some ruffian," Edwina said, but she slowed down as he'd asked. He held out his arm to seal the illusion of them as a couple, and she took it.

The setting sun created a silhouette effect that sank the city into a cauldron of light and dark hues. The buildings' shadows stretched out on the pavement, helping to cloak their presence as the sister walked several strides ahead of them. Ian thought he heard Mary humming a tune to herself, but the sound sailed away on a crosscurrent, so he could not be sure. At the corner, she stopped to let a carriage pass before crossing the street, forcing Edwina and him to feign interest in a handbill about crime in the East End that had been glued to a horse stable door.

Mary, wherever she was going, was not heading in the direction of home. The farther they walked, the more the broken windows in the buildings were stuffed with rags and old newspaper. Edwina tensed at Ian's side when they passed a man staggering in the street from drink, but he patted her hand and held her arm firmly with his own, encouraging her to act natural. Twice he twisted around to look for George's face in the bustle behind them, but if he was there, he did not show himself.

Unlike the neighborhood they'd run to while seeking the safe house, the block of tenements Mary led them to was crowded with stick-thin women watching their children run in the lane, while weary-eyed men milled about in front of a doss-house on the corner. It was impossible to ignore the stench of too many humans living in squalor as the smell infiltrated the people's clothes, their hair, and likely the stale bread they put in their mouths at the end of the day as well.

"She's left the road." Ian pointed to where Mary had disappeared around a corner onto a quieter lane.

Afraid of being seen, he had them hang back at the entrance to the lane. From there they watched Mary walk several yards before passing through a narrow opening in the wall. He took a measurement with his watch and found only the three of them in the vicinity. Wherever George was, he hadn't followed. "Come on, let's see where she's gone."

Catching up, they came to a narrow, damp corridor that led to a rectangle of gray light at the far end. There appeared to be a courtyard ahead surrounded by more ramshackle tenements. Ian paused, waiting and listening.

"Let's not stop now," Edwina said.

Bricky lass. Ian pressed forward with a grudging smile on his face, even as he fought off the anxiety he felt at the sight of another cramped nook made for murder.

Inside, the corridor was sour with the reek of curdled milk. Edwina whispered she wished they had a torch, then risked a little fire to better see where to set her feet by blowing on her fingertips. She held the small flame aloft, scaring a pair of pigeons from their roost above. In the orange light, the puddle causing the sour smell was made more obvious, resembling the leftovers of a drunkard's rebellious stomach. Letting go of Ian's arm, she lifted the hem of her skirt until they were through to the other side.

Unlike the busy road they'd left full of people sorting out their lodging and food for the night, the courtyard was abandoned. And hastily so. A fire burned in a communal pit with a fish hovering above on an improvised spit. The split flesh was still pink from too little time in the heat. Edwina blew out the flame on her fingers as they left the passageway. Surrounding the courtyard were a dozen flats, upstairs and down, that formed a U shape around a muddy common area. Laundry hung like flags from the upper rails to dry. A brick wall enclosed the far end, and a second corridor continued out the other side. Ian realized too late that anyone entering from either passage could be seen from every window in the building. But where was Mary?

A curtain snapped shut on the upper level as a door clicked closed at their right. "Why do I feel like a mouse trapped in a dead end?" Edwina said, surrounded on all sides as they were.

"Because we were led here deliberately." Ian realized now how blinded by curiosity he'd been. "She knew we were following her," he said, taking note of the exit on the other side of the courtyard, where the alley appeared as dodgy as the one they'd just come through.

He was considering their limited options when Mary emerged from behind a grungy bedsheet that had been hung on a rope strung between the stairs and the single lamppost. Almost coquettishly, she swung out to show her face as she braced her feet on the base of the lamp and held on to the post with one hand.

"Sister, what a surprise to see you here, and with your new beau," she said, letting the sarcasm drip sweetly off her tongue.

"You've taken us on a jolly expedition," Edwina said. "What a lovely location you've chosen." Though he could not be certain, Ian thought he detected a note of charmwork in her voice. As if she was accustomed to calming her sister. "Perhaps now we can go home so we can talk about how you came to know this place. You know I understand everything. I forgive everything. But you need to explain the details to me so we can make things right again." Edwina attempted to take a step closer, her hand held out to clasp her sister's, but was forced to stop when the false smile fell away from Mary's lips.

"Stay where you are," she snapped. In her grip she held a small, gleaming orb with a gold vein running through a sea of blue. "Or I might be tempted to crush his precious memories to dust."

The area above Ian's left ear throbbed at the sight of the orb, and he had no doubt the memory in the witch's hand was his. All the intricate, interstitial moments of his life, the ones Hob could never replace, she now held up as leverage, threatening to destroy them forever.

"Aye, and what about all the others you've taken?" he asked. "We found the memories of the men you helped murder."

Mary's brows tightened and she shook her head. "I didn't murder anyone. Ask Edwina. I merely followed the scent of death." She locked eyes with her sister. "Tell him."

Edwina flinched when a baby cried out in a flat above and then quickly hushed, as though the whole of the tenement building were eavesdropping on their family secrets. "Let's go home. I'll tell him every-thing there."

"You're too much like Father." Mary shook her head, disappointed. "Thinking you can make it all go away by plastering over the ugly parts with a few apologies." She tossed the orb in the air, catching it again like a child's plaything. "What would you have me do? Move somewhere far away again where nobody knows us or our pathetic mutant tale?"

"Yes, we can go somewhere else, if you like," Edwina said with the inflection of someone trying to talk a cat out of a tree.

"You know this was the last best place for us to go. A city of millions where no one looks each other in the eye. Everyone hip to shoulder in the street, all covered in the same muck. Don't you see?" Mary stepped down from the base of the streetlamp. "I can finally breathe here. I can stretch and be myself among the filth."

Suddenly, she charged, closing by half the distance between her and Edwina, her eyes fierce and wild. "Death thrives in this city's back lanes. And with it, so do I. More than anyplace we've ever lived."

Ian stepped protectively nearer to Edwina, wondering now whether Mary had lost a part of her mind to madness. "What is death's attrac-tion?" he asked.

Mary turned her smoky eyes on him. "You should have died," she said frankly. "Fortunately, I harvested your memories before you woke, or I'd have made sure you ended up just another body for the papers to shout about." She held his orb up again, skipping backward and twirl-ing around as she held it out teasingly in her palm. "Oh, the tales you could have told if you'd been allowed to remember."

Edwina pressed her fingers over her mouth. "Mary, what have you done?"

Her sister dipped her head and smiled. With a slow, even breath, she blew on the orb until its shell expanded in her hand, glowing slightly as it grew to the size of a globe on a gas lamp. Inside, shadows of people and places Ian recognized swirled beneath the iridescence—his mother and father standing on a lakeshore on holiday, Hob smoking his pipe by the fireplace, the shepherd dog he'd had as a lad, and the faces and bodies of women he'd loved and lost. Mary lifted her hand, turning the orb slightly to give a different view. "Concentrate," she teased.

Peering closer, he saw an image of George on the street, mumbling to himself about a woman as he sat in the gutter. His neck was covered in dried blood, and he complained about the woman stealing something from him, but he couldn't remember what. The pin on his lapel was missing. The memory swirled out of view and a new one animated. Ian saw himself checking pawnshops and trinket carts until he spotted the thistle pin under the glass at the sisters' shop. And there, the mermaid match safe, not yet squirreled away in a cloth sack, on display too! Missing items from the murder victims. The woman behind the counter—he'd spoken to Mary—explaining she'd found them while scavenging on the foreshore. *Evidence. Proof. Lies.* The orb's interior clouded over. The images inside shifted.

Now his memories showed him hidden in an alcove across the lane from the shop in the middle of the night, watching and waiting. Drizzle coated his clothes and skin until his nose and mouth were nearly numb from the cold. He cursed the need for surveillance when he could be sleeping in a warm bed, but he was so close to the truth! The image changed. The clouds had vanished and the stars shone above. He was on the embankment now, shivering as he followed Mary and Edwina in their flowing black shawls toward the river. *Suspicion. Murder. Blood magic.* Ian could almost feel the images inside the orb as true memories again, so closely they cleaved to his mind and nature. The sisters walked down the stairs to the river's foreshore, then meandered up shore as they scoured the ground. Getting ahead of them, he took the ladder by the bridge several hundred yards away, dropped to the riverside, and hid by a stranded boat as the sisters made their way toward him. A noise at his back, but he paid it no mind. Only a gull or rat scurrying after prey at that hour. And then a piercing, shattering pain at the base of his skull. Sand in his mouth. Blood on his neck. The glint of metal in the starlight. A knife flicking open. A struggle. A last breathless defensive spell to throw off his attacker before consciousness faded.

Mary dimmed the orb so that it shrank in her palm again, and with it the last glimpse at his lost memories. "Did you see it? The knife?"

"It was never mine," he answered, still half-drunk on the effect of watching his displaced memories. "The knife was his. He dropped it because of my spell. After he'd followed me following you."

"I got in so much trouble when I stole it back for him." She tilted her bruised cheek to better show it off in the lamppost's light. "You'd have thought I'd stolen the crown jewels straight off the queen's head after I nicked the knife from your pocket while you had your fit in my father's bed. But I thought the knife best belonged to him after all the good work he'd done with it. How he fretted about the coppers coming for him, though." She touched her cheek lightly and shifted her lower jaw from side to side.

Edwina's face paled under the quarter moon. "Who hit you, Mary?" She cast her eyes up to the dark windows of the surrounding flats, searching for movement. "Where is he now?"

"Oh, he's coming. He wants to meet you properly." Mary walked up to the firepit and pinched off a chunk of fish from the spit. "I do hope you'll get on," she said and popped the undercooked flesh in her mouth.

"How do you know this man?" Edwina's frustration bled through her questioning. "Where did you meet? Who is he?"

While Edwina badgered her sister for answers, Ian slipped his watch out of his pocket as discreetly as possible. A quick glance suggested a second presence was nearby. Very near. He eyed the alley behind them and found it empty, though the rattle of a glass bottle hitting the stone pavement echoed not far beyond.

"You didn't really think we used up that much milk, did you?" Mary lifted her head and took a deep breath with her eyes closed. "We crossed paths in the street one evening, and that's when I caught the scent of death clinging to his clothes." She shrugged, as if her next choice were obvious. "So I followed him and watched from above as he struck down his prey. Then he watched as I took my bauble." Mary licked her bottom lip. "I let him lift my skirts afterward in the next alley over."

"Edwina, we need to go now," Ian said. He put his arm around her shoulder, hoping to lead her safely out of the courtyard. If he was right and George was on his way, there would be a bloody confrontation. One he wasn't sure he could win, and one he no longer believed worth the risk to her or any of the tenants hiding in their rooms. They needed to get out and summon the Constabulary.

Edwina stood in wretched shock at her sister's admission.

"Edwina!" Ian turned her around so they faced the exit. They'd take a cab to the headquarters. Let Singh and her department handle it. But before they took their first step, a taunting voice echoed out of the corridor.

"Edwina and Mary, quite contrary. How does your garden grow? With silver bells and cockleshells, and bloody lads all in a row."

The boy emerged from the narrow passageway, dragging a stick along the wall. His face was smudged with dirt, making the whites of his eyes appear almost luminescent from the contrast as he stared at them and grinned. Ian felt a sigh of relief it was only the boy until his intuition climbed up his back and clouted him over the head in warning: *Damn fool.*

Chapter Twenty-Three

"What you want here?" the boy asked.

As many times as she'd had to pass the filthy child in the street after one of his ruthless taunts, Edwina had never acknowledged or addressed the boy directly. Until this moment she'd never truly looked him in the eye. As she did so now, she was met with cunning intuitiveness. The sort formed from watching and studying people over time with the understanding everyone around him lived in a world indifferent to his existence. She nearly withered under his icy gaze.

"I . . ." she began to stutter, still knocked off-kilter by the vile things her sister had admitted, but she lifted her chin, regaining her composure. She refused to stumble in front of this odd specter of a boy. "I came to talk my sister into seeing sense, but it appears I'm too late."

Beside her, Ian had his watch out again. His face had gone slack after studying the reading. She had an inkling why, now that she'd paid proper attention to the boy. But curse it all, they needed answers, so she addressed him again. "You were at the pub earlier."

"So were you," he replied.

"And what are you doing here?" she asked the boy. "You do spend a lot of energy watching my sister and I, don't you?" Her question seemed to sober Ian again as he looked up from his watch to hear the boy's answer.

"It's my home, then, innit."

"I've told you before. His name is Benjamin." Mary sat on the bench by the firepit eating the rest of the fish with her fingers, as if she were on a picnic. "Come over and sit with me, Ben. You don't need to answer any of her questions. There's a good lad."

Edwina and Ian watched the boy respond to her sister. It was uncanny how they'd missed the telltale signs before, the way he clung so closely to Mary. He was a bright lad. Shrewd. Sharp. But looking deeper into the hollow of his eyes, it was obvious he was tangled up on the wrong side of the veil between life and death. Where his feet ought to have been buried in one world and his spirit in another, the two remained together in an ethereal ghostly form intense enough to manifest on Ian's sensitive timepiece.

"It isn't George who's coming, is it?" she asked.

"Nae." Ian snapped his watch shut and tucked it out of sight. "We really should go," he said to Edwina with more urgency.

"Yes, I think you're quite right." She lifted the hem of her skirt, ready to flee, when two young men emerged from the damp and sour corridor at their rear carrying a wooden club and a stout stick. One wore a crushed top hat, while the other smiled with crooked teeth too big for his mouth. A second pair of ragged lads showed their faces in the alley opposite. The first swung a police truncheon in his grip. The second flashed a bowie knife. The metal glinted in the starlight for Edwina as bright as quicksilver.

"Don't be leaving yet," the young man with the knife said. "We still got some unfinished business after that stunt you pulled on the embankment." He stared with eyes as pale as winter and raised the knife.

The youth who'd tried to rob them on the foreshore!

"Ian, it's them."

"So it is," he replied. He shifted their position to better keep track of where everyone stood. The four young men advanced as the boy grinned beside Mary as if he were at a carnival.

"I see you've still got that lovely gold watch," said the hooligan in the smashed top hat. He banged his club against the chipped bricks to punctuate his intentions.

They'd been surrounded, drawn into a secluded courtyard by her sister's coordinated and deliberate escape. But what was she doing with these street thieves?

"Don't know about you," Ian said in Edwina's ear, "but I'm starting to think it's no coincidence we've been set upon a second time by these ruffians."

He was being facetious at a most inopportune moment, but the point struck home. It was no coincidence. Not the boy, not the lads turning up, and not the bloody items they had found in her sister's trunk.

"Mary, what is this?" Edwina called out. "Do you know these young men?" The lads did not advance, yet the feeling of threat grew, much as it does when a dog begins to snarl before the bite.

"Oh, they live here." Mary licked her fingers so that her lips shone from the oily fish residue. She flicked her eyes toward the landing. "Up there somewhere."

Seeing as they were in much the same situation they'd been in before, caught between one bad option and another, Edwina deferred to Ian. "Well, what poem shall you recite to keep them at bay this time?" She cast a wary eye at the thief holding the knife and took a step closer to Ian. "Somehow, comparing them to a summer's day doesn't seem quite fitting."

"Have you more fine words for us, then?" The lad in the top hat shook his head and gaped at his partner. "Go on, you nutter."

Ian had squared his feet, ready to give him what he wanted, when an upstairs door swung open. The dandy, the lad who fashioned himself the leader of this ragtag gang of thieves, slammed the door shut and stepped onto the landing, strutting as if he were an actor entering the stage. He buttoned his plaid jacket like a man going off to work, squinting at them below in the gloomy soot of the courtyard. The late evening twilight betrayed him, revealing the sparse stubble of a young man perhaps in the last year of his teens, but his worn countenance was one of a life lived ten times that.

"Oi," he shouted. "That's no way to treat our guests." The young man came down the stairs, stopping at the bottom to let his eyes trail over Mary before facing Ian and Edwina. The boy lit up, smiling and waving, but the mortal could not see him.

"Nick's my brother," Benjamin said proudly, pointing with his thumb. Mary patted him on the knee to shush him.

"What we got here, then?" Nick, as he was called, smoothed his hand over his chest, drawing attention to the mother-of-pearl buttons dazzling his jacket front. Edwina recognized the buttons at once from the shop. The ones Mary had claimed to have sold. She feared they, too, had likely been snapped off a dead man's coat.

"You're the brute who struck my sister."

He raised his brows at her accusation. "What? That?" He took Mary's chin in his hands and turned her face so her bruise faced them. "Yeah, might have done. But it's only half of what she deserves for leading you lot here. Only I'm going to assume you've come to make amends." Mary kissed the palm of his hand before he let go of her chin. The disturbing exchange made Edwina's head reel. Something was so very wrong.

Edwina's cheeks blazed with shame and embarrassment at Mary's indiscretion. Her sister hadn't been meeting with George. The man Mary had described was this conceited dandy still too young to grow a full beard. A thief who robbed people in broad daylight. What was she thinking, taking up with this common back-alley rake?

"Amends?" Ian asked. "For what, not letting your gang of reprobates rob us blind?"

"Nah, mate." Nick took a step closer so the light from the firepit put the heat of recklessness in his eyes. "For not doing the courtesy of dying proper-like when you should have done." He removed a knife with a staghorn handle from his pocket, the collapsible sort that flicked open with the release of a spring. The same knife that had flashed in the stolen memory Mary had held in her hand.

"That was you on the shore that night." Ian looked down at Nick's boots while the young man ran his thumbnail over the blade. Brogues with a stitched toe. "And it was you in the alley. You murdered Jake Donovan."

"You?" Edwina watched Mary put her arm around Nick's waist and lean her chin against his shoulder. The sight of them touching so blatantly frosted her blood.

Nick grinned, knowing the tragic conclusion they'd come to. "Ah, now, that right there is why my girl had to pop your brains out and take her trinket," he said to Ian. "See, me and Mary got a nice thing going. Suits us both." He looked at Mary and gave her a squeeze. "What'd you call it again?"

"Symbiotic," she said, pressing her finger against his lower lip before sitting down beside the boy again.

"Isn't going to work having you lot coming around and mucking it all up for us then, is it?"

"You mean murdering people?" Ian very subtly changed his stance.

"Aye, well, that part's for her, innit. We used to just crack 'em on the back of the head and clean out their pockets. Done all right for ourselves, too, with only the one bloke what croaked. Ain't that right, lads?" He snorted when they nodded and banged their clubs against their hands. "Until our Mary showed me a better way. The kind that don't leave no witnesses to go crying to the coppers."

"What about all the people who live here?" Edwina asked. "They know what you are. They're all witnesses now."

"Them?" He laughed. "None of 'em's got a word to say against us. There'd be nothing on the table but a stale loaf of bread if it weren't for us. Feed 'em meat and gin once a week. Ain't that right?" he yelled to the closed doors.

His fellow residents answered with silence and dark windows that should have long been aglow with a lamp burning bright behind the glass.

"By the way, I know what Mary is," he said, closing and opening his knife as if he enjoyed the sound of the blade springing to life. "I even know she talks to me dead brother, Ben. Gives him messages for me, she does. And him to me." The boy nodded in agreement as he listened beside Mary. "And I know what you are too." Nick's voice dropped as he pointed the tip of his knife at Edwina and Ian. "The both of you."

"Mary, I think you should come home. Now." Edwina lowered her voice to match Nick's threat and sang, "I know the compulsion you feel, but there are better ways to bring it to heel."

Mary crossed her legs and leaned back on the bench. "You should gag her now or she'll sing you all to sleep before you know it."

The dandy crooked his finger at the thug with the gray eyes. Before Edwina could utter her next word, a filthy rag came over her head, digging into the corners of her mouth as the cretin tied the ends in a knot at the back of her neck. Bony, vile hands gripped her forearms so she couldn't flee.

Ian, too, had been grabbed from behind. His right arm was bent up at an excruciating angle until his fingertips reached the top of his shoulder. He yelled out in agony as he tried in vain to struggle free.

"Don't gag him just yet," Mary said before they could slip the rag over his head. "We still need something from him. And I don't think his voice is as devious as my sister's."

She had the ruffians drag him over to the firepit, where they leaned him close enough to the flames to make him flinch. Edwina attempted to jerk free from her captor, but the grip on her arms only tightened. Tears flooded her eyes, not only for Ian but for her sister's spiral into depravity.

"Now, I believe this is how it works." Mary put her hand under Ian's chin and made him look into the fire. "Call your imp to you."

"What?" Ian unscrewed his face from the pain long enough to look into Mary's eyes.

"Call that repulsive thing to your side." She nudged her chin at the ring of stones. "This cauldron would be the nearest open portal, would it not? So call him. Into the fire."

Nick's mortal nonchalance reached its limit. "What's this about an imp?"

"It's his hairy servant. It knows everything he knows. That thing has to be dealt with too."

Edwina shook her head, pleading with her eyes for her sister to see sense.

"He's nae but a wee elf," Ian said. "He'll be gone up north by now. Dinna fash yourself over him."

"I don't believe you." Mary released his chin and stood back, holding up the orb containing his memories. "And I rather suspect he knows you're here already, so summon that creature of yours. Or I toss all these precious memories of your family and lovers into the fire."

The thug with the crooked teeth tightened the grip on his arm when Ian took too long to answer. "I'll do it. I just . . . I have a wee spell I use to call him to me."

Mary nodded, and they pulled him back from the fire a fraction and waited without easing the tension on his arm. Edwina struggled and screamed through her gag, but Ian cleared his throat and stared into the flames.

"Ashes denote that fire was," he began. "Revere the grayest pile, for the departed creature's sake, that hovered there awhile." The flames sputtered, dying out as though his words encouraged them to dampen. Edwina held her breath. "Fire exists the first in light, and then consolidates." He lifted his eyes to Mary's. "Only the chemist can disclose, into what carbonates."

"He's gone all nutter again," the thief in the top hat said, laughing.

"Mad as a hatter, he is," said another.

But Mary knew better. "What spell was that?" She looked from the dying flames to Ian in alarm. "What did you do?"

"I did the summoning, as you asked," he deadpanned.

Mary grew agitated. She circled the firepit, watching the flames shrink. "No, no, that was—"

At once the flames burst in the firepit, shooting up as high as the rooftops. Mary covered her face and backed away as fireworks detonated out of the center and exploded in the darkened sky above their heads in a shower of sparks for all the borough to see. Edwina rejoiced behind her gag at Ian's fiery, rebellious words.

The gang stood with their mouths agape and their weapons momentarily forgotten at their sides. Ian used the distraction to free his arm and twist away, even as Mary berated them for being awestruck fools. He lashed out swiftly with a hurling spell meant to disarm, no longer bothering to disguise his conjuring in the open. The lad with the police truncheon had his arm slung backward by the magic until the weapon vaulted out of his hand and across the courtyard, splintering into a dozen pieces. His mate suffered the same, though he hadn't let go of his club and was thrown into the wall. The third lad, who brandished the stick, had his weapon yanked loose only to soar into the blazing fire to become more kindling.

Like Ian, Edwina attempted to twist free, but the thug with the ghost eyes, quick as lightning, drew the bowie knife to her throat. Her mouth and magic remained gagged, so she stilled herself, hoping he had a steady hand. Then Ian's magic found his knife too. The blade slid past her throat, cutting a thin line deep enough to draw a trace of blood, before embedding itself in the nearest door with a thud. Crossing himself, the lad ran off before the sting from the knife rose to the surface of her skin.

Free of him, Edwina removed the rag from her mouth. Sparks from the fireworks rained down from above, landing on the shingle roof of the tenement building. She sucked in a breath and tenderly checked the cut on her neck. Only a trace of blood came away. Shaken, she retreated to the door of the flat on her right.

Somehow unaffected by the disarming spell, Nick circled the firepit with his folding knife in hand, his eyes tracking Ian. But where was Mary? Edwina searched the shadows in the courtyard before spotting her strutting up the final steps to lean on the railing of the upper landing. She was too confident. Too smug. What had she done? Edwina studied Nick's foul appearance. He was being protected, but how? Then she spotted it. The mother-of-pearl buttons gleamed with an iridescence infused with swirling magic. "Ian, watch out! He's using a protection charm."

Nick slashed with the knife, missing Ian's middle by a mere inch when he sucked in his stomach at the last second. Ian took careful steps sideways as the tenement roof smoldered, sending smoke into the sky.

Mary grinned from her perch like some medieval gargoyle. "Careful, sister, your concern for a man is showing."

Unarmed, Ian had no choice but to back up toward the courtyard wall as the final sparks of his fire spell shot into the sky. He was running out of room. Benjamin attempted to trip him, but as the boy was made of nothing more than mist and misery, Ian passed right through him as though he were smoke.

Ian spit out another spell. "With this charm, I disarm!" Yet the magic had no effect on Nick, who toyed with him by jabbing with the knife. Ian dodged until his back hit the brick wall. Mary watched with eyes as wide and black as coals, tapping her fingers lightly against her lips in anticipation of the death that surely must follow.

Edwina had seen hints of the specter of cruelty in her sister before with Freddie and that Thisbury boy, but it sickened her to witness Mary's ghoulish complicity on full display.

As Nick taunted with the knife, relishing his power over Ian's magic, the tenement roof burst into flame. There were children inside, and parents so desperate to feed them they took handouts from a murderer. Edwina concentrated on words potent enough to douse the fire. She stepped into the courtyard and raised her hand to the sky. "Gather in form, gray and frightening. Cloud and storm, thunder and lightning. Wind and rain, lash and blow. Fog and murk, sink below."

She'd made no effort to hide her incantation behind mortal poetry. The spell was a beacon. A gust of storm to rattle the Constabulary to action. But she also needed the cloak of fog to hide her from those who'd soon swarm the yard.

The rain fell, lashing the burning roof with relief. The fog billowed and settled, enveloping the courtyard in a blanket of thick gray mist. Tenants ran out of their flats in a panic, their faces and bodies fading in and out of ghostly view. Ian called out Edwina's name through the mist. Nick answered with a call for his blood. An emergency whistle shrilled in the lane.

Somewhere in the fog Benjamin sang, "Ladybird, ladybird, fly away home. Your house is on fire, your children shall burn."

Mary, she knew, had already flown. And now she must too.

Fog swirled around Edwina as she held her arms out to let her shawl's fringe hang free. She summoned her ancient heredity, letting the magic coalesce inside and flutter up to fill her veins. The grounded weight of flesh and heavy marrow fell away, replaced by broad wings and hollow bones that spread out in graceful arcs. From downy tufts to pinion feathers, from claws to polished beak, her primeval bloodline effused throughout her body, transforming her.

Then she took to the air.

Chapter Twenty-Four

The mortals, who'd been happy enough to stay silent while Ian was being attacked in their yard, streamed out of their upper-level flats, screaming the roof was on fire. And still Nick lunged. The dandy was done playing, but without his club to first render his victim unconscious, his blade kept missing the mark.

Then, from the corner of his eye, Ian spotted Edwina. She'd cast a spell to draw the rain and fog. *Well done, lass.*

She'd done a proper job of it. The mist swallowed everyone in seconds so he couldn't see two feet in front of him, though he knew Nick was still there. He dodged right, feeling his way against the courtyard wall. He could hear men rushing through the corridor, but he'd lost track of Edwina. He called out for her to know she was okay, but it was Nick who answered, rising out of the mist only inches away on his left. Seeing the bloodlust in his eyes reinvigorated Ian's memory of the man found lying facedown in the alley in a pool of his own blood. The fear Ian had felt reliving the man's final moments—the terror, the degradation, the helplessness—all surged within him in an overwhelming desire to live.

Nick grinned, knowing he had him pinned and hidden from view by the fog. He could still stick the blade in and slip away unseen, letting the blood wash away with the rain. Nick's vile thoughts showed on his face as he drew his arm back for a roundhouse slice meant to sever

Ian's carotid artery. Ian raised his forearm to defend himself, cringing in anticipation as the rain spit in his face, when a large bird plunged out of the mist.

The strike came swift and brutal. A raven, with wings as black as coal, dropped out of the fog, lunging with its claws out. It tore at Nick's face, his buttons, his plaid coat. The dandy ducked and covered his head with one arm, but the raven found the vulnerable skin on the back of his neck and tore open a gash that no magical talisman could have deflected. The bloodletting forced Nick to retreat as he swatted his arm and cursed at the mad bird. He jabbed with his knife, stabbing at the air, but the raven only swooped out of reach and circled around for another attack.

Ian watched, awestruck at the viciousness of the bird's attack. Where had the raven come from? What had drawn it to the fight? While Nick tried to defend himself with another wild, aimless thrust, Ian grabbed his wrist midswing and slammed his hand against the courtyard wall to loosen the knife. They wrestled for control of the blade, headbutting and crashing against the bricks, as a pair of glowing lanterns filled with pixie light surfaced from the fog on the ends of long sticks. Two officers in top hats emerged from the gray mist a second later, pulling Ian and Nick apart and kicking the knife away after it finally fell loose.

"Hold him," Ian ordered when he saw Constable Bottomfield among the men. "He's the one the police are looking for. The Brick Lane Slasher. It's him."

The constables stood Nick up and secured him in shackles while Ian swam through the fog, calling out for Edwina when he did not spot her in the courtyard. He looked up to the second floor, where he saw the misty silhouette of the raven. It cawed and flapped its wings, eyeing him from atop the lamppost. The rain stopped and the enchanted fog began to thin. The bird leaped into the air. He watched in awe as it circled over the rooftop until a familiar voice called out his name.

"I told them it was you." Chief Inspector Singh stepped over a mud puddle, holding the hem of her skirt above her ankles.

"I take it your wee spiders jumped," Ian replied.

"About a foot." Singh blew a stream of air into the last of the fog, making the mist dissipate almost as quickly as it had arrived. When the whole of the courtyard was clear again, Ian saw the faces of the people who lived in the tenement. Babies crying, children wide-eyed, men trying hard to hide their fear from themselves and their wives. Nick was flanked by a pair of constables warning him he was under arrest, while the remainder of his gang of thieves were frog-marched back through the passageways where they'd attempted to escape. But nowhere did he see either of the Blackwood sisters.

Singh held out her hand and asked to see the gold pocket watch, which Ian reluctantly provided. "How does this thing work again?" she asked. He pushed the pin at the side and she watched the cogs and flywheels whir into motion, scrunching her face up in confusion when they stopped. "So where are the others?" she asked. "The spiders indicated there were two more witches in this courtyard besides you before we arrived. And the ghost boy, though he's a little past being a concern."

Ian's first instinct was to lie and say he didn't know. He still didn't for sure, but he could make a decent guess. "They left."

"Impossible. We were watching. I've got men searching the flats, but there's no way they could have left except through the two exits. Unless they went over the wall." She scanned the courtyard to see if it was remotely possible, then closed his watch unconvinced. "I understand why magic was used in public against this lot. Hell's bells and a bucket of blood, I'd have done much worse, if it had been me." She waited until he looked her in the eye again when she added, "But whoever the other two are, they still need to come in and make a statement."

She'd spoken as if he were one of her subordinates, convincing him to bring an informant in for questioning. For his sake and theirs.

He supposed he owed Singh that much, but he was uncertain of how much to tell.

"That bloody bird!" Nick Abernathy complained nonstop about the raven as they escorted him out of the courtyard. "Nearly scratched my eyes out, it did. Great big thing with claws like dockers' hooks. It's that bloody dangerous bird you should be after."

Singh watched him go with a shrug. "You all right? Any giant birds try and peck your eyes out?"

"Mary Blackwood," Ian said. "That's his accomplice. She's the witch you're looking for."

"So are you back to thinking the murders were part of some ritual?" she asked.

He shook his head. "Nae, not like I thought at all." As he explained what he knew as well as what he guessed, he tenderly explored the skin above his left ear with his fingers, thinking about the spiral marks he'd seen on the bodies. The temporal lobe. The hippocampus. The place in the brain where memories swam like coil-shaped seahorses. Until they were removed. Drawn out and reduced to a tiny orb of glittering blue and gold. He wondered then if they had shaved his head on the examination table, would he, too, bear the blue bruise on his temple?

And if he'd had his memories extracted by Mary and lived, how many others might have too?

"Elvanfoot," Ian said, thinking out loud.

"Was *he* here? Was George involved with this after all?" Singh grew agitated, ready to send her constables into the streets to look for him.

"Nae, nae, but he may be another victim. I'm fair convinced of it," he said, following his intuition as it burrowed into the truth. "He must be." He glanced in the direction of the city's heart. Was that why George had run? Because he didn't know who or *what* he was? Ian thought of his own confusion and fear when he'd awoken to a world that offered nothing of the familiar.

"What makes you think that? We haven't had any other bodies turn up."

"It's Mary. Aye, she's a witch, but more like in the old stories."

"What do you mean 'like in the old stories'?" She waited a beat for him to answer. "Ian, are you all right? Are you hurt? Did you take another hit to the head?"

He'd been put in mind of the old ones, those who had walked the hills and moors before the world had been taken up with steam and coal and steel. The ones who'd breathed in unity with the earth once upon a time. "Mary takes people's memories," he said. "She's attracted to their corpse lights. Only the victims don't always have to be dead for her to remove them. But that's what made the mark above the dead men's ears. It wasn't ritualistic; it was compulsion. A witches' coroner should be able to confirm it, now that we know what we're looking at."

"You're telling me we have a murderous witch out there stealing people's memories?" One of Singh's constables gave her the sign that the City Police were snooping around. "Bloody hell, Cameron."

"Aye," he answered, though he remained silent about Edwina. They may yet discover she'd been present in the courtyard, but they'd not learn it from him.

Singh shook her head and walked away to brief her crew about a witch who'd invented a spell for stealing memories, leaving him alone to ponder the night sky and all the secrets it oversaw. He knew Edwina had gone after Mary. To a place he could never follow. He also knew Singh wouldn't believe the sisters needed no spells to do what they did. They simply were. Kith and kin, with something far older and more magical than what a few rhyming incantations could do. Magic like his father had told him about on firelit nights when the wind howled outside and the veil between worlds thinned enough to fear for your soul should you sit too near the window.

Chapter Twenty-Five

Moonlight rippled on the river's surface, drawing Edwina back to the water. But even in the still of the evening, the chugging of machines at the river's edge, whether from train or barge or the ungainly work of dredges and hoppers, kept up a constant droning of man-made noise in her ears. The din interfered with her natural senses, so she soared higher until there was enough room between her and the ground that she need only abide the soft sighs of nightfall. At such a height she'd have to rely solely on her night vision to find her sister. That and an educated guess about where to search for Mary when she was upset.

The glint of moonlight on the water would have attracted Mary too. Since they were girls, they'd had a fascination for all things shiny. So curious, their mother had oft remarked of them. So bright and quick and clever the way they could find lost buttons and dropped needles. Their mother had hoped they'd both grow up to be dedicated witches practiced in the art of weaving and stitching like herself. But then their maturity came, arriving on their twelfth birthday. With it came the shape-shifting.

Clumsy and awkward at first, their bodies struggled to know what to do with their newfound gift. Sometimes a wing flapped in place of an arm through a will of its own; other times they stood at the river's edge in frocks and aprons as their raven heads poked out of their lace collars. It was only after their mother took out her magic loom and crafted their shawls that they learned to control the odd compulsions that sometimes overtook them. The shawls settled them, easing the anxiety that came with being so different from every other witch they'd ever met until they learned to control their magic. The unkind sort called them freaks, while a mystic or two called their magic a gift, and that was what their parents clung to during times of turmoil.

Until they each left in their own time.

Dipping a wing, Edwina thought about checking the clock tower in the heart of the palace borough, but it was too near the top of the hour, and the noise the bell made when it struck could rattle body, soul, and spirit all at once. Instead she banked toward the thousand-year-old abbey. Occasionally, Mary slunk off to sit atop the spires when the moon was full, but a quick glide over the top revealed an abandoned rooftop. Thinking again of the moon and the water, she turned around and followed the bend of the river back toward the city center. Her sister was lost both mentally and morally, but Edwina didn't think she'd stray too far for fear of being caught out alone. That was always the problem with Mary. She craved everything being different brought her—the power to surprise, to be abhorrent, to render tender mercy when it was not expected—yet she detested being an outcast and couldn't bear to be shunned and left alone.

The two towers of the bridge loomed ahead. She'd circled above an hour earlier but went in for another look, knowing it was a favorite haunt of her sister's. Her wings beat out a steady rhythm as she glided over the roof of the north tower. And there, slumped behind a corner turret facing the river, she saw her. Mary sat deep in shadow with her shawl draped over her head and her knees drawn up to her chest. Edwina swooped down, shifting from bird to woman the moment her feet touched the shingles.

"Go away."

"No." Edwina tucked her skirt in under her knees and sat against the angled roof. "Not until you tell me why."

"Why what?"

"Why you didn't confide in me how bad the need had become. Why you allowed innocent people to be murdered." Edwina felt little room in her heart at the moment for forgiveness, but she needed answers. "And why *him?*"

Mary lifted her face. She'd been crying. She wiped her eyes with her sleeve and looked out at the city, where arc lights kept the darkness at bay on the busy streets. It was only a matter of time before the entire world would be bathed in the harsh white light of electricity.

"You wouldn't understand."

Edwina's anger piqued. "There isn't another being in all the world who could understand more!" Exasperated, she turned her shoulder to Mary, wondering what she was going to do with her sister. There were other cities to flee to, but they'd fare no better there. If they couldn't find peace in the biggest city in the world, there really was no place they could go to escape who and what they were. It was worse for Mary, she knew. It had always been worse for her, but Edwina's charitable patience had run out.

"It was thrilling," Mary said after a moment. "Not like the memories of the old people at the hospital, who'd forgotten half their lives by the time they died. Did you never notice how shrunken and dull their memories were? Like common quartz compared to the brilliant blue-and-gold hue of people still in their prime." She raised her chin, proud of her thoughts. "Throw in the threat of imminent death and the most precious memories come surging to the surface for the taking." She closed her eyes and smiled, as if reliving the sensation of extracting the baubles again for the first time. "Do you have any idea what true euphoria feels like?"

Edwina's intuition drifted on a current of disquiet in the wake of her sister's admission. There was a time she'd convinced herself they were two sides of the same unique coin, but in truth they were different currencies altogether. "There's a moment in people's eyes when they begin to figure out there's something not quite right about us," she said. "They say mortals don't experience things beyond their five senses. Perhaps they don't recognize what's triggering their unease, but their instinct tells them there's something to be wary of." Edwina turned to face Mary. "I say 'us,' but it's really just you they're afraid of. I used to see it in the old people's faces at Saint Basil's before they passed. They feared they wouldn't make it through the veil safely with you sitting so near at their moment of death. I swear they were afraid their soul would be devoured. I'm ashamed now I looked away as if I hadn't noticed."

"You know what the mortals call a gathering of our kind?" Mary asked with a derisive laugh. "An Unkindness. Well deserved, don't you think? Me *and* you."

Across the city, the clock tower chimed the midnight hour, punctuating the rift between them until the final bong rang out.

"I know you're angry," Mary said. "But the life we had wasn't enough for me anymore. Can't you see? None of it. Digging in the mud for dented castoffs, scraping by in the shop every day, and then having to make do with the feeble memories of the sick and the dying. I craved more. And Nick gave that to me."

"By murdering mortals."

"Not always." Mary's eyes flicked to Edwina when she turned to hear more. "Like your Ian on the foreshore that morning," she said. "I saved his life."

"You took his memory thinking he was dead."

"But he wasn't. I made sure I called you over before Nick could find the knife he'd dropped during their struggle and do the cutting. And yet I couldn't have the man remembering all those incriminating details he'd uncovered. I'd grown too fond of my nights with Nick—the killing, the shiny new baubles, the feel of him inside me when it was over."

"You're a monster. You've become the thing everyone always said you were."

"You've never had a man. You wouldn't understand the things you'd do for him."

Edwina rose and stood on one of the minor crenellations. Her hand shook as she leaned against the stonework housing the center tower window. Below, a ship approached, its horn bellowing as the vessel neared the bridge. "I don't know who you are anymore. Maybe I never did."

"Aren't the lights on the water beautiful? Mercy, I wish we had some of Father's sherry right now." Mary spoke as if they were girls again, reminiscing on the roof of some old castle on the north bay instead of confronting demons. "Don't settle for ordinary, Edwina. It wouldn't suit you either, if you're honest with yourself. It's not what we were made for."

This was madness. There was nothing left to salvage. No bright speck of hope left in Mary to catch the eye or change the heart. Except . . .

"Will you give it back?" Edwina spun around and leaned against the wall, trying to present an air of bravery. "His memory is precious to me."

"Did you mean what you said? Do you really think I'm a monster?"

Edwina resisted the urge to lay a comforting hand on her sister's shoulder. She'd once said she would forgive everything. Understand fully. But she was wrong. She didn't understand anything anymore. All those men dead so her sister could feel *euphoric*. "They'll hang you," she said. "Nick. The lads. The police have them in custody already. Soon they'll have you, too, and then you'll all hang for what you did."

Mary looked up sharply. She'd expected the usual comfort. Forgiveness. Perhaps an apology. Never a rebuke. "If I'm to hang, then I guess I won't be needing this any longer." In an instant of retaliation, she let the bauble holding Ian's memory drop from her hand. "Goodbye, sister."

The orb rolled down the tiles, then bounced off the tower roof, falling between the walkways below. Edwina's eye caught the orb's motion in free fall. Without thinking, she jumped after it, transforming in a midair acrobatic. But the change made her momentarily take her eye off the gem. Had it dropped in the water? On the roadway? A wagon drawn by a single draft horse lumbered over the span of road above the water. The bauble had to be there somewhere. *Please don't let it be in the river,* she thought as she landed on the bridge.

The wagon drew nearer. The thought of the memory being crushed underfoot of the horse made her jump about madly and spread her wings, scaring the animal so that it veered away to its right.

"Easy, easy," the driver said, gripping the reins to settle his horse. "Bloody damn bird."

The wagon wheels passed by mere inches from Edwina as she scanned the road, using her superior vision to check every crevice. It couldn't be lost. It couldn't. She thought of Ian and all the stolen moments he would never get back if she didn't find the shiny orb. The tender memories that could never be reclaimed. She would look for it all night, if she must.

And then the bridge shuttered. The noise of an engine rumbled to life. Somewhere a bolt slid open. The road lifted, tilting to let the oncoming ship pass through. And with it the round orb, no bigger than a marble, rolled free of its resting place in a crevice along the railing. The road rose higher and the memory picked up speed, rolling toward the end of the bridge and a certain drop into the river. Edwina spread her wings and swooped under the structure, anticipating the arc of the falling bauble.

But at the last second, the orb hit a rivet, altering its momentum. It bounced once and plummeted off the bridge, where it sank beneath the river's surface.

Chapter Twenty-Six

After leaving the Constabulary headquarters, where he'd been made to give a formal statement, Ian returned to the shop. The clock tower had already chimed the hour by the time he knocked on the front door a few minutes past midnight. He feared the old man had gone to sleep and readied a lock-opening spell on his tongue, but then Elvanfoot and Hob both met him at the door.

"Great blazes, where have you been?" Elvanfoot rushed him inside and through to the back room where Edwina kept her cupboard of herbs. "Come this way, I have something to show you."

"Has Miss Blackwood returned?" Ian asked, making a quick search of the back room.

"I thought she was with you," Elvanfoot said.

Ian's heart sank from guilt as much as worry. "Aye, she was, but she took off after her sister again. I have no idea where."

"I tried to find you," Hob said. "But all I could see of you was fog."

"Sorry, I had to lock you out. You would have been roasted on a bonfire if I hadn't."

Hob leaned in to sniff Ian's clothes. "Smoke and blood," he said and wrinkled his nose.

"We got him," Ian explained. "The Brick Lane Slasher. That's who Mary led us to."

"Yes, yes, we heard all about that," Elvanfoot said, rummaging in the bottom of an umbrella stand.

Thinking he'd brought shocking news, Ian was surprised to find them uninterested in the information. "Wait, you canna have heard already. I only just returned from the station house."

Hob informed him otherwise. "The police were here! Searched the place top to bottom."

"Witch or mortal?" Ian asked. He supposed Singh could have sent a team while he was giving his statement.

"Both," Sir Elvanfoot said as he retrieved one of Mary's orbs out of the umbrella stand and set it on the table. "They came to gather evidence." Then he added softly, "It wasn't my George."

So the old man had had his suspicions too.

"Nae," Ian said and tried to understand the pain it must cause to feel relief at such news, only to still anguish over the missing son's whereabouts. "It was a local hooligan Mary had befriended. Claimed he only killed the poor sods to satisfy her"—he pointed to the bauble in Elvanfoot's hand—"peculiar obsession."

Elvanfoot nodded, taking in his meaning. "Only it's more than an obsession," he clarified. "With Mary, I suspect her odd quirk of nature is as natural as eating, drinking, or sleeping for you or I."

"There's nothing natural about it," he said.

Elvanfoot begged to differ, but he had more pressing matters to get to. "The police left a few minutes before you arrived. They confiscated everything belonging to Mary. They took the items hidden in the trunk. Her grimoire, and the baubles she'd collected." He held up a finger. "All but this one, that is."

"Sir had to keep it safe, so I hid it in the umbrella stand," Hob said.

For a heartbeat Ian held out hope the memory was his, but he knew Mary had taken that one with her. So who did this one belong to? And why hide it from the police?

"We were fortunate to have finished our little experiment moments before they arrived, were we not, Hob? Or we would have been found out."

Hob grinned so wide the corners of his mouth forced his pointed ears to poke up through his scruff of hair. "Show Mister," he said. "Come see, come see, come see!"

Ian watched as Sir Elvanfoot placed the blue orb in his palm.

"It occurred to me that there was little use in taking a person's memory only to shrink it down to stone. There's little fascination in holding the orbs. Light doesn't pass through. And they aren't of true gemstone quality. However," the witch said, holding his hand open, "if one could condense a memory, perhaps one could also expand it."

Sir Elvanfoot had Hob sprinkle water over the orb. The hard shell cracked and swelled, transforming into a shimmering blue light that reflected shadows of people and places.

"Mary did that very thing. I could see images of my thoughts floating inside the orb she'd stolen from me." A strange sort of melancholia ruffled through Ian at the sight of another's memories, knowing he would never really know the extent of what he'd lost inside that orb.

"Simple expansion spell." Elvanfoot shrugged. "Same one I use for turning prunes into plums."

"Sir tested them all before we found this one." Hob's eyes reflected the blue light. "Such strange and wondrous visions they all held."

Elvanfoot raised his hand and they watched the shadows swirl inside the orb. A woman in a green dress laughing. A carriage ride over the River Clayborn. Ian recognized the columns of the philosopher's monument above his city and then the image of a viaduct as a train rattled over, blowing its whistle. "Whose memory is this?" he asked as Sir Elvanfoot's face appeared in the orb's shadows. The wizard was reading a grimoire beside an enormous fireplace. His hair was not yet white. He offered a toffee to the owner of the memory.

"It belongs to my son." Elvanfoot let the orb shrink again. The blue light collapsed.

"It's George's? But then—"

Before he could finish his thought, a noise like a window sash crashing against the sill rattled upstairs. Ian held up his hand to caution Elvanfoot and Hob to stay put while he checked the stairway. If it was Mary, he would strike first and ask questions later. Instead, he found Edwina at the top of the stairs, soaked to the skin and shivering as her shawl hung limp over her shoulders.

"It's gone," she said. "I lost it." Ian ran up to meet her as she spoke between sobs. "Your memory. The orb fell in the river. I tried to get it back, but I didn't know where to look." Her knees folded and she nearly collapsed.

"You're all right. Calm down." Ian put his arms around her and held her tight, helping her down the stairs. "Hob! Tea and warm clothes!"

The hearth elf hovered over Edwina as Ian lowered her gently onto the same chair he'd sat in when she'd helped him. Hob removed a fluff of cotton wadding from his inside pocket and set it in Edwina's hand. He blew out a puff of breath and her sodden clothes dried instantly, restored to their previous condition, though her hand now held a sopping clump of wet cotton.

She sat up a little less bedraggled than before and thanked the elf, who ran off to get her a cup of tea.

When he'd gone, Sir Elvanfoot approached Edwina. "And what news of your sister?" he asked, still holding his son's memory in his hand.

"I think I've lost her for good too," she said and described her confrontation with Mary. "I told her she would hang for what she'd done, and then she dropped Ian's memory in the river and escaped." Though her clothes were now dry, she continued to tremble from the ordeal until Hob handed her a steaming cup of tea, which she drank in small sips between repeated apologies.

It was then Ian truly let it sink in what she'd said. His memories, all the missing pieces his hearth elf couldn't restore, were gone. Lost in the river. Forever. All his most intimate experiences, his reflections on life and love, the thoughts he'd kept only to himself, were gone. What dreams and secret desires had he lost? What fears and regrets? Grudges? Ambitions? Who was he without the private interstices that once existed between the larger memories? It was almost too vast to consider, and yet he knew he was still himself, still capable of rekindling the better parts of the man he hoped he was.

Thoughts on his nature led him to wonder about George and how their fates had crossed on the path with Mary Blackwood. If the man's memory was here, then he was out on the streets without his wits. He would know no one and remember nothing, not even his name. Ian saw the same worried thought surface in Sir Elvanfoot's eyes as he peered at the orb in his hand, as though wondering how he would return a memory to a son who didn't know who or what he was anymore.

"We won't lose hope for George," Ian said. "Not yet." He recalled then what the innkeeper had said about George's appearance. Disheveled, as though he'd been sleeping rough in the gutter. So he was out there somewhere. Surviving on instinct. "Mary may have taken the memories from his head, aye, but there's more to it than that. Before Hob gave me back my past, there was a sort of recognition in my body of things that were familiar. I dinna know why, of course, only that I could feel if something resonated or not. That intuition was all I had to hold on to, even when I dinna remember the magic in me. It was almost like the body held on to its own experience of the mind's memory, ye ken."

"You think George may be feeling something similar?" Sir Elvanfoot allowed himself a moment of hope, holding the orb up for a second inspection.

"He's out there," Ian said. "I know he is. We just have to find him."

"But how?" Edwina asked. "He could be anywhere."

Ian inhaled, thinking about how he'd felt when he had no memory. "Nae, not anywhere," he said. "He'll stick to what he knows, even if it's only subconsciously." He snapped his fingers, getting an idea. "The road between the theaters. Lizzie said he walked the same path every night after his play ended." He pulled out his watch, only this time he really did check the hour. "In his normal state, he'd be walking to her right now from the Belfry Theater. But what if his body held on to that memory and he's been out there the whole time, walking that same path, even if he didn't know why?"

"The Belfry is just down the road," Edwina said.

"That's where we need to be looking," Ian said. "On the road between there and the Wilshire Music Hall in the East End."

"I have a coach in the lane," Sir Elvanfoot said and hurried for the front door.

The wizard summoned his carriage with a signal from a shrill whistle while Ian told Hob to follow on his own and out of sight. By the time Edwina had her shawl around her shoulders and the front door locked, the carriage horses clopped down the road with the sleepy-eyed coachman perched on his box. Ian did a double take at the driver in his top hat and tails, briefly suspicious he was one of Singh's men, then gave up on the notion and climbed into the velvet-covered seat beside Edwina, while Sir Elvanfoot sat opposite.

After urgent instruction was given, the coach took them straight to the Belfry Theater, where they asked him to slow-walk the horses so they could peer down every dark lane and question each face they passed. Twice Ian hopped out of the coach to get a better look at a man sleeping rough in a doorway. Each time he shook his head and jumped back in, taking Edwina's hand in his on the seat beside him, locking fingers and holding on to her and hope in the same gesture. And each time, at the touch of her skin next to his, he wanted to ask about the remarkable magic he'd seen in the courtyard. His mind churned with curiosity about it, but first they had to find George.

"Perhaps it was a fool's errand from the start," Sir Elvanfoot said when they'd reached the end of the lane where the Wilshire Music Hall stood. A small crowd mingled outside, a mix of audience members and performers still relishing the buzz of the performance. Intoxicated on spirits and the aura of camaraderie, a few young men sang out bawdy tunes, then tossed their semi-empty brown bottles of ale into the alley, where they splashed and broke in a void of darkness.

The alley. Damn his stupidity!

Ian jumped out of the coach. Dodging the young men in their frock coats, he ran into the alley to where he remembered a stairwell had led to a belowground entrance. He squinted in the low light, walking softly so his tackety boots wouldn't scrape on the pavement and startle anyone to rash action. He glanced over his shoulder at the streetlight where Hob had hidden himself before, but the glass was still broken, the light not working. There were too many people around to fix it with magic, so he took the risk of snapping a flame on his fingertips to illuminate the stairwell. There in the gloom, curled up on the landing at the bottom, was a man sleeping rough in a dirty gray coat, with three weeks' worth of beard and a smell on him strong enough to raise the dead.

Ian shone the light closer to get a better look at his face. The man groaned and held his hand up defensively to shield his eyes from the light. "George!" Ian called out, but of course the man didn't recognize his name.

"Ian?" Edwina and Sir Elvanfoot caught up to him in the alley. "Have you found him?" she asked. "Is it George?"

Elvanfoot, overtaken by eagerness, pressed in beside Ian on the stairs. "My boy," he said and walked to the bottom for a better look.

Ian shook his head in regret as he looked up at Edwina. "He's been here the whole time. I saw him yesterday and didn't recognize him."

But below it was no happy reunion between father and son. The man who'd been sleeping in his coat on the street in the rain for weeks rebelled at the invasion of his space.

"Get off!" he yelled. "Help! Murder!"

For all George knew, Ian and Elvanfoot were the ones who'd been killing men on the streets. He kicked and clawed at them, screaming bloody murder. Edwina warned the gents from outside the theater had grown suspicious enough to venture into the alley, so Ian ran up the steps to meet them halfway, leaving the father to calm his son. Were it not for the Constabulary, which he wished to keep away from Edwina and her magic for as long as he could, he'd have stunned the gents with a bright flash of white light so all they could see were spots. Instead he took a milder, disarming approach. Before their curiosity brought them too near, he picked up one of the partially broken bottles the young men had tossed and stumbled forward pretending to be as drunk as they were.

"The moon has a face like the clock in the hall," he shouted to the sky. "She shines on thieves on the garden wall. On streets and fields and harbor quays. And birdies asleep in the forks of the trees." He feigned taking a drink while they lost their threatening postures, too bemused at his performance to quarrel. He continued with his poem, growing more animated as the words cloaked his spell. "The squalling cat and the squeaking mouse. The howling dog by the door of the house. The bat that lies in bed at noon. All love to be out by the light of the moon." He and the lads had a laugh as he pointed to the crescent moon slipping in and out of clouds. Then he hit them with the thrust of his incantation incognito. "But all the things that belong to the day, cuddle to sleep to be out of her way. And flowers and children close their eyes, till up in the morning the sun shall arise."

The young men laughed nervously at the change the spell made to their mood before turning around and wandering back to the lane, stretching and yawning and calling for an early night. Ian watched them walk out of sight, then tossed the bottle aside and hurried back to help with George.

In the stairwell, Elvanfoot had had to do much the same to his son, who did not trust who his intruders said they were or who they claimed he was. He fought to the last until he was rendered unconscious with a flick of the old wizard's wrist. At Edwina's instruction, the orb belonging to George was slipped in his mouth to rest on the tongue. Using that lilting quality of her voice, she induced George to swallow the hard stone so it could dissolve inside him. She sang her spell to restore the memories while Elvanfoot cradled his son's head in his lap. Ian watched with a mix of envy and apprehension as the magic seeped into the man's system, returning his most personal thoughts to him. He remembered the fuzzy feeling in his blood before the images had flipped through his mind. He only hoped George's restored visions were of people and places he recognized and welcomed.

When he woke a few moments later, George blinked several times before sitting up and asking what his father was doing in the city. His second question was to ask why they were sitting in the bottom of a stairwell smelling like rubbish, but then the new memories merged with the old and he nodded, not quite understanding exactly perhaps, but acknowledging the strange journey he'd been on after being hit on the head and left for dead in a darkened lane. Ian called for Hob, and the little elf got the man cleaned up as best he could with the help of his whisk broom and chant. There was little to be done about the beard and weight loss, but at least the man no longer smelled like yesterday's fish. And lucky thing, too, as the stage door opened and a young woman with a white gardenia in her hair walked out and caught sight of her missing beau when they emerged from the alley.

Chapter Twenty-Seven

Witnessing the reunion between George and his father had wrenched Edwina's heart sideways, knowing her own family had been scattered to the four winds. She was happy, certainly, that Sir Elvanfoot's search for his son hadn't ended in tragedy. She'd smiled like a loon when the young man spotted his beloved at the stage door and they collapsed into each other's arms. Yet as pleased as she was for them, her sister was still out there on her own. A willing accessory to murder. How could anything be right again?

And then Ian walked over after shaking Sir Elvanfoot's hand and seeing him to the coach, and half her worries fell away. "They're off to the old man's hotel," he said. "Thought it might be a bit crowded if we all piled in. Told them to go on without us. Should I see if I can find us a cab?"

"It's well past midnight. I doubt you'd have much luck. Besides, I don't mind walking." She was exhausted, but the night called for a long stroll to exorcise the mind of all that had happened. "If you'll join me."

"There may be brigands loose on the street."

"Then they'll have met their match with the pair of us," she replied and took his arm when offered.

They strode without purpose along the narrow lane as an elevated train rumbled past overhead. A halo of lamplight shone on the cobblestone road, deserted now but for a few stray cats prowling the rubbish piles. As yet they'd said very little, other than to comment on the quality of the starlight, each keeping silent while ruminating on the events of the evening. But soon Ian came to the point he could no longer keep his thoughts to himself.

He stopped and released her arm so they might face each other. "There's still the wee matter of your magic I have to ask about."

"Ever the detective," Edwina answered.

"Truer than you know," he said with a self-admitting nod. He paused then and gave her a searching look. "How long have you and your sister been able to transform?"

His genuine curiosity was a refreshing change from the grotesque fascination people who'd seen them shape-shift usually displayed. Her father, by necessity, had become quite adept at altering mortal memories himself before she and Mary were through adolescence.

"From the time we were girls," she answered. "And awkwardly at first, but my father was very patient. We lived in the snowy hills then and had ample room to practice our new skill, which he encouraged. Though Mother wasn't always as keen."

"Your parents weren't . . . ?" He gestured to her general being.

"No. Both witches, of course, but neither could recall a shape-shifter in the family before. Everyone teased we must be Merlin's long-lost great-great-granddaughters. Or the Morrígan's. That was another theory."

Ian nodded, evaluating what she'd said instead of laughing or scoffing as most did. He scratched at his jaw as though lost in thought, seemingly searching his memory for some piece of knowledge he'd once known. She felt a twinge of guilt seeing him struggle to remember, but he let it go with the shake of his head. "Well, it's a fair talent, whichever ancient relative the magic comes by."

Next it was her turn to share her innermost thoughts. "You must find me strange," she said. Many did. In truth, Edwina secretly feared he would abandon her on the street, afraid to continue walking beside such an aberration, knowing who and what she really was. Instead, he took hold of both her hands, drawing her closer to him.

"Miss Blackwood, I find you many things—brave, remarkable, enchanting—but strange isn't one of them."

A black cat scurried past their feet with a dead mouse dangling from its mouth. A train rattled overhead, spewing coal smoke and ash that rained down on their hair and clothes. Though far from a romantic setting, Edwina did not object when Ian leaned in to kiss her under the glow of a streetlamp. She could have stood in his arms until morning, and might have, too, if not for the hansom cab that pulled to a stop beside them.

Ian sighed and faced the cab. "Chief Inspector Singh. Impeccable timing as usual."

The inspector leaned her head out of the cab. "You need to come with me. Both of you."

The pair, feeling they had no other choice, climbed into the cab beside the woman who, for the moment, seemed to hold their freedom in her hands.

"We would have come to see you in the morning," Ian said. When Singh didn't answer, he paid closer attention to the direction the cab was going. "Wait, where are we heading?" he asked, but their destination was soon apparent without Singh verbalizing it. The cab veered left and two minutes later drove up beside the northern end of the tower bridge.

A cold foreboding came over Edwina as the cab stopped inside an archway beneath the massive girders. She shivered, remembering the cold water she'd plunged into over and over again, searching for Ian's lost memory. The chief inspector jumped out of the cab and ordered them to follow.

"Riya, what's happened?" Ian demanded she answer before he let Edwina disembark. He seemed to understand something grave had occurred or they wouldn't have stopped at such a place.

Singh did an about-face on the pavement, her skirt twirling in a manner too frivolous for the moment. "A body. About an hour ago." She stared solemnly at Edwina. "I'm afraid I must insist."

Edwina grew queasy. Unsteady. Images came to mind unbidden of ghastly blue skin and seaweed draped over half-lidded eyes. She squeezed her own eyes shut, willing the image to fade as she stepped out of the cab.

"Are you all right?" Ian wrapped his arm around her shoulders. "Lean on me, if you must," he said and nodded at the chief inspector.

They followed Singh inside the bridge's abutment to a room covered in white tiles. The temperature dropped like a winter chill out of the north. A body lay on a table covered with a white cloth. The dripping fringe of a black shawl peeked out below. Edwina covered her mouth with her hand, afraid of the noise that would come out otherwise.

"They fished the body out down there," Singh said, pointing to where a set of steps led to the river from the landing outside the room.

"What is this place?" Ian asked, holding Edwina with both arms now as she curled into him.

"They call it Dead Man's Hole," she answered plainly.

Singh nodded. "So many bodies wash up here because of the current, they added a morgue to have a place to store them until they could be identified or taken for burial." The chief inspector beckoned forward a man standing in the corner, and he came and peeled the sheet back from the body. "I know this is difficult," she said, "but we need you to tell us if this is your sister, Mary."

Edwina didn't need to look to know her sister was the one laid out on the table. The lace-up boots, the black skirt, and the shawl from their mother's loom were all Mary's. But she knew she must maintain composure long enough to verify the face she'd seen every day of her life for twenty-three years. Not another in the world as similar to her own as the one gone gray and blue under a sheet.

"What happened to her?" she asked.

"We think she waded in upriver as the tide came in. She'd filled her shawl with large stones and tied it around her neck and shoulder." Singh gave Edwina a moment to take it in. "Sometimes a sinking spell is used to aid the weight of the stones, but we can't be certain."

A strange paralysis came over Edwina. Her lungs forgot to take in breath, and her legs wanted to collapse beneath her. Singh snapped her fingers, and the man from the morgue grabbed a chair for Edwina to sit on. "I saw her mere hours ago," she said, recovering only slightly. "We fought. Here on the bridge. I told her she would hang for what she did."

There were no recriminations from Singh or Ian. They draped no guilt over her shoulders for what her sister had done, yet the shame and remorse clung to her like sopping-wet wool.

They gave her a moment alone to say goodbye to her sister. Though Mary's flesh was cold and pale, Edwina held her hand in hers. The skin, though slack from death, still carried the softness of youth, and she had to steady herself against denial. Her sister, the one other person who understood what it was like to live with the burden of possessing two forms in one body, was inexplicably dead. The vibrant, rosy youth drained from her cheek, replaced with this still, gray death at the river's edge. Grief, anger, and disbelief braided their knot around Edwina's heart until it hurt to breathe.

She could not forgive, but she would strive to understand the compulsion that had taken her sister from her. She assured Mary that much. And there in the cold, stark white room, she saw the corpse light rise, the first she'd ever seen without Mary's magic to guide it out of the body, shimmering and blue and more beautiful than she'd imagined. In that moment, Benjamin walked up the steps from the river, mesmerized, as she was, by the light floating above the body. He did not come any nearer, satisfied to watch until the light floated out over the water, where it hovered momentarily before flickering out. She and the boy briefly looked each other in the eye one last time before each retreated from the room in silence.

After promising Chief Inspector Singh they would come by the Constabulary headquarters in the morning to make a full statement for the inquest, Ian and Edwina rebuffed an offer of a ride home, choosing instead to linger by the water for a moment longer. When the hansom cab had gone, they took the steps up to the bridge.

"The river tried to warn me," Edwina said, thinking of the skull that had washed up on the rocks. "But I didn't know it would cost so dearly."

Ian leaned on the railing beside her, watching the dark water swirl and eddy in pools along the shore. He had no poetry to offer then. No spell to cast a fog over all that had happened. Only the silent reflection of a man mourning his own loss to the river.

Edwina could never know the depth of forfeiture he'd suffered because of her sister's nature. And hers, if she were honest with herself. She'd have done anything to appease her sister and keep her by her side after their parents had walked away without a word. But murder? People died of natural causes every day in the city. How could that not have been enough for her sister?

"Mary craved the lights," she said, still shocked and bewildered by the night's events. "I think maybe she needed to possess them. Control them. To know they were hers to manipulate and no one else's. But in the end, the compulsion controlled her, didn't it?"

Ian straightened, reeling in the private meditations he'd spooled out over the river. His brow creased in thought. "A little like the wretch who seeks oblivion in the opium den, is it not?" he asked. "I've seen a man go in a place like that looking for escape, only to end up the same as a rabbit caught in a snare, willing to chew his leg off to get more of the stuff. If that's what your sister was feeling, maybe it was a mercy she didn't kill more."

Mary had said as much, denying to the end she was the murderer they'd accused her of being. Ian had been her proof. She'd left him alive when he could have easily been another victim. Edwina gazed at the stars above, shining bright before the dawn. Had his life been spared because of something her sister had seen brewing among the stars? Had Mary left him alive for her sake, knowing she would someday be alone?

The vagaries of such fate were too much for her to contemplate, so she stepped away from the center railing as a barge piled wide with coal floated silently beneath the bridge like a mythical beast slithering past their feet.

"It was just there," she said, pointing near the riverbank. "We might yet search the foreshore for the orb when the water goes down. There's still a chance the memory may surface. I'll spot the sharp blue color if it does. We shouldn't give up hope of finding it."

Ian stared out at the dark water floating under their feet. "Nae, I think those memories are gone for good. And maybe it's for the best." He took her hand as a steam tug chugged by. "There are moments to hold on to forever. The ones you want to cherish, like the love you had for your sister before all this trouble, ye ken. But there are others . . ." He shook his head at something unpleasant. "Nae, you do not mind if the current takes those memories, and good riddance. I have all I need to start again," he said and held her hand.

As they walked away from the bridge and past the old castle, Benjamin's voice rose, alone and mournful, as he crossed the bridge in their place, singing, "One for sorrow, two for joy. Three for a girl, four for a boy. Five for silver, six for gold. Seven for a secret never to be told."

Epilogue

Edwina had avoided the foreshore for three days, the longest she'd gone without setting foot in the mud since her father moved the family to the city. Instead of picking up half-buried treasures uncovered by the tide, she had devoted her days to arranging her sister's funeral.

There'd been a discussion among Chief Inspector Singh and various representatives of the Constabulary who'd suggested there ought not be a public funeral for Mary. Mention of her involvement in the murders had been kept out of the official City Police report, a feat that ironically required altering the memories of all the mortal witnesses present at the residential block of flats where the Brick Lane Slasher was apprehended. As a consequence, there'd been no official mention of her related death either. Yet she had passed through the veil, which caused a number of others involved in the decision-making to argue it would be more burdensome to try to cover up her death. Besides, she was obviously a member of a localized community in which she had daily interactions with customers and hospital staff who would notice her absence, not to mention a sister who wished to publicly mourn.

And so, with approval in place, Edwina saw to the details once her sister had been delivered to the shop in the coffin she'd paid for with the family's long-saved funerary funds.

With no way to contact her missing parents, the final viewing of the body by family was left to Edwina and Ian. And Mrs. Dower, who'd kindly offered to wash and dress Mary's body for burial. Edwina expected a small coalition of mourners within the hour, including Sir Elvanfoot before he caught his train north. Ian was going, too, but she chose to dwell on only one source of grief at a time and so put that out of her mind. The rest of the mourners were thought to consist of various neighbors who'd been prodded to attend by Mrs. Dower, who had suggested to Edwina it might be wise to set out cakes and tea and a spot of sherry in the shop for "them what's kind enough to pay their respects to the odd bird, and no disrespect intended."

Edwina worried it was a plain-looking sort of coffin. Wooden, but with a coat of black paint and gilded handles. The coffin sat in the middle of the shop atop the kitchen table that had been brought down from the living quarters. The display cases and counters had already been moved aside and covered with sheets, as were any visible clocks or mirrors, so that the small space felt appropriately shrine-like. Small cakes and tarts were set on trays as prescribed.

A photographer was due any moment to capture Mary's final likeness. If Edwina ever did hear from her mother or father again, she'd like to have one last photo to show them of their daughters together, and so she planned to have Mary propped up with their heads resting together as they'd always been before the world turned upside down. Mrs. Dower had agreed that the midnight-blue dress from the hope chest was the appropriate somber attire for a memento mori photo.

And now it was time for Edwina to see for herself.

"Ready?" Ian undid the latches on the coffin lid, preparing to open it so Edwina could have a private moment to say goodbye before the others arrived.

Edwina nervously fussed with the crisp black crepe that had been attached to the bodice of her mourning dress before bravely nodding.

Ian pried the top of the coffin open on its hinge. Edwina stood beside him to gaze upon Mary's face a final time and say goodbye. But even before the coffin was fully open, they both knew something was wrong. The distinct smell of river mud seeped out of the confined space. In a single effort, Ian pushed the lid all the way back.

At first, they couldn't make sense of what they were seeing. Mary was attired as she should be, but her dress was soaked with muddy water, and strands of algae clung to her arms and neck. Her hair, which Mrs. Dower swore had been combed into a beautiful pompadour, was drenched and smelled of fish slime. And there, in Mary's cupped white hands, which had been folded neatly over her middle, rested a blue orb with a vein of gold visible beneath a sheen of newly dried mud.

"Blimey, I never," said Mrs. Dower, clutching her chest as she peered inside the coffin. "What's happened to her? She were in a right proper state only this morning, she were. Saw to it myself."

Edwina shivered from a dose of superstition. The orb appeared to have been inexplicably fished from the river.

Ian flicked open his watch, then shook his head when it gave him a negative reading. "Nothing," he said, careful not to confuse Mrs. Dower with talk of ghosts and witches. The thought had occurred to Edwina as well.

Confused, she scrutinized her sister's body from head to foot, trying to make sense of what was laid out before her. Then her eye spotted the corner of an envelope poking out of the lining of the coffin lid. Ian saw it, too, and retrieved a small card, the sort one might send with a bouquet of flowers.

"It's addressed to you," he said to Edwina, then opened the envelope with her approval.

He slipped the note loose of its sleeve, and they leaned together to read the handwritten note:

Dear Miss Edwina Blackwood,
A token of my esteem. Until we meet again.
Yours truly,
An Ardent Admirer

The signature, written in iridescent green ink, was smeared nearly beyond recognition from a misplaced drop of muddy water. Yet the indication was clear.

Someone had been watching her.

ACKNOWLEDGMENTS

As always, I need to thank a number of people for helping deliver *The Raven Spell* into the world. Without their guidance and expertise, it would be a much different book. To my wonderful agent, Marlene Stringer: thank you once again for believing in this story when it was just a single chapter based on *what if.* To my acquiring editor, Adrienne Procaccini: thank you for taking a leap of faith with me on a second series. To my editor, Liz Pearsons, who graciously stepped up to oversee the novel through production: thank you for doing double duty.

I've also been fortunate to work with many of the same developmental and copy editors on this series at 47North as I did with *The Vine Witch*, which made the work feel more like a reunion. To Clarence, Jon, Kellie, and Stephanie: your critical scrutiny of the work is what makes the words publishable, and I thank you all. You are word witches of the highest order! And to the people working behind the scenes—Kristin, Grace, Lauren, Leonard, and the rest of the team at 47North—thank you for all you do. And a final thanks to Shasti O'Leary Soudant for her spot-on cover concept.

APPENDIX

Borrowed Written Works and Poems in the Public Domain

The Pirate by Walter Scott
"The Sick Rose" by William Blake
"Ashes Denote That Fire Was" by Emily Dickinson
"The Moon" by Robert Louis Stevenson

Borrowed Nursery Rhymes in the Public Domain

"Mary, Mary, Quite Contrary"
"Who Killed Cock Robin?"
"Three Blind Mice"
"Ladybird, Ladybird"
"One for Sorrow"

ABOUT THE AUTHOR

Photo © 2018 Bob Carmichael

Luanne G. Smith is the Amazon Charts and *Washington Post* bestselling author of *The Vine Witch*, *The Glamourist*, and *The Conjurer*. She lives in Colorado at the base of the beautiful Rocky Mountains, where she enjoys hiking, gardening, and a glass of wine at the end of the day. For more information, visit www.luannegsmith.com.